"I'm heading to bed."

He punctuated his words by gesturing toward the tent.

"Bed?" Chantelle hugged her knees hard and took a deep breath. "It's my tent. I don't want to share it with you."

"Big girls have to learn to share. I thought your mum would have taught you that."

"My mother didn't teach me to share sleeping accommodations with strange men. Sleep somewhere else."

Grant squatted in front of her. "Chantelle, it's clouding over. I won't risk getting soaked just because of your outdated standards. We're adults. I know that I'm capable of keeping my hands to myself. The question is, can you keep your hands off me?"

Dear Reader,

In a world of constant dizzying change, some things, fortunately, remain the same. One of those things is the Silhouette **Special Edition** commitment to our readers—a commitment, renewed each month, to bring you six stimulating, sensitive, substantial novels of living and loving in today's world, novels blending deep, vivid emotions with high romance.

This month, six fabulous authors step up to fulfill that commitment: Terese Ramin brings you the uproarious, unforgettable and decidedly adult *Accompanying Alice;* Jo Ann Algermissen lends her unique voice—and heart—to fond family feuding in *Would You Marry Me Anyway?;* Judi Edwards stirs our deepest hunger for love and healing in *Step from a Dream;* Christine Flynn enchants the senses with a tale of legendary love in *Out of the Mist;* Pat Warren deftly balances both the fears and the courage intimacy generates in *Till I Loved You;* and Dee Holmes delivers a mature, perceptive novel of the true nature of loving and heroism in *The Return of Slade Garner*. All six novels are sterling examples of the Silhouette **Special Edition** experience: romance you can believe in.

Next month also features a sensational array of talent, including two tantalizing volumes many of you have been clamoring for, by bestselling authors Ginna Gray and Debbie Macomber.

So don't miss a moment of the Silhouette **Special Edition** experience!

From all the authors and editors of Silhouette **Special Edition**—warmest wishes.

JUDI EDWARDS
Step from a Dream

Silhouette Special Edition

Published by Silhouette Books New York

America's Publisher of Contemporary Romance

To the dedicated staff of Dutch Lake School,
past and present.

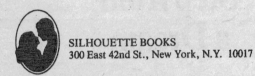

SILHOUETTE BOOKS
300 East 42nd St., New York, N.Y. 10017

STEP FROM A DREAM

ISBN: 0-373-09658-5

First Silhouette Books printing March 1991

Printed in the U.S.A.

Books by Judi Edwards

Silhouette Special Edition

The Perfect Ten #470
Step from a Dream #658

JUDI EDWARDS

was born and raised in Chicago. She spent many years teaching elementary school in remote areas of Canada, and she now lives with four children and her spouse of twenty years in Tucson, Arizona. She prefers writing romances to the software manuals she also writes—the endings are happier, even if they aren't as good for curing insomnia.

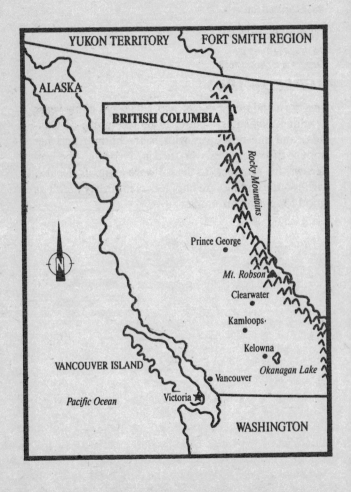

Chapter One

Breath congealed in Chantelle DuMaurier's lungs as her outstretched fingers groped along featureless gray roughness. Finding a lip of rock, she warily tested its strength before inching forward. A lucky thing she did; the limestone crumbled. Chantelle pressed her cheek against the painful rock and watched the precipitous dance of pebbles clattering to the talus ten feet below. Ten feet wasn't much. Enough, though, to be dangerous.

Chantelle exhaled loudly as she edged back to where the path was wide enough to plant both feet side by side. Well, she could always forget about reaching the rock ledge that promised such a grand view of the glacier and Mount Robson, and stick instead to the easy and obvious route along the bottom of the slope. She was sure that most of the infrequent visitors to this spot did exactly that.

Or, she thought with a grin, she could retrace her steps and try another approach. Chantelle shifted the strap of her pack to less sensitive parts of her shoulders and studied the barren rocks. If she clambered up the slope where it broadened out near that pond up ahead and then zigzagged back...

It would be extra work, but worth it. The flat outcrop reminded her of her solitary perches on the hillside behind the DuMaurier family orchard. She had called them her Thinking Places. A good Thinking Place, she'd discovered early in life, had to provide a sweeping overview of everyday life while at the same time—and this was the crucial factor, really—it had to be inaccessible enough to discourage any of her six siblings from invading her privacy.

That rock ledge looked like a perfect Thinking Place. Chantelle headed back along the alternate route.

She was more than ready for a rest by the time she finally reached her goal. Gusting a sigh of relief, she eased her pack onto the ground, then held the hair off the back of her neck as she looked around.

Yes. It was worth it.

It was always worth the effort required to get into the bush, even the relatively tame bush back home near Kamloops. But if the familiar grasslands dotted with pine, sagebrush and cows were Chantelle's church—and they were, but only in a way most people never understood, so that she'd given up trying to explain—then this mountain valley was Notre Dame.

She tried to still her labored breathing, which blocked the sounds of breeze and distant water. Back when she was a child, she'd gone to her Thinking Places not only to think, but to listen. If she was quiet enough maybe she would understand the half-intelligible words of the wind whispering through the ponderosa pines. The words would tell her, she was sure, of her purpose in life. Her destiny, a goal worth devoting her life to, was floating on the next breeze if only she was determined enough and wise enough to catch it.

Chantelle wasn't seeking her destiny in this wilderness, of course. She was a full-grown twenty-eight now, had brazened her way through the embarrassment of the first divorce in the history of her entire family and craved solitude rather than voices. Her current destiny was a live-in teenage sister who'd become the most important person in her life and a small used-and-rare bookstore, the type favored by fanatical book lovers.

In a simpler, less cynical age she might have become a nun, she thought with a tinge of melodrama undimmed by her knowledge that she would have slowly gone mad in a cloister. She rubbed at the freckles on the bridge of her nose as a smile crept across her face. Actually she'd nearly fulfilled that destiny. Her store was the second most quiet place on Earth, after a cloister.

Chantelle abruptly realized she was listening, hard. Another tiny smile nudged her lips. She took a deep breath and let it out in a long, tuneless whistle that drowned out the wind.

The beauty of this spot went beyond the massive peaks and lush forest. No highway scarred the green carpet. No houses pockmarked the landscape. There were no customers, no sisters, brothers, parents, uncles or cousins. No people at all.

Chantelle let her hair fall onto her neck as she leaned back on her elbows and extended her legs. The glacial breeze promptly tossed a ticklish auburn mass across her eye. She blew the hair off her cheek. The breeze volleyed the hair back, which brought a determined smile to Chantelle's face. She scrunched up her mouth for better aim and blew the hair away—only to lose out to the slam of an exceptionally strong gust. "Point, set and match," she murmured with a laugh.

Chantelle gazed to the west. An hour's walk in that direction was the mountain pass that marked the continental divide—and the back door to Alberta's Jasper National Park. Jasper had rules. Rules allowed a person to hike only with others. When she finished visiting this glacier she'd have to cross the park boundary just to know she'd hiked there alone despite their rules.

No, she wouldn't bother. Her pack was light compared to what she'd carried the last two days, but still she rubbed at the ache in her shoulders and stretched her legs like her cat, Trudeau, awakening from a nap.

It was amazing, though, how a few miles had loosened muscles she'd been sure would never function again after the hike to Berg Lake. The most discouraging moment had been on the first day, when two women jogged by her on the very steepest climb, when Chantelle was gasping with each tortured step.

The women had been friendly in the way of people meeting in the wilderness. It had turned out that they were no mere joggers but members of the Canadian Olympic team in training for a high-altitude meet in Mexico City. Talking to them with sweat rolling into her eyes, her chest heaving and muscles screaming, Chantelle had been inspired. That inspiration had forced her into taking this pathless side trip rather than groaning the whole day in her tent. And now, the memory of that inspiration roused her from her pleasant lethargy. After slipping her arms through the pack straps, she stood.

She was pivoting when it happened.

Loose rock slipped underfoot—only a few, small, glacially rounded marbles, she noticed with a spurt of annoyance. Annoyance burst into shock when she failed to regain her balance. Then, as if in slow motion, her boot lodged against a stubborn root, arms flailed but grasped nothing, pain exploded in her ankle. She fell backward. Hardness knocked the wind from her. She braced her arms wide, but handholds flashed by before she could reach them. Pebbles felt like boulders as she rolled over them. Helpless, she slid down the rocky slope.

Not far. A pond cushioned her fall. Water, fresh from the ice, stung her skin and invaded her eyes and mouth and threatened to trickle into her lungs. Shrieking and sputtering, Chantelle rose to her knees and wiped a cascade of hair off her face. The air tasted good, so good, and she strug-

gled to get her fill of it. Finally on hands and knees she tot-
tered to the shore. She lay there, hugging barren rock, as her
breathing gradually returned to something approaching
normal.

Her first rational thought was for her tape recorder. Ignoring the pains her movements sparked, she twisted till her
pack lay beside her. Her hands encountered a flood of wetness inside her pack, and at the bottom, her tape recorder
and camera. The camera didn't matter because she'd bought
it too recently to have become attached. But the recorder... She allowed herself a moment's silent mourning
for the friend that never refused to listen to her wandering
thoughts.

Wincing, Chantelle sat up to take stock of her situation.
Tomorrow she would undoubtedly be sore and speckled
with bruises, but the skin wasn't broken except for a trick-
ling scrape on her shoulder. Her twisted ankle was worse.
Though it throbbed in the tight confines of her boot, she
thought she could probably walk. All in all, she'd been
lucky. A real injury would have meant trouble since no one
here or back home knew her whereabouts within two
hundred miles.

The worst effect of the fall, aside from the tape recorder,
of course, was the soak in icy water. Wet clothes, combined
with a glacial breeze that had seemed refreshing only moments before, sent an ominous chill rippling along her spine.
Well, there was nothing she could do but wait for the sun to
dry her clothes, then begin a four- or five-mile hobble back
to the main provincial park trail where someone would
eventually come along to help. As for her ankle—well, a bit
of rest would do it good. The pond's cold water would help
control the swelling till she got to the stream where she'd
pitched her tent. It wasn't a pleasant prospect, but at least
the walk was downhill and the sky stayed light till after ten
o'clock.

Chantelle looked in all directions before she pulled her
knit top over her head and spread it on the rocks. The

northern sun glancing off her shoulders seemed weak and pitiful against the cold that frosted through her. Back in arid Kamloops, her jeans would sun-dry in an hour or so, but how long would it take at six thousand feet in the British Columbia Rockies? She glanced around again as she loosened her belt. At least there was little danger of anyone stumbling upon her like this.

Come to think of it, that wasn't very reassuring.

Grant Van Arden concentrated on keeping his stride the same length and speed on the slopes as on the flats. Concentrating on something mechanical like that transformed the steady rhythm of hiking into a peace and contentment that soothed his mind. Take three steps, then breathe. Three steps, breathe.

Grant didn't care about the glacier up ahead. He just didn't want to sit around camp all day like his weary trail mates. The trek from Jasper town to Mount Robson, a hundred and twenty rugged, wilderness miles, was nearly over. Grant didn't want it to end. The fifteen-miles-a-day springiness of his legs would deteriorate. His soaring spirits would slowly settle under the weight of responsibilities and civilization. When he got back to town he'd gladly resume his life and be grateful for these weeks of renewal, but right now he simply didn't want it to end.

He crested the loose rock of the ground moraine—a jumble of rocks and dirt deposited as the glacier melted, dotted here and there with turquoise pools—and breathed deeply of the fresh, crisp air. There was something immortal about secret mountain strongholds like this. Apollo, he thought, would have thrived in the splendor of this valley. Mount Robson, the loftiest peak in all the Canadian Rockies, would have made Zeus a more regal throne than puny Mount Olympus.

When he rounded a stone outcrop, surprise rattled through him. As if on cue, Venus lay just ahead.

It took Grant a startled heartbeat to comprehend that she was real. The woman was almost too perfect to be flesh and blood. Well, flesh, certainly, though not much more than could be seen on any beach. She lay on her back by a pond, with one arm covering her eyes. Her delicately rounded figure was showcased by matching, baby-blue underwear. Pale skin contrasted with dark hair whose reddish highlights seemed to dance and shimmer in the sun. One long, enticingly tapered leg dangled in the water, while the other was suggestively bent at the knee.

The casual eroticism of her posture jarred Grant to the realization that she didn't know he was watching.

No, he admitted to himself with a shake of his head. He wasn't just watching. He was staring at Venus's beauty like a boorish youth who knew no better. The lady obviously wouldn't appreciate it, either, since she had the modesty not to sunbathe in the nude despite her isolation.

Grant turned to leave, then stopped. Sunbathe? Here?

That made no sense. His gaze flicked back to her sensuous yet rather pale body. Well, he supposed that was all the tan a person could get in a place like this, but it was still strange to choose this exact spot. In a forest clearing, a couple hundred yards from the brisk, glacial down draft—maybe there. But not here.

Was she a member of the Polar Bear Club, that group that plunged into Vancouver's English Bay each New Year's Day? Was she simply hot after a day's hike? There was a story behind her pose, and to his annoyance—because he of all people valued privacy—he itched to know what it was.

Again, Grant turned to leave, then glanced back over his shoulder. This wasn't a crowded street where you ignored a stranger. In the bush, people were enough of a rarity that even city people saw fellow humans as allies. Grant rubbed his hand along the stubble of his jaw with an uncertain shake of his head.

He didn't see this woman just as an ally. He saw her as a highly desirable female, period. Maybe he'd been out on the trail too long.

Whatever the reason, he was irritated. He ran his knuckles along the prickly trail beard on his jaw and tried to stifle the involuntary glances that brushed her shapely legs despite his best intentions.

What the heck. With a grunt he began stalking toward the woman, not bothering to muffle his approach. He stopped and squatted down a scant six feet from her. She had to know he was there, yet her forearm remained over her eyes.

From this close, her garments were mere transparent wisps of low-cut lace. As he looked away, his lungs emptied in a long gust. Though it had never occurred to him before to wonder what underwear women chose for backpacking, he never would have suspected slinky things like these.

Slowly, through the haze of desire that held him motionless, Grant noticed details. Not just the scattering of freckles on finely sculpted cheeks or the mesmerizing fall and rise of lace as she breathed, either. Details, instead, about the precise way her jeans and striped top were stretched across rocks to allow air to get underneath them. Details about sunlight glinting off a microcassette recorder opened to the air. Details about a trickle of water running from the corner of an orange nylon pack to the edge of the pool.

With a guilty jolt Grant realized the story behind this pose. He grabbed for the pulse at her wrist and stared grimly at her full lips.

They were turning blue.

Everything looked fuzzy. Chantelle wasn't surprised, because that was how dreams were sometimes, especially when she was close to wakefulness. There was nothing fuzzy, however, about the arms that cradled her or the hard male chest that moved against her cheek with every step the man took. His chest was naked and her thighs were bare; so, it was one of *those* dreams. Well, that was fine. Dream-men were safe to love. Dream-men disappeared in the morning, but they left your heart intact.

Should she be thinking about that in the middle of a dream itself? This was a strange dream. Long-denied needs moved through her body, not like a warm blast of passion but like the north wind whistling through a cold void that was eager to be filled with warmth and love. She snuggled against the comforting heat of his flesh, prepared to follow her dream wherever it led.

It seemed to lead nowhere, though. Despite the almost-real friction of flesh against flesh, he just kept carrying her. It was frustrating, but then dreams were like that, too, sometimes—running desperately yet never getting anywhere, that sort of thing.

The stranger's skin was warm and inviting, while she felt so cold and separate. Why didn't he consume her with the raging fires of passion, make her feel safe and alive and comfortable? She wanted that. Wanted *him*. His male nipple appeared before her. She seized it between her lips, then ran her teeth provocatively along it to urge him on. She wanted to get to the good part before she awoke or the dream transformed into something less appealing, like a giant green ape ravaging her precious first editions.

But the man just walked. She wriggled her hand free and rubbed it pointedly across his abdomen. Amazing how *real* the woolen texture of his pants felt. This was a marvelous dream.

She felt a bounce as the man shifted her in his arms so that she could no longer caress him. Darn. With a frustrated sigh, Chantelle snuggled her face against his shoulder and drifted back into nothingness.

Her dreams after that were vague and disjointed. There was more walking, then shifting shadows and hard ground. At one point the harsh croak of a jay seemed to say something crucial, something important, something about ice and loneliness that was just beyond her comprehension.

She half awoke when the man placed her on something soft. He loomed over her, blocking out the darkening blue of the sky, then bent to stroke her face. A masculine, strong touch. Nice. Strange, too. Instead of caressing her he held her eyelid open wide and leaned close. Very close.

Maybe he wanted to play doctor? She giggled. Delighted at having a second chance, she draped a heavy arm around his neck and urged his lips to hers. At first his kiss was cold, but after she slipped her tongue between his lips he finally responded with the fervor and skill only a dream-man could possess. The kiss seemed to go on and on, with delight following delight. This dream-man knew every nuance of pleasure the female mouth was capable of, including many that were new to Chantelle. And, she suspected, to womankind in general. Wonderful. Too bad in a way that she was enjoying it too much to remember all of his techniques. There was a book to be written about this kiss. Books. How was Ricki doing with the bookstore?

She never knew when the kiss ended.

There was confusion and darkness, followed by leaping brightness and warmth. Fire, or passion? Passion, she guessed. The lean heat of his body against hers was too vivid for anything else. The man covered her with a blanket. They must be finished making love. She should feel more satisfied than this, more cozy. Not so cold. You couldn't trust dream-men. Dream-men were lousy lovers. Good kissers but lousy lovers. The story of her life.

A hot, tasteless drink dribbled down her throat. Hot water? Strange. She coughed viciously, but wanted more. After several sips she turned her lips from the cup.

And then there was just hazy sleep, broken by wild, frustrating bouts of almost passion that were quelled by firm, gentle hands on her shoulders and forehead.

Something was moving toward her. Chantelle's eyes opened blearily. A gray stellar's jay was in the act of snatching a crumb of breakfast from near a burned-out fire.

The bird seemed significant, almost but not quite familiar. Certainly no threat. Reassured, she closed her eyes.

Only for a moment. Her eyes flew open and darted around, though she kept her body rigid. A crude but effective lean-to sheltered her from the morning sky. A camper's reflective blanket was wrapped around her. Her clothes were folded neatly, more neatly than she ever bothered, on a fallen log.

Where was she? She remembered falling and soaking her ankle and trying to dry her clothes. She remembered being cold, very cold, and yet too drowsy to do anything but drift into numbness. She must have been delirious when she was rescued.

Rescued? Something about being rescued. Yes, she remembered a fire. Remembered the croak of a jay.

Chantelle squeezed her eyes shut as a moan escaped from her soul. Unfortunately she also remembered a man.

She remembered making love.

A cheerful whistling announced that she was not alone. A muscular man stepped into view from a sparse clump of evergreens, carrying an armload of sticks. He wore no shirt, which seemed familiar. His pants were a dark gray wool. That seemed definitely familiar. The details were vague—except for the texture of his pants, which was crushingly vivid—but with a burning, boiling flood of mortification Chantelle realized that she had already thanked her rescuer, thoroughly and brazenly.

The man noticed her stare. "Hello, Venus. You're awake." He stepped over a fallen log with the easy grace of a mountain lion. When he laid the sticks beside the burned-out fire he beamed at her with a smug grin that confirmed her worst fears. "Feeling better, I trust."

"No thanks to you," she spat.

His blue eyes narrowed, yet his smile remained in place. Despite his light blond hair, his skin was deeply tanned. It was the kind of tan a fashionable businessman might sport, yet on him it was the brand of the wilderness. Perhaps it was the hint of a beard on his face, or the casual way he sat on the ground that showed he was totally at home out here. Whatever it was, this stranger, and her memories, made her dangerously aware of her vulnerable femininity.

"I'm glad you're feeling better," he said in a commanding baritone. "Would you like breakfast? All we have is dried fruit, I'm afraid."

"I'd like you to put on a shirt. You do have a shirt, don't you?"

His answering chuckle was a sensuous rumble. He pointed to her with an intimate, insulting smile. "As a matter of fact, you're wearing it."

Chantelle pulled the blanket up to her chin. He was right. Not only that, she wore almost nothing *but* his shirt. The tight swathing around her ankle didn't count. She managed to clamp her jaws on a hysterical screech of rage, but her voice bristled with tightly controlled forcefulness. "Give me my damn clothes."

The smile vanished from his rugged face. A frown dashed across his features before submerging under a mask of neutrality. With one hand he casually began to build a meticulous pyramid of kindling atop the cold embers, stick by maddening stick. He made building a fire look easy, though Chantelle knew from experience it wasn't. His macho attitude and outdoors skill infuriated her more. Each time he moved a certain way she could see three scars running parallel across his shoulder blade. Probably, she thought, gouged by some woman's fingernails.

"It seems to me," he said at last, "that you ought to ask more politely than that."

"Give me my clothes!"

"Now, that wasn't polite at all." But then he glanced at her with a sudden concern that bounced off the armor of her anger. "Are you cold?"

Chantelle propped herself on one elbow, still hugging the blanket. Neither bone-deep weakness nor masses of aches and pains could blunt her outrage. "No, I'm not cold. Not that you care, you creep."

He struck a match against the sole of his boot, making a noise startlingly like a human sigh. Chantelle wouldn't have been surprised if he'd struck it across the expanse of his chest. No expression showed on his face as he flicked his hand out to light the fire—which, unlike her attempts, blazed with the first match. "Lady," he said slowly, almost negligently. "I just saved your life. Where I come from it's customary to thank someone who saves your life."

This, from a man who'd taken advantage of her delirium? God save her from waking dream-men! "Where you come from, mister, people have nasty, perverted customs."

She thought he'd get angry. Instead his bare chest shook, and his granite face relaxed into a smile as he rumbled out a laugh. The rumble grew to a roar that filled the wilderness with the unmistakable presence of Man.

It was the last straw. Chantelle pushed herself from the lean-to and tried to stomp toward her clothes with as much bare-legged dignity as possible.

She managed less than a step. She wobbled immediately, and as soon as her left foot touched the ground she crumpled cruelly to her hands and knees.

Damn. She'd been planning to walk five miles on that ankle? Damn, damn, damn.

She wanted to crawl through the sticky mass of exhaustion and pain toward her clothes. She sank to the harsh ground, instead. All the tiredness and agony that her anger had camouflaged cascaded out, inundating her will and leaving her helpless to struggle. She hated being dependent, yet she knew beyond a glimmer of hope that she had no choice. Hate it or not, she needed this stranger.

That thought should have made her angry but instead it drained her anger away. At the moment, without her stubborn pride she was nothing. A bundle of jelly. A stuffed scarecrow. She lacked the energy to fight or argue or defend herself. She wanted to crawl into her own bed, away from this horrid man, pull her grandmother's quilt up to her nose and sleep till August. That wasn't too much to ask, was it?

In a minute, she thought wearily. I'll get up in a minute.

"Help me," she whispered.

The man was at her side instantly. He enveloped her in his arms and guided her back to the pallet of branches and boughs. "I apologize," he said gently as he pulled the blanket around her. "I should have known better. You've had a bad shock, you're bruised, your ankle is sprained and you just woke from a nasty fever. Hypothermia is worse than people think." He felt her forehead with his palm, then nodded in approval. "Do you still insist on getting dressed?"

Chantelle nodded her head. Now that her brief burst of anger was over she felt drained and hollow. Though she felt pain, it was the unutterable weariness that bottled the words inside her.

The man disappeared for a moment, then placed her jeans and blouse on her stomach. "Here you are."

When she didn't move, he asked her gently, dispassionately, "Do you need help?"

Of course she did, but that didn't mean she'd take it. She didn't answer for a long time. Which was worse, she wondered, the indignity of allowing a lascivious stranger to dress her, or lying out in the open in boudoir panties and a nightmare-lover's shirt? And if he tried something now, while she was conscious and aware...

She made an effort to sit up. Her body decided for her. "Okay," she grumbled. "Help me."

"That's a good girl," he said with a reassuring smile.

Chantelle gritted her teeth at being dismissed as a girl, then looked away as he pulled the blanket off her, not quite daring to see the expression on his face. To her surprise, though, the ordeal of letting him put on her jeans and shirt passed with impersonal efficiency. He touched her no more than was necessary, and when she peeked at him his eyes were behaving themselves. If she didn't know what a reprehensible creep he was, the brushing of his thumb against her skin might have felt halfway reassuring. The man's bedside manner was good, she had to admit. Almost as if he'd had practice.

Words fell from her tongue before her weary brain could censor them. "Have you done this before?"

He glanced at her as he buttoned the waistband of her jeans. "Done what?"

Chantelle bit the inside of her lip. Of course he'd done this sort of thing before, at least once before to her, personally. But then, she'd rather not think about that. "Saved someone's life."

His shoulders rippled in a small shrug. "I guess so."

"You guess so?"

He didn't elaborate. If he had, she might have scoffed. Instead she believed. He was the type, she realized, to march around saving lives. It was one thing his type might actually be good at. Saving lives and, she recalled, kissing.

She turned her head toward the airy shadows of the pines. "I feel like taking a nap."

"That's the best thing for you." He sat back on his haunches and looked at her seriously. "But first, tell me your name."

"Chantelle DuMaurier." He nodded, then looked at her as if expecting her to ask his name. Instead she yawned.

"Where are you from, Chantelle?"

"Two hundred and fifty miles down the highway, on the British Columbia side. Kamloops."

"Hey, I do my shopping in Kamloops. I'm from Clearwater. We're almost neighbors."

"Seventy-five miles hardly makes us neighbors, mister."

He shrugged, as if her rude tone meant nothing to him. Chantelle turned her face from the sight of his bare torso, but not even exhaustion could exterminate all the tingling in her skin.

Damn. With a frustrated sigh that turned into another yawn halfway through, she forced herself to look back at him. From the way his eyebrows were drawn together, she figured a lecture was coming about hiking alone in the wilderness. A small surge of anger echoed through her at the thought of an unprincipled man like him lecturing her about anything—and, worse, having the right to lecture her.

"Chantelle, I need to leave you for a little bit, and if you take a nap that will give me the chance. The people I hike with will be getting worried, and I need to pick up food and a tent and sleeping bag. If you tell me where you camped, I'll get your things, too. I'll hurry back, I promise."

"Okay." A tent and sleeping bag. That meant he realized she wasn't ready to hike out of here, and was willing to help her. She tried to staunch her near teariness, but had a harder time than she expected. At least he decided to skip the lecture.

In as few words as possible, she described where she'd pitched her tent. As much as she hated it, she did need this man. Being pleasant to him was no big price to pay for his help. Though of course she vowed never again to be as nice to him as last night.

Well, she thought, now was as good a time as any to start being pleasant. "I don't have any relatives in Clearwater."

He paused in the act of picking up his shirt. But of course that remark must sound silly.

"We're even," he said. "I don't have any relatives in Kamloops. Big family, eh?"

Chantelle nodded. The long scars on his back rippled as he slipped on his shirt. "How did you get the scars?"

"A bear." He added wood to the fire, oblivious to her startled intake of breath.

"Did it happen here in the Rockies?"

He looked at her then, alarm clouding his clear blue eyes. "No, Chantelle. Don't worry, you're safe here. It happened two years and two hundred miles from here. A garbage-dump bear with no fear of people wandered by my house one evening as I was cooking. He invited himself to dine and took exception to my complaints about his table manners."

A shiver raced along Chantelle's spine, and she wasn't sure if it was because of her physical condition or his tale. "What happened?"

He shrugged. "I had bear meat that winter. Bearburger is passable with lots of ketchup."

His blue eyes were warm and forceful, and when he took her hand in his it felt surprisingly gentle for a hand that had conquered a wild beast. "I don't want you to worry, Chantelle. That was a dump bear. He was so used to people that he became contemptuous. Bears like that are the most dangerous kind. Bush bears are more scared of you than the other way around." He held her shoulders and locked his gaze with hers. "I'll only be gone a few hours. Maybe less. It's important that someone know where we are and that we get food. Do you understand?"

The bed of boughs rustled as Chantelle nodded. Anyone born and raised in the B.C. Interior, where wilderness was inevitably visible through the living-room window, knew about bears. Kamloops-area rattlers posed as much of a threat as bears, yet she never let them deter her.

Actually, after the way she'd exploded at him, she was more concerned that he might not return than she was of bears. "Do you mean to say that the great Northwoodsman can't forage off the land for the two of us?"

He stood, and his legs stretched long and firm over her. The corners of his mouth bobbed into a brief but hearty smile. "Precisely," he said. "The berries aren't ripe yet, so anything edible up here isn't worth eating. Take my word for it."

Chantelle settled back against the surprisingly soft bed he'd made for her. She was so exhausted that she doubted she'd even notice he was gone. "I'll be fine. I'm used to taking care of myself."

"Yeah, sure." His skeptical tone and the lifting of his eyebrows would have started an argument at any other time. She let it pass.

Before he left, he gave her water and dried apples. He also gave her his pocketknife, a clublike stick and two tin cups to bang together to frighten off bears. He then insisted a bear wouldn't venture closer than a mile. His concern for her fear—she wasn't frightened, but he refused to believe that—was rather comical.

Also, she decided reluctantly, rather touching.

Chapter Two

What did she remember for certain? Not dream things, but real happenings?

Chantelle gingerly rolled from her back to her side, seeking without much success a comfortable position. She had slept for a long while, and the mattress branches were re-emerging as branches. On top of that, the sun was hot on her face. The heat reminded her that the sunscreen was in her tent, which reminded her of where she was and why, and of what she thought had happened, and of the nameless man and what she'd said to him.

Chantelle flung her arm over her forehead, then regretted the rash gesture when her muscles shrieked a protest.

What, exactly, did she remember?

Fact 1: He had carried her. That much she not only remembered but could deduce from the fact that she was away from the scene of the accident.

Fact 2: She had made a shameless pass at him as he carried her. That part was too vivid to be dream. It was embarrassing, considering that he turned out to be real rather than a dream, but it was totally excusable given the circumstances. Wasn't it?

Fact 3: The man had ignored her blatant intimacies and tended to her needs. Instead of ravaging her then and there he had carried her to safety, wrapped her ankle expertly and built shelter and a fire.

Fact 4: She had kissed him. As she recalled, his was a good kiss. A great kiss. A world-class, Olympic-quality kiss that had stirred dreams of a marathon. Of course, that could be delirium, because after the kiss everything was vague. She remembered *thinking* they had made love. But— and this was a key point—she didn't remember actually doing it. As a matter of fact, every surviving memory after the kiss did not include making love.

Fact 5: In the first hazy minutes after awakening she'd jumped to conclusions and then been impolite, boorish, ungrateful and downright improper.

So, fact 6: The man was perhaps a great kisser, but on the basis of the evidence he probably hadn't done anything else, aside from saving her life. At the very least, she owed him the effort to find out what had happened before condemning him. At the most, she owed him an abject apology, and her life.

A new thought roused her to full wakefulness. If he was a hero, a thank-you kiss would be in order and she could learn if he kissed as well in real life as in a dream.

Chantelle smiled under the secure cover of her arm. She could almost hear her sister Ricki challenge her to find out how well the stranger could kiss. Last year Ricki, the youngest DuMaurier child, had left the orchard to live with her while attending Cariboo College. Her baby sister had all the social instincts and bravery that Chantelle herself lacked. In truth, Ricki was as much of a social kamikaze as...well, as she herself had been with this mountain. But with men? Chantelle's idea of a good date was to curl up with a book that had a dashing hero. Or even one without.

Chantelle wondered how her sister was managing with the bookstore. Not that her used bookstore was so busy Ricki couldn't cope. At times—surprisingly many times, actually—Chantelle appreciated the advantages of a large family. Summer holidays, for example, when she didn't have to worry about the quality of the fill-in help.

Now if she could only convince Ricki to spend less time socializing and more time studying...

A noise from behind jerked her eyes open wide. Without moving, she strained her ears. She heard it again. A footstep. Not a bird this time, either. Something big, shuffling toward her with irregular steps. Exactly the way a wary but curious bear might approach.

Chantelle's hand was beside the club the man had left behind. She grasped it, then waited with a pounding heart and a thick, salty taste in her mouth. The steps came closer, halted perhaps ten feet behind her, just out of sight. She tightened her grip.

Another step. Too close.

Chantelle hurled the stick blindly. She heard a fleshy thump and a yelp, then she struggled to sit up.

The blond man was rubbing at his knee. The huge pack on his back made him appear to be on the verge of toppling over as he glared at her. "Are you trying to kill me?"

Relief washed the fear from her system, leaving behind a light-headed sense of safety. It was good, she realized, not to be alone in the wilderness.

She propped her head on her hand and watched as he squatted to slip the pack from his shoulders. The gray crags of Mount Robson framed his unruly blond hair.

"I told you I could take care of myself," she said.

His brow furrowed and the corner of his mouth hardened into a rigid line. "Yes, and I can tell that you enjoyed this demonstration of your competence. I bet you're going to claim you thought I was a grizzly."

"That's right. I did."

He nodded his head, but his hard blue eyes pierced her with obvious disbelief. "Sure."

Chantelle knew she'd made a mistake in throwing the stick, but if he'd been a bear it might have been a mistake not to throw it. Though she was sorry she'd hurt him, his attitude halted words of apology. Still, she kept her voice civil. "What do you expect when you sneak up on me like that?"

"I was trying not to disturb you." He held the club she'd thrown in one hand and tapped it against the ground as if it was a drumstick. "Next time, I won't bother to try."

"That's fine with me, mister." Chantelle disliked men who had to flaunt their strength as he was doing with his stern voice and his menacing clubbing of the ground. Who did he think he was, Tarzan?

She crossed her arms over her chest and stared at the sky. This reunion wasn't going the way she wanted. Not at all. Darn. She wanted to explain and apologize and be pleasant. Instead the man sat there with a face like a summer storm, and the words clogged inside her.

He crossed the campsite to stand near her. From her position he loomed like a giant, his arms crossed so that the muscles of his forearms stood out lean and corded past the rolled-up sleeves of his plaid shirt. The view would have been an intriguing study in virility if his face wasn't so stern and overpowering.

"Look, Chantelle," he said in a voice as cool as yesterday's glacial breeze, "despite what I've done, you've been rude to me, sworn at me, shouted at me and tried to break my kneecap. Well, I'm not stupid. I've received your message loud and clear. For some reason you don't like me, and I, for obvious reasons—well, let's just say the feeling is mutual."

Chantelle swallowed hard. She opened her mouth to speak, but before she could figure out what to say he was plowing onward.

"You are one of the most exasperating, ungrateful and uncooperative females it's ever been my misfortune to meet. You deserve to be left here to fend for yourself till your ankle heals, but I'm not going to do that. Do you know why?"

Though he didn't wait for an answer, Chantelle shook her head mutely.

"Because I refuse to have you on my conscience. No matter what, I'm going to make sure you get out of here in good health." His gaze shifted to the dark trees behind her as his face tensed in a sudden hint of sorrow that, she felt, had nothing to do with her. He paused only briefly, but long enough for Chantelle to wonder what memory had caused that flicker of pain and determination. "You might as well get used to the idea that we're going to be together whether you like it or not. I know I sure won't like it."

He squatted beside her, so that his face filled her vision with an unflinching granite that brooked no contradiction. "So we need to get a few things straight. I'm in charge. Period. If you do any thinking you'll probably get us both killed, so plan on disconnecting your brain. Preferably your mouth, as well."

A lump collected in Chantelle's throat as she narrowed her eyes and glared at him. Ignoring her expression, he leaned forward to take her shoulders in his hands. She wanted to bury her face in those strong hands and shut out everything that had happened in the past two days—the accident, her foolish behavior when she was sick, his biting anger. But his relentless voice held her motionless.

"A trail partner of mine will drop off your gear later today. When you're able to walk I'll help you to the Yellowhead Highway. If I can still stand the sight of you by then I'll expect you to drive me to my place, since my friends will have left already. After that you can go back to Kamloops and complain about the way I treated a helpless tourist who bungled into a life-threatening situation by sheer stupidity."

He jerked to a stop as if his soaring anger had abruptly spent its momentum and fallen to earth. It wasn't just that he paused for breath. As he shook his head, his whole expression softened and his grip eased on her shoulders.

Chantelle's eyes felt watery as they gazed into his, mesmerized. Though she still said nothing—what could she say, when he was partly right?—she searched for understanding with her eyes. A strange lassitude kept her silent, kept her from fighting back. She was exhausted and ill and a bit ashamed. More than anything else, though, she simply wasn't capable of dealing with his anger. Not now. Later, she knew, her anger could match his, spark for spark. Later, but not now.

Then he did something totally unexpected. He kissed her.

Chantelle was so surprised that her eyes remained frozen open as his face swooped toward hers. She saw the determined set of his jaw and the parting of his lips. She saw his eyes close just before his flesh touched hers. She saw, fuzzily and out of focus, the furrows on his forehead disappear as he pressed his demanding mouth on hers. With an insistence that she couldn't overcome—though she didn't try very hard, she realized—his tongue probed and thrust at her lips, teasing them into surrendering the tender secrets of her mouth.

Then and only then, with the deep caresses of his lips and tongue sending urgent messages catapulting along her nerves, did Chantelle's eyes slip closed. Without sight to distract her, she knew only the hunger of his kiss and the foolish hammering of her heart as it sent blood coursing through her veins like an awakened river. She heard herself whimper and realized she was bobbing without willpower on the flash flood of sensations hurtling through her. Surrendering to the passion, she raised her hand toward the back of his head to urge the kiss to eternity. She felt a single strand of hair tickle her palm—

And then he pulled away from the kiss as abruptly as he'd begun it. His eyes were cloudy and troubled, not the eyes of a lover. She dropped her hand to the blanket, thankful she'd been saved the embarrassment of completing that small gesture of intimate capitulation.

"I don't even know your name," she whispered.

The man sat back on his heels. The sudden distance between them was like a splash of cold water, shocking Chantelle to reality. Never in her life had she been kissed by a man before she knew his name, or even before she'd known him for weeks. She simply didn't do things like that.

But then, never in her life had she been kissed quite so thoroughly. Name or no name.

"Grant Van Arden," he said.

"I'm glad to meet you, Grant." Chantelle nodded, then extended her hand toward him. It felt like a strange thing to do, considering that they had just shared something far more intimate than a handshake, yet Grant shook her hand solemnly and without comment. Chantelle shifted her eyes away from his when he continued to hold her hand longer than custom dictated. Sparks of awareness shot along her palm from the point where his flesh touched hers. Finally she slipped her hand away and tucked it beside her.

Grant's mind was reeling as he crossed the campsite to put as much space as possible between him and this bewitching beauty who had dropped into his life with a backpack full of complications. Slowly and deliberately, he began to sort things from his hastily packed bag. Pan. Camp stove. Foil-wrapped dehydrated meals. Miniature plastic salt and pepper shakers.

He kept his gaze off Chantelle, though his peripheral vision told him she watched as he worked. She was silent, too. Maybe they both needed time to digest the fireworks that had rocketed between them.

To his surprise, Grant felt an almost overpowering desire for this difficult and provocative young woman. Ending that kiss had called for strength that went beyond muscles and sinews. Ending that kiss had been astonishingly difficult.

Astonishing was the word for her, all right. Oh, she was an attractive woman, and their first encounter had emphasized her feminine charms. But he was astonished that he couldn't appreciate her freckled face and sensuous body as another example of nature's perfection without losing control. Yet he had lost control, and not just when he kissed her. He had lost control as well when his temper flared, glazing his desire under a veneer of anger that was, in retrospect, an excuse to kiss her.

He unpacked the nested silverware that they would have to share, unless Chantelle had planned this trip better than she'd so far indicated and brought silverware. In that case, Ariel would bring it up with the rest of Chantelle's gear.

Ariel had never confused him. Whatever promise of desire existed between him and his trail partner had sprouted naturally out of the fertile ground of friendship. Ariel had helped him through rough times, had become his confidante, had goaded him into rebuilding his life rather than wasting away as a bitter hermit. But she had never confused him.

The desire he felt for Chantelle was confusing because casual sexual encounters held no attraction for him, and never had. There was no virtue involved, in the same way that there was no virtue involved in his abstention from tobacco or alcohol. He disliked both and saw no reason to bother acquiring the taste. In the same way, the woman beneath the skin had to be worth the bother of acquiring the taste. A strange woman could stir his senses, but never his heart.

Except for Chantelle, who was his responsibility. Who needed his help without the unfair attachment of sexual strings. Who was, in a very real sense, his patient, with all the ramifications for honor and decency and sacred trust that this entailed. Who might feel obligated to him—though obligation certainly wasn't apparent—and give in to his desire out of fear of abandonment or out of gratitude.

He chuckled and shook his head. Out of gratitude? He was kidding himself if he thought that. Give her time and she might show verbal gratitude—maybe—but she was obviously too much her own woman to give sexual favors casually.

No, it wasn't Chantelle he had to worry about. It was himself, as that unfortunate kiss had proved. He was surprised she hadn't scratched his eyes out after that unwarranted bit of overfamiliarity.

Her ankle was only sprained. He'd felt neither broken bones nor torn ligaments. A couple of days, then; he needed something to keep his mind and hands busy for a couple of days. Something to get his mind off the scent of attraction that wafted from this fractious female.

Well, she would need a crutch to help her walk. In the past two years he'd become a passable whittler. After starting water for soup he took the club she'd aimed at him and began shaping the pine with his hatchet.

The blows of the hatchet chipped at Chantelle's nerves. After an hour of chopping, Grant must still be angry. He'd said little throughout lunch, and she'd reacted with silence of her own. It had been a tense silence, because the memory of the kiss hung in the air between them like a veil that distorted everything Chantelle observed. His long, graceful fingers, more suited to a pianist than an outdoorsman, had seemed to weave seductively as they performed the prosaic chore of fixing soup. The deep, incisive cadence of his speech, which tended to brisk commands and firm utterances, had seemed almost musical as he complained mechanically about the sameness of trail food.

But that kiss...

He had answered all her idle questions about whether the real Grant was as sexy as the dream Grant, then left her dangling in irritating silence. After lunch, she'd promised herself, she would get her mind off him.

But after lunch Grant had resumed chopping that stick into short pieces, till she wanted to chop him into pieces, as well.

The distant sound of a human voice cut through both nature's and man's noises. Chantelle shaded her eyes with one hand and pointed with the other. "Someone's coming."

Grant waved to the newcomer, then eagerly strode toward the woman. The two of them stood talking with many a gesture toward Chantelle, maddeningly just out of earshot so that all she could hear was the buzz of their words.

Grant's trail partner? Chantelle's irritation grew sharper. His so-called *trail partner* was not a burly man with a four-day growth of beard, but a sturdy-looking woman whose lustrous brown hair seemed to rebel against confinement in a ponytail. She looked to be a few years older than Chantelle, perhaps early thirties. As the two of them started to walk toward the campsite, Grant took the woman's arm with an easy familiarity that made Chantelle rue that kiss all over again.

Grant's friend smiled in her direction. Despite travel-worn clothes and lack of makeup, her high cheekbones and even features were as outstanding as her buxom figure. Chantelle would normally find herself drawn to a woman who looked this good yet wasn't afraid to sweat, but not now.

The woman extended her hand in friendship. "Hello. I'm Ariel Johnson."

"Chantelle DuMaurier. Pleased to meet you."

Ariel slipped a familiar green packsack off her back. "I brought your things. At least I hope they're yours." Her laughter was simple and unforced, the kind of laugh that invited you to join in. "Otherwise some poor camper is going to go crazy trying to find a policeman to whom to report a robbery."

"It's mine," Chantelle replied. "Thank you very much."

Grant made an unintelligible noise, as if to point out that she'd never said those simple words to him. She ignored him as she rummaged through one of the pockets on the outside of the pack. With a sigh, she pulled out a small comb and mirror.

Excluding Grant from her conversation, Chantelle talked directly to Ariel as she started to pull at her hair, grimacing occasionally as she encountered a tangle. "Ahh, the joys of civilization. I can't tell you, Ariel, how much I've been wanting a comb. My hair got wet yesterday and I couldn't do anything about it."

"Yesterday," Grant said, "you weren't in any condition to do anything about it."

Ariel smiled over at him. The gesture had the same practiced ease as Grant's fire-making skill. Chantelle felt like an interloper.

"I think," Ariel said, "we can safely say the lady is on the mend, since she's becoming concerned about her hair. How long do you think it will be before she can walk out of here, Grant?"

"Well, I haven't examined her yet—I thought maybe you could give me a hand with that, Ariel—but I'd say another three or four days. Then we'll have to take it easy on the way down, make the trip in three days instead of one and a half."

The comb stilled in Chantelle's hand. A week? A whole week, with a man who kissed like that? She didn't know whether to cry or laugh.

Then, as another thought occurred to her, her eyebrows pulled together and her lips tightened. Examine her? Who did this fellow think he was, a hotshot doctor? She'd best get in on this discussion, instead of letting him decide everything on his own. "Are you going to be staying with us here, Ariel?"

"No. I'm attending summer school down in Kelowna next week, and I need to leave with the rest of our group. I guess it will just be you and Grant."

"I see." Chantelle hugged her arms around herself and withdrew from the conversation. She looked from Grant, who appeared totally and yet unconvincingly disinterested, to Ariel. The other woman's forehead was wrinkled in a frown, as if disturbed at the prospect of abandoning a fellow woman into a stranger's clutches for a week.

Or more likely, Chantelle thought as she watched Ariel laugh and joke with Grant, it was the other way around. She was worried about leaving Grant alone with a strange female.

In any case, the idea was unsettling to Chantelle, too. She wasn't sure she trusted herself around him, and she wasn't certain Grant was trustworthy. Oh, he probably was, though she had grounds for doubts, but a week of enforced togetherness would wear veneers thin and expose the real man underneath the civilization. She doubted any female would feel totally safe around a man such as Grant.

But mostly, the idea was unsettling because of the tingle that seemed to linger on her lips.

Chantelle ran her hand over her eyes, shutting out the sight of Grant and Ariel examining her stock of freeze-dried food with the eagerness of campers too long on the trail. Seven long days when Grant would be her only companion, her nursemaid, her protector. The very thought made Chantelle panicky to be back in her own little house, in her own environment, where she was in charge and the world behaved as it should.

Wishing wouldn't make it so. Chantelle took a deep breath and turned to the older woman. "While you're here, Ariel, I wonder if you could help me get changed. I've worn these clothes for two days now." She probably didn't need the help because she was feeling so much better, but it gave her an excuse to get rid of Grant for a few minutes.

"Certainly." Ariel moved the green backpack so Chantelle could search for a change of clothes. Then the older woman began shooing Grant away with both hands. "In case you didn't get the hint, men aren't welcome for the next few minutes."

He rubbed his hand along his jaw. "I need to shave, anyway. I'll be over by the creek if you need me." He pointed in the direction of the thickest growth of trees. "Oh, Ariel, while you're at it check the scrape on her shoulder to see if it's getting infected."

Ariel stared at Grant's back as he left, then shook her head. "The man is going to shave? I don't believe it." She glanced over at Chantelle, a brittle smile pulsing across her mouth. "Or maybe I do."

Chantelle chose to ignore the implication. She glanced nervously to ensure that Grant had disappeared into the trees before she pulled fresh clothes and underwear from the pack. She didn't want to hear hints that he found her attractive. He already seemed threatening enough.

"When I get back," Ariel asked, "is anyone you want me to contact for you?"

"I live with my sister. You could let her know I'll be back in a week or so, but don't worry her. Just tell her I'm delayed."

"You live with your sister?"

Chantelle nodded, wondering why that information brought a smile to Ariel's face. With a careful shrug, she removed her blouse. "Is Grant one of those men who walks around like an unshaven caveman?"

Ariel's laugh held gentle amusement. "Grant, a caveman? Hardly. He's quite dapper when the occasion demands." She helped Chantelle untangle her arm from a sleeve and carefully folded the blouse. "Here, let me look at that scratch on your back. Ah. It seems to be fine."

Ariel's face turned in the direction of the clump of trees where the man had disappeared. "I guess that's the problem. Grant dresses to the occasion, and lately he must have felt there was no reason to dress up. He wouldn't have shaved for another couple of days out on the trail." She paused briefly, then tore her gaze away from the trees and laughed again. "Until this trip I never would have believed that Grant, the only teacher on our staff who wears a tie every day, had a bit of the slob in him."

"He's a *teacher?*"

"High-school science, and I'm the head of the English Department."

"A teacher?"

"Yes. Why, what's wrong with being a teacher?"

"Nothing's wrong with being a teacher." Chantelle abruptly remembered what she was supposed to be doing, and squirmed into the last of her clothes. She sat up as straight as possible and looked Ariel in the eye. Grant, a teacher? "They sure didn't have teachers like him where I went to school."

Ariel laughed gently. "Nor anywhere else, I'd guess. We assign Grant all the problem children, and he never notices because they never even start to act up for him. The boys don't dare, and the girls all fall in love with him. It's safe to say Grant is the best-loved man in Clearwater." She glanced up from folding Chantelle's clothes. "He's quite oblivious to the effect he has on people, you know."

Chantelle stared at the dark pines where Grant had gone. "It's just that . . . well, he doesn't seem like a teacher."

Ariel's brow wrinkled. She nodded as if Chantelle had said something sad and profound. "I'd hoped he could be content with it, but I'm afraid you're right." She lifted her head, and her serious expression was swept away by another quick, gentle laugh. "I'm curious what you thought Grant did for a living."

"I didn't have anything specific in mind." Chantelle waved her hands in the general direction of the trees that carpeted the lower slopes of the valley, as if that explained something. "If I had to guess, though, I'd say he was a logger."

"Grant, a logger? That's priceless! I can just picture him with a double-bit ax slung over his shoulder." Ariel curled her feet under her thighs and leaned forward. "What would you guess is his favorite drink?"

"Oh, I don't know. Moosehead beer."

"Try tea with a strong twist of lemon. What about his favorite TV show?"

Chantelle smiled at the other woman's eagerness. *"Hockey Night in Canada."*

Ariel clapped and shook her head. "News shows and—" she wrinkled her nose "—boring CBC sagas. What's his favorite pastime?"

Wild, passionate sex with bewitched young ladies.

Chantelle momentarily found it hard to breathe. Had she said that aloud? No, thank God. She shoved away the vivid image as being outside the spirit of the moment.

Chantelle ran her tongue lightly along her lips, thinking. For some reason she was willing to play along with this game about Grant Van Arden, even though she noticed the not-so-subtle sparkle that danced in the other woman's brown eyes as she imparted her intimate knowledge. "Hunting and fishing."

"Wrong again. Reading."

"Reading?" Chantelle cocked her head in the direction of the creek, but the band of trees still hid Grant from view. She had once joked that instead of going to pubs to meet men she should go to bookstores. Ricki had laughed and said that she'd assumed that was why Chantelle owned a bookstore.

"My," Ariel said. "Grant certainly gave you a wrong first impression. I won't let him live this down. But you see, dear, Grant isn't the gruff hooligan you've imagined." She placed a hand on Chantelle's arm and leaned forward to stare earnestly into her face. "He's the most honorable man I've ever known. You're safe with him."

"Safe?" Then why did she feel the exact opposite of safe around Grant?

"Completely." Ariel smiled again, then her face grew serious. "Chantelle, you seem to be a lady. Grant won't allow himself a serious relationship, and he has old-fashioned standards about toying with a lady's affections."

Ariel paused, studying her hands as if flustered, then glanced up and smiled quickly. "On top of everything else, Grant used to be—" she glanced back down at her hands

"—well, let's just say he's capable of caring for you. We talked about this, the other four hikers in our party, that is, and there's no question but that Grant is the ideal person for this job. If we didn't believe that we'd cancel our plans and stay with you. Don't worry. You'll be safe with Grant."

Chantelle nodded in surprise and gratitude. Though Ariel wore her heart on her sleeve, that little game about Grant hadn't been staged only to stake Ariel's claim, but to allay Chantelle's fears as well. With a smile at her new friend Chantelle absently trailed a knuckle across lips that still tingled.

Grant tossed one last pebble into the creek, then studied the patterns of the cascading water. The snow-fed creek leaped noisily over its bed of rocks in the extroverted manner typical of the Rockies. Under other circumstances he would have enjoyed the sight, but now his attention kept shifting in the direction of the trees from which he'd come.

It was unnerving having Chantelle and Ariel alone with each other. Besides, he'd much rather study the beauty of sunlight glowing red in Chantelle's hair than this creek. He shoved himself away from the boulder where he'd been sitting and stared in the direction of camp. No use. He couldn't hear a thing over the babble of the water.

Grant gathered up his shaving gear and headed back. When a dead branch cracked underfoot he smiled and began looking for noisy underbrush to blunder through. A man had to be careful not to sneak up on Chantelle Du-Maurier.

When he caught his first glimpse of her through the pines he paused. She was now dressed in a plaid, western-style blouse and faded denim cutoffs that invited his gaze to devour her long, slender calves. As Ariel described the rigors of a two-week camping trip, Chantelle drew a comb slowly through her shoulder-length hair. The smooth, languorous motion and the rich, shifting colors in its wake—from dark brown to red to auburn—made his breath catch in his throat. He stood there, entranced and motionless.

Ariel's soft laugh nudged him from his silent reverie. "We know you're there, Grant, so come on out."

A slight twist of pain on Chantelle's face as she turned to watch his approach reminded Grant that she was his patient. With a wordless oath he stomped into the clearing and squatted beside her open packsack. He began pulling things out and laying them on the ground in three separate piles. Canteen: no, her desert-size container was too cumbersome for this water-rich land. Camp stove: smaller than his. If it worked well, it was a maybe. Extra socks: definitely a yes.

Chantelle, he noticed, crossed her arms over her chest and watched him with an open mouth. "Just what do you think you're doing?"

He ignored her. Next in her pack was the baby-blue lace panties she'd just changed out of. He dangled it on one finger while his stare pierced her soft, vulnerable brown eyes. "Do you have any more of these?"

Ariel stifled a chuckle under a discreet cough, but Grant kept his gaze on Chantelle. The clenching of her hands warned him that the blush creeping up her neck was more anger than embarrassment. A small part of him wondered at his strange urge to provoke a reaction, any reaction.

"My lingerie is absolutely no business of yours."

Ariel spoke softly. "Grant means that the others and I will take nonessential gear down with us, because he'll be carrying supplies for two as well as helping you walk. Will you need those clothes, hon?"

Neither of them gave any indication of having heard Ariel. They continued to glare at each other, and Grant admired the way Chantelle's gaze never lowered from his. She was, however, the one to finally break the silent deadlock. "I repeat, Mr. Van Arden. My lingerie is no business of yours."

Grant chuckled at the fire flashing in her eyes. What a handful Chantelle would be for any man crazy enough to try to tame her willfulness. Though she was bruised, sprained and convalescing, she was uncowed. Energy and determination sparked from her voice. Without breaking eye contact, he tossed the intimate lace onto the pile to keep.

He patted the orange roll tied to the frame of the pack. "How big is her tent, Ariel?"

"Two person. It's top quality, Grant."

"We'll keep it," he said. "You take my tent down with you."

Ariel's habitual smile drained from her face, but she nodded.

"Hold on, you arrogant son of a bitch," Chantelle growled. "If you think I'm going to share a tent with you for the next week you're sorely mistaken. Not a chance, mister. Absolutely no way!"

Chapter Three

The orange tent flapped in the breeze. Chantelle glared at it, her arms folded tightly across her chest.

Ariel had left sometime while Chantelle was napping. Chantelle hadn't wanted to sleep—not with that overbearing male poised to make unilateral decisions—but even Ariel had insisted she try. To Chantelle's surprise, she had dropped right off to sleep.

Now she wished she hadn't. By the time she awoke, the tent was up. *Her* tent. The tent that was cozy for one, and would be downright intimate for two. The tent she had refused Grant permission to use.

Chantelle shifted her gaze from the tent to Grant, whose hair flashed in the late-afternoon sun as he sat on a log with his back to her. He whistled a bright and snappy tune as he worked intently on something hidden from her view. His right hand moved in small, controlled jerks that corded the muscles on his forearm as if to remind her of his strength and, by extension, of her own current weakness.

Her eyes narrowed. Grant's cheerful whistling was so far from her mood that it grated on her eardrums despite the fact that the whistling was, in fact, quite good.

There. A sour note.

Keeping her voice frigidly polite, she said, "Would you please stop that horrendous caterwauling?"

Grant half turned. In his hands he held a pocketknife and a roughly whittled piece of wood from the club she'd thrown at him this morning. A faint smile dusted his lips. "You're awake." He bent to pick up a sturdy, fairly straight tree limb that had been recently stripped of branches. "I found a walking stick to help you hobble around camp, and I'm carving pieces for a real crutch. That'll take a while, though, so you might as well use the walking stick till then. Have a good nap?"

"Yes." She averted her eyes, unable to meet his friendly expression when she had just gone out of her way to be nasty. The fact that he was working to help her again made her more angry with herself, not less angry with him.

Then the flapping of the tent made her realize that her lips were tingling again. "I was fine until you started that noise."

Grant sighed and fixed her with a stare that never wavered. For a long time he said nothing, yet Chantelle somehow felt more shamed by his silence than by anyone else's outburst. He stripped her soul and left her naked to the world. It was almost as if his glance was a mirror that reflected herself in X-ray form to reveal emotions and motives that she herself scarcely knew. Her anger, his gaze reflected, wasn't real. It was a feeble defense against a fear that sprang not from him, but from inside herself.

Finally Grant shrugged one flaxen eyebrow and bent to gather his tools. "Sorry." Without another word he carried his work toward the trees, whistling as he went. The sound faded almost but not quite to nothing. Chantelle was alone.

Grant's abrupt departure took her by surprise. When she realized her hand was trembling, she forced her fingers into a rocklike fist. She'd gotten herself all primed for a battle over the tent, and he hadn't let her say a word about it. Well, just wait till it got dark. She'd have plenty to say then.

But it took hours to get dark; a long time to be alone. As she sat there with nothing to do, she occasionally saw Grant moving among the trees. She could still hear his whistling, so she knew she hadn't been abandoned. He seemed to favor old show tunes, working his way through *Porgy and Bess, West Side Story* and *Man of LaMancha* before adding numerous contemporary tunes that she couldn't name. Hearing Grant whistle wasn't the same, though, as having another person around. Usually she liked being alone, but not right now. Being alone brought loneliness.

She spent a long time just staring around, trying to ignore Grant's music. In her present mood the majestic scenery barely registered, and in any case it was hidden on most sides by the trees around the campsite clearing. Only the brooding peak of Mount Robson transcended the forest, a stern, gray monolith against the darker gray of the clouds. She filled time studying its massive layers of limestone with the determination and detachment of a scientist.

When she'd finished with the mountains and forest, she memorized the campsite. The "bed" where she lay, with her foam sleeping pad now added for comfort, was at one corner of a triangle. The fallen log that served Grant as a chair was at another corner, and the blasted tent at the third. In the middle were the rocks ringing the charred remnants of the fire. It was a beautiful setting, really, and she should have been enthralled.

She wasn't. She was bored. When she'd decided to hike around Mount Robson she hadn't planned on a period of enforced idleness or she would have brought a book.

She glared in the direction of the forest. If she'd brought a book, that arrogant so-and-so undoubtedly would have trashed it in the name of weight. How dare he?

A part of her was instantly contrite. Grant was, Ariel assured her, an honorable man. Chantelle owed him her life.

Carrying supplies for two people was indeed too much to ask, and she should be willing to forgive him small things like whistling or a touch of arrogance.

The breeze flapped the tent, as if to remind her of its presence. Chantelle felt her chest rise and fall with renewed speed. She wasn't ready to forgive a major arrogance like the tent, though. The tent represented a vulnerability and loss of control that cut too close to her core. If he thought she would meekly share it with him, her body pressed full-length beside his while memories of his kisses nibbled at her composure, he was insane. The thought of lying next to him in the hushed intimacy of the tent, forcibly aware of his every breath, of the heat of his body, of the touch of his knee through the sleeping bags as he turned in his sleep—the very thought made her cheeks burn from embarrassment and anger.

And also, she was honest enough to admit, from something else.

Though Grant materialized as soon as she tried to move around or shift position—he hovered like a mother hen, without being the slightest bit of company—he disappeared as abruptly as he appeared. She saw little of him the remainder of the day. Only as the western sky dimmed to a hint of red did he finally return to camp for good. By then, she was thoroughly glad to see his rangy, confident gait. With few words, he boiled water on her camp stove to cook a freeze-dried casserole and handed her a plate and cup. He silently wolfed down the mediocre food with a misplaced look of enjoyment on his face, then disappeared again with a brief explanation that he was going to wash the dishes in the creek.

The long northern twilight was casting a vague pallor of light when he returned. Eager for conversation, Chantelle sat up and watched attentively as he moved like a shadow, putting away dishes and food and camp stove. He still said nothing. She was about ready to talk to thin air, though, and so she spoke first. "Aren't you going to make a camp fire?"

"No."

"I see." Disappointment at his terse response clutched briefly at her throat, only to be pushed aside by a thrust of impatience. "May I ask why not?"

"It's too late to bother. I'm heading to bed." He punctuated these words by gesturing toward the tent.

"Bed?" Chantelle hugged her knees so hard the kneecap bit into her forearm. She took a deep breath. "It's my tent. I don't want to share it with you."

"Big girls have to learn to share. I thought your mom would have taught you that."

"My mother didn't teach me to share sleeping accommodations with strange men. Sleep somewhere else."

Grant crossed the campsite and squatted in front of her. The dark shadow of his presence filled her vision, though only vague hints of his face were visible: the light blur of his hair, the finely sculpted prominence of his cheekbones, the whites of eyes that peered at her. "Chantelle, it's clouding over. I won't risk getting soaked just because of your outdated standards. We're adults. I know that I'm capable of keeping my hands to myself. The question is, can you keep your hands off me?"

"What? How dare you suggest that I—you infuriating, insufferable, infuriating..."

"Ah, ah. You're repeating yourself. I take it that means you won't take advantage of me in my sleep."

"Count on it, mister."

"Then it's settled. You go in first and get ready."

Chantelle let out an exasperated sigh. Before she could decide what to say, Grant stood and extended his arms to help her up. Well, why not? She realized with a renewed touch of annoyance that she knew all along he'd get his way.

With his help, she stood. His touch was so gentle and careful that she momentarily forgot her annoyance as she concentrated on standing without putting weight on her left foot. To succeed, she had to lean heavily against his sturdy torso. When he slipped his arm around her waist to help her walk, she realized just how far along the road to recovery she'd come. She was more aware of the firmness of his body than the achiness of her own.

At the front of the tent he helped her kneel. He loosened his grip on her waist but didn't quite let go, and the touch of his hand at her side loomed on Chantelle's consciousness more than the soft gesture demanded. Breath seemed to gel in her lungs as she waited for his next move. At first, he did nothing. His stillness calmed her limbs but not her pulse, which seemed to grow in loudness as it grew in speed. Despite the darkness, she was aware of the steady rise and fall of his chest, mere inches from her face.

After a wait that tightened her nerves to full alertness, Grant finally broke the spell of the moment. Slowly, as if giving her time to move away, he raised his other hand to her cheek and feathered his fingertips from temple to jaw along a tingling trail of intimacy. He rested his fingers on her jaw in a position that could at any moment lead to tilting her face upward for another of his devastating kisses.

"I thought—" Chantelle stopped to clear her throat "—I thought you said you could keep your hands to yourself."

He chuckled, and the sound reminded her of the deep, dangerous purr of a mountain lion. "Just checking."

"Checking what?" She held up a hand to ward off his reply. "No, don't answer. Good night, Grant."

Chantelle shook her head as she crawled into the tent. These little moments of physical attraction kept happening, catching her by surprise. Surprising, too, was that she was able to smile when she heard muttering from the outside of the tent. At least she wasn't the only one struggling. Feeling around for the opening of her sleeping bag, she crept gingerly to a sitting position.

"Chantelle?"

Startled, she glanced behind her to see if he had closed the tent flap. He had.

"Yes?"

"Ariel put your pajamas on top of your sleeping bag. She also put a change of clothes inside the bag by your feet. That way they won't be cold in the morning." After a pause, he continued in a quiet voice that had lost all trace of a predatory lion. "Can you manage by yourself or do you need help?"

"No! I mean, I'll be fine." She began to undress, aware of each tiny rustle that Grant could surely hear through the negligible wall of the tent. She usually enjoyed a tent's closeness to raw nature but when the raw nature was Grant Van Arden... Chantelle was tempted to sleep in her clothes, but she was experienced enough to know the clammy coldness slept-in clothes gave a camper. Between being careful of her ankle and trying to be silent, however, undressing took twice as long as usual.

"I'm ready," she said at last. She zipped the sleeping bag up to the very top and tried to feign sleep.

It was useless. The tent was so small that Grant brushed against her despite obvious efforts. Worse, when he sat up to unbutton his shirt the pitch of the roof forced him to the middle. Though she shifted away, she was still aware of his every movement as he bumped against her.

"Excuse me," he whispered.

"That's okay," she whispered back.

His shirt fluttered from his shoulders and landed atop her sleeping bag, filling her nostrils with his virile presence. She could almost but not quite see him as a moving shadow against the roof of the tent. As soon as she realized what she was doing, watching a man undress, she felt heat rise to her cheeks and she averted her eyes.

It didn't help. Her mental image of the man beside her actually grew sharper. As if in broad daylight, her mind's eye saw the rippling of his shoulders as he moved. Each well-remembered plane of his chest appeared vividly in her mind. The warmth in Chantelle's cheeks spread down her neck to lodge with disconcerting insistence in her breasts.

This was ridiculous. The more she tried not to look the more clearly she could see him. With a harsh sigh she turned toward him and concentrated openly on his shadowy form rather than on the erotic imagery his rustling clothes conjured. Watching him was less provocative than having her mind roll an X-rated movie. Besides, in the dark he'd never know she was watching.

Grant was in his sleeping bag now, raising his hips and removing his pants. He rolled up the pants, stuffed them under his head for a pillow and relaxed.

After a moment Chantelle realized her chest was still rising and falling rapidly as if she was waiting for something that hadn't happened. She licked at lips suddenly gone dry and tried to rein in her galloping heart with a long, slow breath. "Mr. Van Arden," she whispered, "didn't you forget something?"

"I don't think so." His voice seemed shockingly loud in the dark. "What do you mean?"

Chantelle shifted in her sleeping bag. She shouldn't have brought this up. "I mean your pajamas."

"Sorry," he replied in a cheerful tone that sounded not the least sorry. "I never use the things."

Oh, God. She was lying beside a naked man. Grant was so close that she could reach mere inches in order to touch him, touch his warm, bare skin. . . .

Chantelle rolled on her side, her back to him, and fought the new images that engulfed her mind. Grant was no longer just a dream-man she could fantasize about in safety. He was flesh and blood—warm, vibrant, virile flesh. Thoughts of him choked her mind with a startling panic that drove her to concentrate on something, anything, else. But she wasn't surprised that she remained awake despite her best efforts to ignore the rhythmic breathing sounds of the man beside her. Though hampered by the sleeping bag and her injuries, she tried several different positions, all to no avail. That didn't surprise her, either. The problem wasn't in the hardness of the ground or confinement in the narrow sleeping bag.

Grant heard and felt Chantelle turning as he lay staring up at the faint light of the never-quite-dark northern twilight that gave the tent a colorless glow. The poor kid was in pain. Intellectually he knew that while her injuries weren't life threatening, a degree of pain was inevitable and even useful. Emotionally, though . . .

The quiet moan that accompanied her turns filled him with feelings that were both new and old, both forgotten and yet bitterly remembered. On the other hand he was totally aware of the here and now, of Chantelle's aura of warmth bathing his right side, of the desire this intimacy stirred in him. On the other hand, he felt as though he was traveling back in time. This whole incident with Chantelle had an element of déjà vu, resurrecting memories of painful months that were best forgotten.

"Grant?" Her whisper was like the wind testing the leaves to see if they were awake. "Are you asleep?"

"No."

"Oh. Well. I can't sleep, either."

Grant folded his hands behind his head and kept his gaze away from Chantelle's shadowy form. In the distance, the rushing sound of the creek played hide-and-seek with his ears, dodging now and again behind the cover of the breeze in the pines. "Did you want to talk?"

A rustling sound, like a shrug. "I guess not."

Grant smiled in the darkness. Sometimes, when he was hit over the head, even he could figure out what a woman really meant. "Where do you work in Kamloops?"

"I own a bookstore, new and used, on the north shore. It's just a small shop."

"Second Thoughts?"

"Yes."

"I've been there. A cute young brunette waited on me."

"My sister, Ricki. Did she ask you for a date?"

"No, but was quite talkative. She seemed like a nice kid."

"Darned right she is. I wonder how she's doing." Chantelle chuckled like a parent admiring a kindergarten painting. "I wonder how many parties she's thrown while I've been away."

"She didn't strike me as the wild kind."

"Who said anything about wild? Ricki's just sociable."

"Not the kind to go hiking by herself, eh?"

Chantelle's sleeping bag rustled. Grant turned his head and became aware of her shadowy form looking at him.

"You understand," she said.

She said nothing more, yet the silence seemed somehow friendlier. What was he supposed to understand, though? He understood almost nothing about this irascible female, let alone her riddles. For several breaths he lay without answering, listening to the portentous secrets of the wind that teased his brain with their near-comprehensibility. Those messages he might eventually understand, but Chantelle?

He realized that she was quiet beside him, listening also. Listening to the voices in the wind? "Maybe," he said, "I do understand."

Grant thought she'd drifted into sleep by the time she spoke again. "Have you really saved someone's life, Grant?"

"Yes."

"Tell me about it."

"Nothing to tell. It was my job, that's all."

"Oh." She paused, as if waiting for him to elaborate, then finally continued speaking. "My family has an orchard in the Okanagan Valley near Kelowna. When I was ten or eleven my dad saved a fruit picker who had a heart attack by giving him CPR. From then on, we had pickers seeking our farm by the truckload. Lots of them were from Quebec, and they liked working for a family named DuMaurier even though we stopped using French long before I was born. Some of the young men tried to teach me French, in between trying to teach me to French kiss."

Grant forced down the extraordinarily sharp image her last sentence produced. Though it took him a heartbeat, he succeeded.

"What I'm trying to say, Grant, is that aside from my father I've never met a real hero before. I'd like to hear about it."

"Go to sleep, Chantelle."

"At least tell me why you won't tell me."

Grant punched his pant-pillow flat. He took a deep breath, then gathered his slacks into pillow shape once more. "Because once," he said, "one very important time, I failed."

He gritted his teeth, as if to take back his words. If this insistent female said she was sorry, he knew his restraint would snap. If she said anything, he'd do something he regretted. But as if she understood that some things were better left unspoken, she said nothing. He listened to her gentle breathing, and remembered.

"Grant?"

"Yes," he answered tersely.

"Thank you. For saving my life, I mean."

He chuckled, and memories scattered. "You're welcome."

Several minutes passed. "You're really a very nice man, you know."

"No, I didn't. Thanks for telling me."

Her laugh was low and incredibly sensual to his ears. "Good night, Grant."

"Good night." And then, because he enjoyed the musical sound of it, he breathed her name. "Good night, Chantelle DuMaurier."

After a long time, he realized she'd finally fallen asleep.

Chantelle awoke gradually, nudged from a restless sleep by sunlight and the growing stuffiness of the tent. With her eyes still closed she rolled over and stretched her arm. The dim surprise she felt when her hand touched empty sleeping bag made her realize that some sleep-drugged part of her had hoped to touch Grant, instead. Her eyes flew open.

The gentle hiss of a camp stove and the faint, stomach-rumbling smell of coffee told her that breakfast was in the works. Chantelle dressed much faster than the night before, conscious that at any moment Grant might look in to see if she was awake.

When she stuck her head out of the tent, he was sitting on the log with plaid-shirted elbows propped on the knees of his jeans. His long fingers caressed a tin mug with the firm gentleness that the flesh of her waist remembered so well from the night before. Strange. It was as if she could still feel his touch lingering at her side.

She stifled the feeling. If Grant remembered the tenderness of the night before, he certainly didn't show it. His face was a blank as he looked at her through the steam rising from the mug.

"Good morning, Chantelle. How do you feel?"

"Better, actually. Not so stiff and sore."

"I'm glad to hear it. Your walking stick is right there. Maybe today you'll be ready to use it."

Chantelle crawled out of the tent and picked up the sturdy, weathered branch that he pointed to beside the tent. Before she could try to stand, Grant was helping her to her feet.

Maybe she wasn't fully awake, or maybe last night's quiet intimacy had left her with a sensual hangover that blurred her judgment. Whatever the reason, she expected him to pull her close and as she stood, she leaned toward him, her thigh touching his and her chest brushing like a match stroke against his ribs.

Grant froze. Chantelle, realizing her mistake but powerless to correct it, froze also. With each quickening breath, her breast rubbed his chest, rousing the nipple to hard attention and alerting her expectant nerves that something important was about to happen.

Grant cradled her chin with his long fingers just as he had last night, then tilted her face toward his. Chantelle's lips parted. Her eyes closed to mere slits.

"Chantelle," he said levelly, "would you like some coffee?"

When the words sank in, her hazy mood of arousal shriveled under a frigid blast of humiliation. She pulled away, balancing heavily on the pole. What kind of woman must he think she was, offering herself so easily after scarcely more than a few words of morning greeting? What kind of woman was she turning into? How could she have done it?

She limped over to the log, casting him a baleful glare. Part of her anger, she thought with disgust, stemmed from disappointment that he had ignored her advances.

Without further comment, Grant poured her a cup of coffee. The scalding liquid settled her nerves and the cup gave her something to do with her hands.

Grant's mind was whirling as he squatted beside the camp stove to turn it off. He tore his gaze away from the woman who'd plummeted through the carefully structured texture of his life. The lingering imprint of her body left him with a confusion that he did his best to hide. He wondered if she realized how open her face was, revealing all her emotions. Resentment. Uncertainty. Desire. All so open and exposed.

Without looking at her, he scooped powdered scrambled eggs onto a plate for her breakfast. "We need to get a few things straight," he said. "You're recovering from a nasty fall. Right now your job is to get better so the government doesn't have to send a helicopter for you. My taxes pay for that helicopter, so I aim to protect you from any physical activity—" Realizing that he was botching this explanation, he kept his glance from her face as he handed her the plate. "Any physical activity that might endanger your ankle. Understand?"

Chantelle took the plate from him, held it motionless for a few seconds and then slammed it down, showering the ground with yellow speckles. Her face assumed the texture of a storm cloud, but not before he'd seen the hurt on her face as if he'd slapped her. "You arrogant bastard!"

Grant let out a breath, then shook his head in frustration. "I didn't mean that the way it sounded. Think of me as your doctor."

She answered that with a string of epithets.

When she paused for breath, he asked, "Why do you swear so much? It isn't ladylike, you know."

"Well, I'm no lady, am I? According to you I'm a senseless hussy who'd make a pass at my mortician."

"I didn't say that. And I was warning myself as much as you." He groped for words, then chopped the air with his hand. "Why is everything so difficult with you?"

"Because I'm an ill-tempered, foul-mouthed nymphomaniac, obviously!"

He rubbed his hand along his jaw. "True. I forgot about that."

Grant was half expecting it when she threw the walking stick at him. Her aim was so much worse than the day before that he suspected she didn't want to hit him, only release anger. With an inward chuckle he retrieved the pole and held it out to her. "If I give this back to you, will you promise not to hit me?"

Chantelle swayed from side to side as she glared at him. She took a long time to answer. "Yes."

"Good." He backed away from her. He saw her draw back her elbow, and he leaped just in time to miss the stick as she whipped it at his feet. Her aim had been better this time. He picked up the pole, matched her angry stare with a bland one of his own, slid it across the ground to her, and then started to chuckle. With a rueful shake of his head, he picked up his wood carving and headed into the forest.

Last night in the tent, Grant thought, talking had been so easy. In the daylight, all he did was provoke her. Not deliberately—well, maybe sometimes, because he had to admit that she was the most bewitching creature imaginable when her eyes smoldered and then abruptly burst into flame.

He would spend as much time as possible away from Chantelle. It was the only way, it seemed, to avoid arguments. Or worse, to avoid sweeping his charge into his arms in a caress that would not end innocently. She deserved better care than that.

He seated himself on the soft forest floor, close enough that he could keep an eye on her. When he saw her hobbling around the camp he hurried to put yesterday's clothes in the backpack and carry fresh ones into the tent for tomorrow so she wouldn't bother. Then he returned to the woods.

From a distance, Grant could look at her without being obvious. Like right now, with the sunlight glowing like incandescent embers in her hair as she hobbled to the log. Fire and heat, that was Chantelle. She was a creature of barely contained fire, dazzling and warm and dangerous.

He wanted her.

Grant forced his gaze back to the near-perfect smoothness of the wood in his hand. At night, with her fire banked, he could talk to her easily, but during the day she blazed so brightly that she seemed unreal somehow, as if she was a creature of the elements rather than the real world. He couldn't imagine her shopping at Clearwater's one and only grocery store, for example, or hurrying frantically in the morning, wearing only underwear and curlers in her hair, worrying about the wrinkled blouse she'd planned to wear to work.

The knife stilled in his hands. He was wrong. He could imagine that last one. Vividly.

Baby-blue underwear it would be, with lace that hugged and shifted and revealed as she got out the ironing board, lace that hid just enough to make a man yearn for more, to make a man yearn to pull her into his arms and make her forget all about a wrinkled blouse.

Pain jerked him from his reverie. Shaking his head, he sucked salty blood from the finger the knife had pricked. Fire, he reminded himself, burned.

His lips curved into a smile as he resumed his carving.

By late afternoon, peace had reigned long enough that he figured he could broach a subject too long avoided. He tucked the knife into its sheath, ran a hand through his hair and stood up.

When he emerged from the woods, Chantelle was leaning back against the log, listlessly twirling stems of yellow Indian Paintbrush around her finger. Her big accomplishment this morning was mastering the art of bending and wrapping the supple stems into perfectly round rings—a skill that would be terribly useful in her late life, she was sure. She watched his approach with narrowed eyes and straight back, yet her body leaned forward in telltale eagerness.

"Hello," she said with an attempt at cheerfulness. "Isn't this a beautiful afternoon? The clouds are so big and fluffy that I don't think we'll be threatened with rain tonight. What have you been doing?"

"Carving."

"I figured that. How is it coming?"

"All right." Grant shook his head as if to cut off her chatter. He knew he was going to irritate her again, but he didn't know how to change things. "Do you remember what I said this morning?" Her lips hardened, but he took his time to explain. "I mean about thinking of me as your doctor."

"Yes." The solitary syllable was cautious. She crossed her arms across her stomach and hugged her elbows.

"Well, I meant it. I want to take care of you as best I can. Do you believe that?"

She stared at him for several seconds behind the fortress of her arms, then nodded her head.

"I'm glad. You see, Chantelle, to take care of you I need your cooperation."

Fire rippled through her hair as she slowly nodded again. "I guess you can have it."

"Good. I'm going to see how your ankle is coming." Grant smiled impersonally at her, the way he might smile at a reluctant child.

He knelt in front of her and undid the wrappings that immobilized her injured ankle nearly as well as a tensor. The warm, smooth feel of her skin forced him to take a deep breath as he traced ligaments in her ankle. The lateral ligaments felt normal and unswollen, as did the articular capsule. He shifted to the puffy skin atop the deltoid ligaments. "Let me know if this hurts."

"It hurts!"

He smiled at her reassuringly, continued his examination more carefully, and then refastened the wrappings and pulled the backpack under her leg to elevate the ankle. "That's healing nicely. It's not nearly as puffy as yesterday. Now, would you please take off your blouse?"

Chantelle's expression remained frozen for a heartbeat, as if she couldn't believe what she'd heard. Abruptly, however, her eyes narrowed and her chest swelled with a long, deep breath.

"The cut on your back," Grant said. "The dressing has been on two days, and it's due for changing. I'll turn around. When you're holding your blouse in front of you, let me know."

"Well...all right."

Grant smiled. For once he hadn't alienated her.

He tried to ignore the warmth of her body as he yanked the old bandage off, examined the scrape and told her it had healed enough that a new bandage wasn't needed. Then, before she had a chance to put her blouse back on, he stomped off to the forest. He whittled furiously, without care for fine lines, till the peace of the wilderness slowly repossessed him.

Chantelle turned her back to the woods as she slowly put her blouse back on. Grant had been so...so cold. Well, maybe not cold, but certainly distant. Professional, at best. Robotic, at worst.

She hugged her knees and, with nothing better to do, sat and tried to think of what she'd done to make him treat her as he did.

She was still sitting like that when a glimpse of distant movement caught her eye. It was a person, heading her way. Chantelle lifted herself onto the log and began waving her hand. "Over here."

Grant emerged from the woods. "Someone's coming," she told him.

The someone was a darkly bearded man wearing the green pants and khaki shirt of the B.C. Park Service. His name was Trevor, he told them, and he'd come because Ariel and her companions had stopped off at the Park Service outpost near Berg Lake to report an injured hiker.

"Miss Johnson's directions weren't too specific," Trevor said, "or I'd have found you sooner."

Grant was sitting on the other end of the log from Chantelle. "I appreciate it. Everything's under control now, though."

"That makes my job a lot easier, then. How are you feeling, ma'am?"

Chantelle rubbed at her neck as she considered her answer. In all honesty, what could she say? That Grant's sex appeal was reducing her temper to adolescent levels? That he insisted on sleeping in the tent without touching her? That he hadn't kissed her all day? "I'm surviving," she muttered.

"Glad to hear it. Miss Johnson said you folks came over the Snake Indian River trail from Jasper Park." Trevor nodded a tribute to Grant and then, surprisingly, to Chantelle. She was glad in a way that he thought she'd been a member of Grant's party. This way she didn't have to hear a lecture about hiking alone.

"That's a long, hard trip," Trevor said. "Fantastic, but hard. Over a hundred miles."

"With all the side trips, I figure we covered over a hundred and fifty miles."

Trevor nodded again. "Only a couple parties a year come to us by our back door."

Grant nodded back.

Trevor unfolded a map and held it out toward Grant. "Did you take the side trip to the Ancient Wall? I've been meaning to get there for years."

"I think so. Let's see." Grant studied the place Trevor indicated, smiled and enthusiastically began to describe the rock structures in a remote valley.

Chantelle looked from Trevor to Grant as she listened. These two woodsmen understood each other with an ease that was totally lacking from her communication with Grant. Trevor had, by mentioning the trail, acknowledged Grant's ability to handle any emergency. The compliment had been given and accepted with typical male understatement.

Trevor rummaged through his packsack and spread several packets of freeze-dried food on the ground. After just a few days, Chantelle was already sick of the sight of the packets.

"Here's some food," Trevor said. "Hopefully there's something you've been dying to taste again. No filet mignon, I'm afraid, but there is some bannock mix. Flashlight, with fresh batteries. Spare waterproof matches. Rope. A can of stove fuel." He looked up from the pile he'd pulled from his pack. "Anything else you want?"

"Tensors," Grant said immediately. "Chantelle's ankle is wrapped with old socks and an undershirt."

"Please," she said with a laugh as she wrinkled up her nose, "get me a real elastic bandage."

"I have one of those." Trevor pulled a beige cylinder of elastic from his pack.

Grant glanced up at the sky. "An extra poncho in case it rains. We each have one, but mine's in use as a ground sheet under the tent."

Trevor gave Grant a small, folded square of vinyl rain gear from his pack. Then he handed Chantelle a tube of lipstick. "Hardly an essential of life," he said with a shrug. "One of the summer crew wanted me to give it to you, though. Can you believe she actually carried it in for fifteen miles?'' He shook his head in a mixture of wonder and disgust.

"I believe it," Chantelle said. The lipstick was flame red, but it was still lipstick and a token of civilization and femininity. She pursed her mouth and spread the bright red over her lips. She smiled at Grant, catching him in the act of staring at her intensely. "How do I look?''

His answer came slowly. "Good.''

Chantelle pulled her gaze away from the rugged strength of Grant's face, and turned to Trevor. "Do you have any books?''

"Books?'' Trevor stroked his beard and then unzipped a pocket on the side of the pack. "Maybe. Ah, here it is.'' He handed her a well-thumbed pocket-size guide to the flora of British Columbia.

The margins of the book were filled with corrections to the text and notes about locations of different plants in the park, and a list of jobs to do—shape timber for bridges, cut firewood, radio for supplies and so forth—was scribbled on a blank page. A woman's name and phone number, underlined, filled the back cover. "I can't keep this, Trevor.''

"Borrow it, then. You need something to do while you're laid up. If you get the chance, drop it off at the cabin on your way out, at the east end of Berg Lake a quarter mile north of the main trail. You two are welcome to spend the night, if you like.''

"That's awfully generous of you, but we couldn't impose.''

"You've been out on the trail this long and you're turning down hot water and a real bed?'' Trevor smiled at her and shook his head. "Don't worry, you wouldn't be imposing. The place is crawling with summer help anyway. Students, mostly. There must be eight, ten people.''

"A regular traffic jam," Grant said.

"Yeah, I might as well move back to Edmonton. I'd like to continue chatting but if you folks don't need me I'll hurry home before dark. Anything else I can do for you?''

Grant and Trevor talked together for several more minutes, spreading out a map and discussing routes and camping spots. After Trevor slipped his pack onto his back, he turned to Chantelle. "Will you be all right, ma'am?"

"Yes." She held up his book. "Now that I have something to read I'll be just fine."

"Good. Injured hikers are usually a lot more trouble for me than this." Trevor took Chantelle's hand and shook it. "I wish everybody was as smart as you, ma'am, and had the foresight to hike with an honest-to-goodness doctor."

Chantelle looked at Grant with her eyes wide. Confusion made her repeat the word, though she'd heard clearly. "Doctor?"

Chapter Four

Chantelle expected Grant to protest. When he didn't, she squinted in confusion. "A doctor?"

Trevor had already turned to Grant, so he couldn't see the surprise on her face. "Dr. Van Arden, it's been good to meet you."

"Call me Grant."

"Grant." Trevor stood and shook the hand Grant extended. "See you in three or four days." Trevor walked away, turning once to wave.

Chantelle waved back, then tapped the worn field guide against her hand as she watched Trevor stride quickly away. Within minutes, the fragile contact with the outside world had disappeared. She was left alone once more with a handsome, frustrating enigma. *Doctor?*

Chantelle stared at Grant's pantherlike grace as he began putting away the food and other articles Trevor had left. He hadn't shaved yet today, the cuffs of his plaid wool shirt were rolled to different heights on his corded forearms, and his weather-worn face could have stared down a bull. "He called you a doctor."

Grant didn't answer immediately, as if he was more concerned with stacking the food packets in his arm. "I believe he did."

"Why did you tell him you were a doctor?"

"I didn't. You were here the whole time, and you heard everything I said." He stood up and began to walk past her.

Chantelle's ankle made her wince as she scrambled on hands and knees to grab hold of his arm. She hardened herself to the concern written on his features. "You're not going to walk away from this conversation."

Grant bent to ease her leg back into a sitting position. "You've got to be careful of your ankle, Chantelle."

"Thanks, *Doc*." She offered sarcasm rather than gratitude, then immediately resented once more the knack this man had for bringing out the worst in her. "Why did Trevor call you Dr. Van Arden? I mean, you're a teacher, aren't you?"

"Yes, though I don't remember telling you that." His mouth curled into a casual smile. "Ariel's more talkative than I am."

That smile at the mention of Ariel's name made Chantelle's grip tighten on the flannel of his shirt. Her next words came out harsh and disjointed. "Are you and Ariel lovers?"

Again his answer took longer than it should, though his voice was firm and unemotional. "No, but she's my best friend. And, yes, I used to be an M.D."

A feeling of cool uneasiness slipped over her, almost as if a storm cloud had hidden the sun. Ariel was instantly forgotten. Chantelle's fingers slipped from his arm. "Used to be?" Her voice was soft, compassionate, almost hesitant. "Were you disbarred, or whatever they do with doctors?"

"Nothing like that. I just gave it up for a while." Grant finished carrying the supplies to the tent and sat down to put them away.

Chantelle again tapped the book against her palm, harder and more quickly. She didn't understand this man and his imperturbable exterior. He rarely gave a clue to his thoughts and feelings. Did he even have thoughts and feelings? "People don't just give up being doctors."

"People make career changes all the time."

"Giving up medicine isn't a career change. It's like a priest abandoning his congregation."

"I have news for you, Chantelle. Out in the real world men leave the priesthood all the time. Some even marry nuns."

"You know what I mean," she argued. She looked toward the dark green shadows of the forest and continued in a more reasonable tone. "Being a doctor is a calling, not just a job."

"I have a new job now. Besides, I didn't say I've given up being a doctor forever. If it makes you feel better, think of me as being on sabbatical."

His calm, reasonable voice was too dispassionate to satisfy her. "But why?" When he didn't answer she leaned forward, holding her hand open toward him. "There must be a reason, Grant."

She watched his face as he closed the Velcro of the pack and dangled it easily in one hand, a husky leg resting on the log. His expression told her nothing, however. He was a mountain man, rugged, wild and totally capable of handling any challenge without even lifting an eyebrow. A surgical mask on his face would be as incongruous as a top hat on a grizzly—and his face would be no less readable than without the mask.

Last night he'd said... Chantelle sucked in a deep breath and held it. "You said that one time you failed to save someone's life. That's it, isn't it?"

"Truth is always too complicated to fit into one neat sentence, Chantelle. Now, if you'll excuse me, I have to continue working on your crutch."

"You can tell me—"

"Chantelle," he interrupted without turning to face her, "tell me about the first time you went to bed with a man."

She sat bolt upright. "What?"

"Tell me about your first time. Tell me what he did. Tell me about the excitement and guilt and pleasure you felt."

"Well..." She shook her head in confusion, glad he was still facing away and couldn't see the warm flush creeping up her neck. "No."

"Why not?"

"Grant, I... Well, you have no right to know. That's personal."

He looked at her over his shoulder. His ice-blue eyes grabbed hers in a long stare that seemed to clog the breath in her lungs. "Exactly," he said.

Chantelle swallowed when he finally broke off the gaze, startled at how easily he could seize her mind and drain her of willpower. She licked her lips. "Grant, I didn't mean..."

But he was already halfway to the woods, and he didn't look back. She never did learn how she would have ended her sentence.

The pattern of the previous evening was repeated. They ate in tense silence. Grant's face, of course, showed neither tension nor any other emotion. After dinner, the campsite faded into a gloomy twilight, which signaled time for bed. Chantelle crawled into the tent, got ready as quietly as possible, then suffered the breath-quickening agony of lying there while Grant crawled in beside her.

Her tension took on a new dimension as his clothes rustled in the darkness. Was she oversexed?

Ridiculous. Being thoroughly aroused said more about Grant's sex appeal than about her. Oversexed? By contemporary standards her love history was downright meager, though she'd enjoyed it while it lasted.

It was her upbringing, of course. In the isolated mountain valleys of B.C., the future arrived slowly. The lush coast was Canada's Lotusland, where anything went, but not so in the dry, small-town Interior. According to her upbringing, love was followed by marriage, which was followed by physical love. Chantelle had gotten the order wrong; she'd lived with Garrett before getting married. Worse, she'd mistaken sex for love and the marriage had collapsed upon itself after passion withered to a hollow core. Divorce wasn't supposed to happen, not to a DuMaurier. Why, she wondered, had she never found true love?

Grant's elbow nudged her as he crawled atop his sleeping bag. Not another X-rated daydream. Please. She filled her lungs with as much air as possible, then let it out slowly.

Well, there was nothing she could do about true love out here in the middle of nowhere. The solution was simple, of course. Accept the attraction to Grant for what it was— hormones—ride it out, maybe even enjoy an innocent flirtation. Nothing more.

Grant bumped her shoulder, jarring her thoughts. Enjoy? Innocent flirtation? She wasn't enjoying it at all. How could she enjoy this knotted feeling in her chest? A heavy sigh escaped her as she heard and felt Grant settle into his sleeping bag. Settling down wasn't possible for her, nor was she capable of demure silence. She'd had silence all day long.

"I took a few steps without the cane before dinner," she said in a tone that successfully feigned lightness. "My ankle hurts a little, but I'm beginning to think that one more day should do it. Maybe tomorrow afternoon we can start back. Even if we just go a couple miles it would feel great to be on the move again."

Grant didn't answer, though she could dimly see that he'd turned his head toward her. Chantelle didn't let his silence stop her. "What do you think, Doc?"

"I think that tomorrow afternoon is too early. If the ankle swells because you hiked too soon the trip will take longer, not shorter. Besides, you need to rebuild your strength."

"I suppose you're right." She almost didn't care what he said, as long as he said something. "Tomorrow may be too soon. But if we're going to be here another night, could you make a campfire?"

"I don't see why not."

"Thank you." Chantelle found herself smiling in the dark. "Waiting for sunset is so desolate. Everything fades from sight, till you're left alone with nothing but sounds and smells and imagination, in the middle of gray nothingness."

To her surprise, Grant touched her cheek. He spoke in velvet tones that matched his gentle, almost apologetic touch. "I haven't taken care of you very well, have I?" His fingertips stirred restlessly along her smooth, sensitive skin, sliding from her jaw to the abruptly alert nerves at the corner of her mouth. Chantelle's lips parted of their own accord, but his fingers left her face.

"I'll make a fire tomorrow," he said. "Is there anything else you've wanted to ask me while I've been..." He paused, as if searching for the right word.

"Avoiding me," she finished for him.

He didn't dispute her choice of words.

"Talk to me," she said. "Tell about yourself. About being a doctor. About how you became who you are. Please."

"Sure."

Chantelle was surprised that he agreed so easily. She turned on her side toward him and folded her hands under her head as a pillow.

"Shall I start at the beginning?"

"You could skip the 'poor but honest' part," she said with a smile in her voice.

"No, that part's important. If my parents' families hadn't lost all their money and status in World War II I'd be a different person. For one thing, I'd be speaking Dutch."

"I'm sorry, Grant. I didn't mean to make fun of your family."

"Don't worry about it. My parents are wonderful people, but they need to take themselves less seriously."

If they were as stone-faced as Grant, she believed him. "What was it like being their son?"

"Pretty good. They didn't have much use for playing, though, unless it had some higher goal. Like the game of Scrabble they bought me one year for Christmas. My other present was a dictionary to use with the game. 'So you improve your English and speak like the Canadian children, not the Italians or Portuguese,' Mother said. They never played Scrabble with me, because they felt their English wasn't good enough. I had to live up to the standards they wanted to reach, but couldn't."

Chantelle had an image of an expressionless blue-eyed couple pinning all their hopes on a miniature version of the man beside her. The humorless picture was very different from her own riotous childhood. "My family never worried about how we spoke," she said. "My father was always contemptuous of English. I think we all suffered in school because of it."

"My parents insisted I get top grades."

"At least you could live up to their standards."

"But not without cost," Grant said.

"What cost?"

"My childhood." He said nothing for a few heartbeats, then continued in a determinedly neutral tone. "My parents moved to Toronto because they liked the Canadian soldiers who liberated their hometown."

Chantelle felt the need to do something to drive the rigidness from Grant's voice. No matter what he said about his parents being good, no one should be this controlled and impassive about boyhood.

She spoke in a teasing voice. "Too bad you don't have that Scrabble game in your pack. We could play to pass the time—but only if you promised not to slip any Dutch words past me."

"If you promised not to use any French."

"Don't worry about that," she said with a laugh. "My family gave up French long ago when they moved to an English-speaking part of the country." Chantelle paused. She turned to study the faint outline of his profile, which appeared ghostlike against the faint background of the tent. "Tell about being a doctor."

She was looking at him, he realized. He liked it when she looked at him, as if bathing him with her gaze. "Being a doctor." He repeated her words to give himself time to think, to give his mind the chance to move back in time. "Well, I used to have a lot more patients than I do now."

"Seriously."

"You mean you'd nurse a grudge if I made more puns?"

"Darned right I would. If I'm trapped in the woods with a punster I'll take my chances with the bears."

"Oh, you want serious," he said in a mock-somber voice that soon softened. "Well, I was an only child, and I came late in life, so I guess my parents doted on me quite a bit. I was expected to make something of myself, to become the success they felt they should have been."

He took a deep breath and filled his body with the quiet intimacy of this moment. Chantelle was a benevolent wraith of sexiness hovering at the edge of his perception. "When I was fifteen I expressed interest in medicine, so they devoted their lives to making me the best doctor possible. The original idea was mine, but after that I was thoroughly programmed to become a doctor. I never realized till years later the sacrifices they must have made to send me to McGill, or how much it must have bothered them when I took a job as surgeon in Calgary rather than in Toronto."

"I bet you were a great doctor."

Grant curled his hands behind his head and digested her statement. A great doctor? Hardly, though hospitals had bid for him when he finished his training, almost as if he was a prized athlete. "I guess I had all the knowledge and all the techniques. Do you like music?"

"Anything but heavy metal. What does that have to do with you as a doctor?"

"Bear with me. Do you know a piece called 'Flight of the Bumblebee'?"

"Yes."

"It's relentlessly fast and difficult, a technical tour de force. As a doctor, I'd have been great on 'Flight of the Bumblebee.' But give me a piece like the 'Moonlight Sonata,' where compassion and empathy count, and I'd have been useless."

Chantelle was about to say that he must be exaggerating, but then she recalled the briskly efficient way he'd examined her ankle and back. Was that how he'd practiced medicine, and not just a reaction to her? "You're hard on yourself."

"No. I'm realistic. A couple of years ago I took an extended holiday at a cabin in Clearwater I'd bought from another doctor. While I was there I took a good look at myself and I didn't like what I saw. I wasn't my own man. I was what my parents wanted me to be."

Chantelle turned to him in the dark.

"I never went back to Calgary."

He was silent then. They both were. She reached across the distance between them, but lowered her hand to the softness of her sleeping bag. Tiny, soft sounds of the night signaled quietly that the world outside the tent still existed. That realization almost startled Chantelle, so engrossed was she in the man beside her. Her eyes, straining in the darkness for every shadowed glimpse of him, were moist.

And he'd still said nothing about the person he'd failed to save.

Did she even have the right to ask? She hadn't treated him very well. The need to apologize in some way filled her mind, yet she hated to shatter the stillness. She stretched her arm farther, till it reached his. As she curled her fingers around his hard biceps, a sharp flash of feminine awareness temporarily drove away simple intentions of compassion. Her breath quickened.

"Grant," she whispered, "earlier today you said my swearing was unladylike."

"Oh, that. Forget whatever I say when I'm trying to needle you, Chantelle. Please."

Her voice held apology, but she was pleased he seemed to feel none was necessary. "No, you were right. You see, I'm not a lady. Not that I'm a pub crawler or a logger," she hastened to add, "but I'm not a lady."

He chuckled. "All right, you've got me hooked. If you aren't a lady, what are you?"

"I'm a farmer's daughter. My family has owned the same orchard for nearly a hundred years. My roots are in the dirt, and my fingernails were always dirty from the day I was born until the day I moved away. I worked with men out in the fields, men who swore at hot sunshine and at cold rain. My young ears were there when Dad got the news that, in the year of our best crop ever, Washington State farmers had dumped trainloads of apples into Canada and the price had fallen to nothing. About the only French I know is swear words."

"That doesn't mean you aren't a lady, Chantelle."

"Well, I'm not. A lady is at home with silver tea services and embroidery. A lady has lace and a hope chest."

Grant's hand covered hers. Slowly, with paintbrushlike strokes that soon had her face glowing red, his touch progressed up to her shoulder. "You have lace, Chantelle. And it looked marvelous."

"Lace? What do you mean?"

"Lace was all you wore when I first saw you."

"Oh. Yes." This intimate reminder fed the warmth spreading from his soft touch, seemingly unmuted by her cotton pajamas. Her chuckle came out throaty and deep. "See what I mean? A lady wouldn't lie around in her underwear when a man comes to visit."

"That's debatable."

"Not a ladylike lady, the kind who marries a pillar of society—" like doctors, she thought "—and breezes through the obligations and commitments that go with status. You know the type I mean."

"Yes," he agreed slowly. "In fact, you've caught the essence of my wife."

Chantelle's heart jumped. She forced her fingers to uncurl from his arm. "Your wife?"

"Former wife, if you prefer."

She preferred. Not that it really made any difference, of course. "I didn't know you'd been married."

"You never asked."

"I did, too—get married, I mean." Chantelle wished she could see his face so she could have some idea what his expression said about his ex-wife. On second thought, light would have been wasted. This was Grant, after all. "I'm asking now," she said. "Would you tell me about your wife?"

"Not right now."

He silenced any further argument by moving his hand up to her neck, making her insides squirm when his fingertips reached flesh. She stretched, baring the full length of her neck to his whispering, scintillating touch.

His fingers resumed their exploration, sliding upward from her neck to her face, rousing sensations Chantelle had never known could spring from her features. Somehow letting him touch her like this—along her cheekbone, her temple, then behind her ear, with the almost-tickle leaving her skin more alive and yearning than ever before—seemed more intimate than an overtly sexual caress.

"Anything else you want from me, Chantelle?"

She swallowed hard. What a time to ask.

His hand was brushing along her neck, eliciting a delightful trickle of sensation from each nerve ending and setting up a clamor of anticipation in those nerves expecting, hoping, to be next. How easy it would be, she thought, to flow with his caresses wherever they might lead.

Just hormones, remember. "Tell me about your trip."

His palm cupped her cheek with pressure so light as to seem a mere promise. "What do you want to know?"

Chantelle swallowed. The movement of her jaw whisked her cheek against his palm. "Tell me about whatever was important."

"It was a totally uneventful trip, until I found you."

She stopped breathing.

"Look, Chantelle, I didn't mean that the way it sounded. I apologize."

"Apologize? For what?"

He shrugged and gestured with his hand. It was too dark to see the motion, but she could sense his frustration. In a flash of inspiration, she guessed that he didn't know why he was apologizing, except that in some vague way he didn't want to embarrass or offend her. Sometimes Grant was very sweet. She smiled in the darkness and waited for his touch to return and drive the coolness from her cheek.

After a moment he put his hand on the edge of her sleeping bag, with only his finger brushing her chin. "Go on," she urged.

Grant was motionless for several heartbeats. "By ordinary standards it was an uneventful trip. We hiked, we camped, we hiked and then hiked some more. Most people would call it boring."

"But you don't."

"No."

"I wouldn't have found it boring, either."

He said nothing, but his fingers stirred. Lightly, gently, he explored the flesh of her neck.

"Tell me something about your trip, Grant, something you'll remember years from now."

His fingers paused. "I'm not sure there's any one thing. More like everything, the whole experience together. A chance to listen to the wind in the trees tell you what you're really thinking." His laugh was a self-deprecating whisper. "I find it easier to pay attention to what I'm really thinking when I'm away from people."

For a few seconds, silence filled the tent. Chantelle took a deep breath. "I understand, Grant. At least I think I do."

"You know, I believe you. At the moment anything seems possible."

She sensed his full attention on her. Her heart seemed to swell with the knowledge that underneath all their arguments and differences, their souls were kindred. "I need to get away, too. Even more so when I was growing up."

"Problems?"

"No, not really. Even if we aren't cultured, my family is nice. Nosy, perhaps, but nice God-fearing people. It was just that there were always so many of us—two older brothers, two younger brothers, two younger sisters, three live-in cousins. On top of which, I was related to half the people within a ten-mile radius."

"It sounds cozy. Safe."

"It was—for everybody else. My brothers and sisters loved being around people. When I got up in the middle of the night I had to step carefully to avoid walking on their friends sprawled on sleeping bags. Every weekend, Mom would cook up a huge pot of stew or soup, enough to feed not only us but the half dozen people who would drop by at the last minute. Our living room was the official meeting place for the fruit farmer's co-op. Something was always happening, someone always stopping by."

"To an only child with no extended family, it sounds great," he said.

"Well, I was shy."

Grant laughed skeptically. "You, shy?"

"Yes, me. Painfully, paralyzingly shy." But she knew why he laughed. Shy people weren't supposed to have feelings. "Shyness isn't the same as meekness. Sometimes I frothed with indignation, but I couldn't express it."

"Unless you lost your temper, right?"

"You catch on quick. I've outgrown the worst of my shyness, but I still remember how it felt." Chantelle took a deep breath, forcing her muscles to loosen up. "I didn't have time to make sense of all the people—they were a blur in front of my eyes. My family was great but I needed space. I still do, and that's why I moved a hundred miles away from them. Do you know how steeply the mountains rise from the floor of the Okanagan Valley?''

''I've been there.''

''They aren't like the Rockies, of course, but when I was young they seemed just as big. I'd climb the hill behind the orchard till I found a Thinking Place where I could look down on all the activity. From there, I had enough distance that I could make sense of things.''

Grant was quiet for a moment. Then a word burst forth. ''Stars.''

''Stars?''

''Late at night, on the trip.'' His hand rested on her nape. ''Thousands of stars, more than you see even from a small town. The Milky Way so bright against the blackness that I understood, not intellectually but in my gut, why the ancients chose that name. Milk, splashed across the sky. And the stars, giving me a sense of connecting to something we've lost in our cities and civilization, scurrying around so immersed in our own lives and our own cleverness that we never search for anything greater than ourselves. Wondering how many men and women of centuries gone by, shepherds and soldiers and farmers and cavemen—people whose lives and language and thoughts I couldn't begin to understand—had looked upward and felt exactly what I was feeling.''

His voice dropped off into a silence that seemed bottomless. Stars. Yes . . . she could see them, thousands of them, through his eyes. And, through his eyes as well, she could sense all the countless others. The wonder he had felt flowed into her and through her like a life-giving river that nourished and cleansed her soul. Yes, the stars . . .

Chantelle said nothing of how his words reverberated inside her. Words felt unnecessary. The tent had become a cocoon of tenderness, cradling the two of them in a primordial bond. She scarcely dared to breath, hoping to prolong the magic. Who would guess that a rugged, silent man like Grant had the soul and tongue of a poet? Who would believe it?

And he was touching her, connecting with her in a way that went beyond the warmth of his hand on the back of her neck. She lay there, seeing the stars through his eyes, wondering how many other women throughout time had lain beside their men and shared this kind of incredible closeness.

Wait a minute. He wasn't her man.

She pulled away from him. He moved his hand to his side. The silence was again normal silence, and a barrier between them.

He was quiet for such a long time that she thought he'd fallen asleep. "I'm amazed," he said in a voice that had softened to match the gentle murmur of the distant creek, "that I told you this."

She said nothing, but the hiss of cloth on sleeping bag as she turned toward him whispered urgently.

"It must be the darkness," he said.

Though she realized he couldn't see the gesture, she nodded. "Darkness helps. I remember when I was a teenager, sometimes my mother would come into my room before I fell asleep and we'd talk. About boys. About the inadequacy of my figure. About all the things I'd rather die than discuss in the daylight."

"Chantelle," Grant said in a wistful voice, "your family sounds... I don't know. Perfect, I guess."

"They aren't, believe me. But thanks anyway." She paused for a deep yawn that she didn't feel she had to hide from him, such was the closeness of the moment. "Darkness is kind of like being alone, and I open up when I'm alone." She shook her head. "I guess that doesn't make much sense."

"It makes sense to me."

Chantelle nodded silently. The quiet seemed friendly now, and she was content.

"Grant?"

She heard the soft, fluid sounds of his yawn. "Yes?"

"Tomorrow night," she said with a tentative note in her voice, "I'll tell you about my ex if you'll tell me about yours."

"What is this—I'll show you mine if you show me yours?" He was flirting with her, in a sleepy, bedroom voice that sent chills flitting along her nerves. "Next thing I know you'll want to play doctor with me."

"Hmm." The sound came out almost like a purr, but she didn't regret it.

"*Hmm* what?"

"I'm thinking about it. Playing doctor, I mean."

"Don't," he said with a chuckle that was low and sensuous. "I'd only palpate your ankle, you know."

"Palpating sounds downright kinky. I'm not so sure about the ankle, though. Is it a deal?"

Suddenly his voice sounded alert and firm, Entirely unlike the sleepy flirtation of seconds before. "When—or if—I palpate you, Chantelle, it won't be a game."

Chantelle's heart began pounding. The chills shooting down her back switched to warm currents that threatened to melt away any resistance she felt. "I meant," she said in a soft voice, "a deal to gossip about our ex-spouses tomorrow night."

Grant was quiet, as if he regretted the burst of truth that had snuck into their verbal play. "I'm not going to get out of this without making some commitment, am I? Okay, it's a deal."

"Grant, I—"

"Leave it, Chantelle. Time for bed." His face descended toward hers till she felt the warm intimacy of his breath on her cheek. And then his lips were on hers, banishing words from her mind. Without conscious thought her lips parted to welcome the taste and thrust of his tongue. For just a moment, Chantelle thought she could see the starry splash of the Milky Way through her closed eyelids. Too soon, Grant ended the kiss.

"Go to sleep, Chantelle."

But she didn't. Not for a long time.

Chapter Five

When something woke Chantelle, her palm was spread on Grant's waist in a flagrant embrace. Her cheek nestled against his chest, so that her lungs were filled with the heady aroma of male warmth. The coolness of early-morning air made his skin under her cheek seem hotter.

She'd never felt more secure, more at ease.

A band of coolness made her realize what had wakened her. Grant had removed his arm, which had been draped around her shoulder. Without withdrawing, she shifted her head so she could see his eyes. He was awake and squinting at her with a look that was startled and curious at the same time.

So, he wasn't sure how she'd react to holding and being held. Too bad, she thought with the mental equivalent of a stretch and a yawn. Let him wonder. She lowered her chin onto his shoulder and snuggled into the deliciously natural warmth of flesh on flesh.

When she closed her eyes she could still picture his disheveled hair and sleep-softened face. As her mind floated toward alertness, she marveled at how handsome he was. At night he was faceless—though his soul, she acknowledged with a satisfied yawn, was beautiful. His daytime magnificence seemed almost superfluous, an embarrassment of riches that was grossly unfair to other men. The wrinkles that crowded together at the corners of his blue eyes added to his impressive looks, proclaiming that someone lived inside that beauty, someone unique and intelligent and intriguing.

Chantelle used his shoulder to muffle the beginning of a laugh of happiness. She almost felt as if she was falling in love.

"Good morning, Chantelle."

She resisted the urge to run her hand across the warm flesh of his stomach. Instead she stretched and removed her hand from his waist. "Your voice is beautiful, too."

The gentle shaking of Grant's chuckle caressed her cheek. "Did you sleep well?"

"Yes." As if to prove her point, she stretched again.

Grant searched her face, as if looking for the reasons behind her calm acceptance of their embrace, then pulled back to his side of the tent. "Maybe I should wear pajamas after all," he said in a smooth baritone that seemed more sensuous because of the hint of sleep it still carried.

Her gaze flicked across the hair of his chest. As he pulled on his shirt and began rummaging around under the covers, she noticed him glancing at her with a strange expression on his face. Then she realized why. She was already so accustomed to the intimacy of the tent that even in the daylight she was staring openly.

Embarrassment shattered the spell of quiet intimacy, and Chantelle exploded to total wakefulness, rolling on her side and pressing her knuckles to the bridge of her nose. Grant's every movement registered on her sensitive ears until he left the tent to start breakfast.

That day seemed to pass more quickly, partly because she was feeling well enough to move around and partly because Grant spent more time in camp. Several chores seemed to have piled up that required his presence, though Chantelle hoped that the communication of the night before was a factor as well.

Not that they shared soul-baring confidences in the daylight. By mutual, unspoken consent, personal topics were put on hold in favor of the mundane things that needed to be said. For one thing, they discussed the crutches he'd finished except for a final fitting. Chantelle was impressed by the carefully carved surface and by the way her fingers fit the handgrips as if they'd been molded to her hands, but when she tried to thank Grant he admitted to nothing more than a quick job. The crutches weren't hastily thrown together, however. They were the work of a careful craftsman who'd devoted hours to the project. She was deeply touched.

Glancing at the overcast sky, Grant announced that he was going to the creek to wash clothes that would be clean and dry before it rained. Chantelle insisted on going with him. He agreed only when she pointed out that she needed to practise using the crutches before they started hiking tomorrow.

They exchanged casual words as they walked, the kind of words trail buddies had always shared. "Watch out for this rock, Chantelle."

"I see it. You can let go of that branch now. It won't hit me."

And when they came to a dry rivulet strewn with heart-size cobbles hazardous for crutches, Grant carried her across even though an easy detour was available.

The creek was lively and gorgeous, with pockets of beauty lurking around every moss-covered rock. The change of scene refreshed Chantelle's spirits and made her feel less like a captive. She found the short walk so easy that she insisted Grant return to camp so she could give herself a sponge bath. The creek came directly from melting snow, and so it was a very quick bath, but by the time she hobbled back she felt like more of a woman and less of a trail buddy. That was worth a few shivers.

Grant had been busy, too. He was worried about the likelihood of rain, and Chantelle could see why. More clouds had closed in, obscuring the surrounding peaks.

While she bathed, Grant had started the skeleton of a wide, shallow lean-to. Within an hour of eating lunch, the framework had a back, two ends and a roof, all of woven pine and spruce boughs, and an open side facing a fire that crackled crisply. Damp clothes lay on rough frameworks of sticks ringing the fire, sending small wafts of steam rising heavenward. Grant went from frame to frame turning the clothes so they dried rather than roasted. Chantelle sat back and enjoyed the homespun domesticity of having a man worry about the laundry.

The lean-to was finished none too soon. Rain began to fall so lightly as to be more a heavy mist than a shower. Grant clucked about the clothes, gathering up those that were dry and bringing those few that weren't under the shelter of the lean-to. Visibility shrank still more, so that even the treetops were gray and shrouded in wisps.

Chantelle stuck her hand into the steadily increasing drizzle, then glanced up at the roof of the lean-to. "You did a good job, Grant."

"I think I got most things in before they got wet."

"No, I mean the lean-to. It doesn't leak."

Grant shrugged his shoulders. "Not yet."

Despite his modesty, the camp was a haven of warmth and light. The lean-to trapped the fire's heat and reflected it onto Chantelle's back, and the bough roof was thick enough and sharply enough pitched that amazingly little water dripped onto the hood of her poncho. Though the rain should have been miserable it instead felt cozy, like a curtain that shut out the world and left only the two of them, alone with a crackling fire.

Chantelle stretched out in front of the fire, glancing occasionally at the strong profile of the man who whistled as he carefully sharpened his knife on a small whetstone. She studied the intense concentration on Grant's face, aware that he was stretching the task to its limits of time and perfection. This was meditation, not a chore to be hurried.

Chantelle watched but didn't intrude. Moments like this, when weather dictated that human activity be put on hold, happened sometimes in the bush. They happened to farmers, too, so she understood how much had been lost when the modern world forsook such pressureless respites. It was a rare moment of utter peace, and she felt privileged to share it with someone who wasn't compelled to ruin the tranquillity with chatter.

The afternoon passed with a slow deliberation that nonetheless seemed too fast for Chantelle. Grant whittled aimlessly, as if not worried about producing anything. Chantelle was content to enjoy the sight of Grant's profile, the smells of wood smoke and dampness and the background hiss of rain sizzling on the roaring fire. She used Trevor's book to identify all the plants within close sight. The rain let up, then started again just before dinner.

The evening was less pleasant. The rain increased, soaking the bough roof till it dripped like a dog emerging from a bath. The clouds grew darker, intensifying the murkiness till Chantelle could no longer read her book and Grant could scarcely whittle. Distant rumbles warned of worse weather to come.

When the wind sprang to life, whipping occasional sheets of water into the open end of the lean-to, they gathered their things together. A sudden gust snuffed the weakened bonfire as if it was no more than a birthday candle, and the sky began dumping buckets instead of drops.

Grant half carried Chantelle in a splashing dash to the tent. She knelt in a puddle as Grant opened the tent flap, and didn't object when he pushed at her buttocks to urge her inside. She sat as far from her sleeping bag as she could, dripping and panting. The guttural rumble of thunder bounced from one mountain to another, giving the sound an immediacy and menace she'd never before felt.

Then she realized Grant was still outside.

Chantelle peered out from under the flap of the tent. Grant was squatting just outside, huddled like a khaki lump under his poncho. She motioned for him to come in.

The lump spoke. "Are you decent yet?"

He was waiting on her modesty, at a time like this? Chantelle shook her head in amazement. "Get inside before you catch pneumonia."

As she crawled across her sleeping bag Chantelle leaned the wrong way, and pain stabbed through her tender ankle. She gave up trying to keep her sleeping bag dry. She sat on it, dripped, and hugged her ankle till the pain subsided.

For several minutes they said nothing. When Grant turned on the flashlight, it cast stark, eerie shadows that complemented the storm. Chantelle sat at one end of the tent, pulling her fingers through the tangles in her hair. Grant sat at the other end and struggled out of his poncho. She did the same. The closed-in air of the tent was musty with the smell of wet clothes and hair.

"This is quite a storm," she said.

"Medium. If you were inside a house rather than a tent it wouldn't seem so bad."

"Well, it will do till a bad storm comes along."

"Believe me," he said fervently, "you don't want to be camping when a bad storm comes along."

"You've been out in bad storms?"

"Yes."

He launched into a series of tales about weather, humorous in the telling though not, she was sure, humorous at the time. A tent blowing down at 2:00 a.m. was slapstick humor at best, as was a desperate need to use the latrine in the middle of a wild thunderstorm, yet he told the stories so well that her sides hurt with laughter.

The humor was at his own expense, casting himself in an exaggerated role of the dumb, inexperienced greenhorn. She knew that he was neither dumb nor inexperienced, so chalk up one more point for Grant Van Arden. She admired men who didn't take themselves too seriously.

"I don't think this is going to let up for a while," Grant said at last. "I'd offer to go out while you dress for bed, but even my stupidity has limits."

"I wouldn't think of letting you do that," Chantelle said quickly. She reached for the flashlight and turned it off. "There, instant privacy. Besides, we're trail partners now."

Before she could think further, she began unbuttoning her shirt. Despite the harsh drumming of rain on the tent, every rustle of clothing seemed loud in her ears. By the time she'd folded her shirt, Grant had also begun to undress. As she slipped her bra off her shoulders, she realized that her eyes were becoming accustomed to the darkness, and that Grant was now a visible shadow. She rose to her knees. Her fingers hesitated after unzipping her pants, as the zipper seemed so loud and conspicuous that she had to summon her nerve for the next step.

Lightning flashed, with an explosion of thunder immediately after. Startled by the sudden illumination that was as bright as daylight, Chantelle looked at Grant. He looked at her, too, and his lips parted as his surprised gaze fell to her breasts. The lightning flickered, then renewed. Chantelle threw her arm across her chest and lowered her eyes. The tent returned to darkness as abruptly as it had streaked to daylight.

Grant's shadow crawled halfway across the tent toward her. "Are you okay?"

"Fine."

The shadow retreated to the far end of the tent, more slowly than it had advanced. "Sorry about that," he said. "I didn't mean to peep."

"Don't be silly. We're trail mates." Her nipples were rock hard against the soft skin of her forearm as Chantelle slowly lowered her arm. Raising her eyes to the moving shadow at the end of the tent and facing him openly, she sat motionless in the dark with her hands at her sides. She took a deep breath, then another.

No more lightning came until after she'd finished undressing and was safely in her sleeping bag. Grant stretched his arm underneath her, like a warm and inviting pillow, and urged her close. The embrace was chaste—with two thick sleeping bags between them, it could hardly be otherwise—but she relished its comfort nonetheless.

There was a short period of abundant thunder, during which she huddled against Grant and said nothing. Without warning, lightning would turn the glow of the tent from dark gray to orange, as if the devil was taking snapshots of the mountain creatures' misery in his storm. After each flash, the mountains crashed and shook with the raucous laughter of the thunder. The harsh peaks had never seemed so close, nor she so small and helpless, as when the thunder ricocheted from rock wall to rock wall.

Soon, though, the thunder grew less frequent. As Chantelle lay there, staring up, the main noise became the gray sound of rain sheeting over the tent, punctuated occasionally by the sharp white flapping of the tent material in a gust.

"This is nice," she murmured.

"I like the rain." Grant listened to the drops, made uneven by the capriciousness of the wind. "When I lived in the city rain used to be a nuisance, nothing more. Now it's an excuse to stop what I'm doing and listen."

"I know. That's what you were doing this afternoon while you sharpened your pocketknife, wasn't it?"

"I guess. I don't recall hearing anything, though."

"That doesn't matter. You just have to keep listening."

Grant curled his hand so that it cupped her shoulder. She felt his gaze on her. "It took me the worst part of my life to realize that. You're a wise woman, Chantelle."

"Hardly." But she smiled in the dark.

Lightning flooded the tent with its unsteady brilliance. By the time the thunder splintered the mountainside Grant's arm had tightened around her, pulling her close. She turned her cheek into the warmth of the crook of his shoulder and closed her eyes.

"Now that I'm getting to know you," she said in a soft drone that subconsciously patterned itself after the rain, "I realize that you aren't at all what you seem."

He chuckled. She was coming to love that deep, warm sound. But then, many things about this man were beginning to seem compelling and extraordinary.

"And what do I seem, Chantelle?"

She shrugged. "You're a hard person to get to know. At first I thought you were a northwoods Tarzan. When I learned you were a schoolteacher, I had to revise your image. But all the time, I thought you were a cold bastard."

"I believe your phrase was 'arrogant bastard.'"

"Well, arrogance is a definite element of your personality, you know." As soon as the accusing words left her tongue, she wished she could call them back.

But Grant accepted the criticism as if he'd earned it. "You should have seen me back in the operating room. I'm downright humble these days."

Didn't this man ever take offense at anything? Chantelle stopped her lips just before they opened to lay a kiss on his chest. She licked her lips, instead, and tried to remember what she'd been talking about. "Last night, when you talked about the stars, I realized you have the soul of a poet."

"A poet? Heaven help the poets of the world, then. I couldn't write a poem to save my life."

"I said the soul of a poet, not the pen of a poet. Anyway, the more I know of you it seems the more there is to know. You're a doctor." She emphasized the last word as if it was something incomprehensible. "And you gave it up. I just don't understand."

"Not everything is open to our understanding."

"Maybe." Chantelle was quiet then, thinking.

"The rain seems to be letting up."

In answer, she snuggled in his arms. He was right that a person couldn't understand everything, of course. She might go crazy if she succeeded, but for sure she'd go crazy if she didn't try. Still, his personal life was just that—personal. Private.

She suddenly recalled the private question he'd asked when she inquired why he left medicine. She took a deep breath and stared straight ahead, the way she might when readying to dive into a pool. Except she wasn't sure there was any water in this particular pool.

"You may not believe this," she said in a dry whisper, "but I actually tried to save myself for my wedding night."

She felt his head swivel toward her. Thunder crashed, without lightning this time, and more distantly. He said nothing.

"I was twenty-two. The first time I made love was in the front seat of my future husband's pickup truck, parked on a hill beside Okanagan Lake, looking for Ogopogo."

"You're losing me, Chantelle. Ogopogo? The sea monster?"

"Yes." She could still remember her youthful surprise when she'd realized that every lake didn't have creatures similar to the Loch Ness monster; myths of Okanagan Lake's Ogopogo had been part of growing up. By the time she was seeing Garrett, of course, she no longer believed in Ogopogo, despite the reported sightings every few years. "In high school that's what we called necking by the lake. Looking for Ogopogo."

"You don't have to tell me this, Chantelle."

She paused as she rubbed her hand back and forth across her neck. "Garrett and I had looked for Ogopogo before. We would kiss, and . . . touch. But that time, for no reason I understand, I didn't stop him."

"Chantelle," Grant whispered, "why are you telling me this?"

"Because one of us had to take the first step. I want to have the right to know about you."

"Chantelle, it's not necessary."

She was silent for a while then, reconsidering her rash words. "You're wrong," she said at last. If not this, she thought, then something. Some token of faith, some baring of vulnerabilities, some whispering into the silence of the heart. "Grant, we spent the entire day together without saying anything real, anything important."

His chest heaved in a sigh. "You sure pick a startling way to break the silence."

Chantelle settled back in his embrace. She wasn't sure what else to say, so eventually she continued where she'd left off. "I was out of school by that time. When I was still in high school, I told other girls I'd done it already, even though I was so shy I'd hardly even had a date." She laughed shyly in the dark. "Being a virgin wasn't the 'in' thing, though I suspect most of us were."

"I thought only boys lied about that sort of thing."

"Did you, when you were in high school?"

"Well, no. But a lot of the other guys did."

No, she thought, Grant wouldn't lie. He might break a woman's heart in other ways, but he wouldn't lie. He wouldn't laugh, either, or embarrass her or throw nighttime words back at her. All that made him no less dangerous—more dangerous, in some crazy way she didn't dare examine right now—yet at the same time, it made her want to continue.

"Garrett made me feel exotic, special. I moved in with him for a year. Later, after we got married, I realized it wasn't Garrett but sex itself that had made me feel special. I should have just had an affair with him, but I was a good girl in the old-fashioned sense of the word, and good girls got married. Garrett was a good lover, I guess, but—" She halted, embarrassed. Taking a deep breath, she went headfirst off the end of the diving board. "He's the only man I've ever made love to."

Grant tightened his grip on her shoulder, urging her to turn toward him. She buried her hand in the warm haven under his arm, then pulled it away when he jumped at the coldness of her fingers. "I guess that makes me some sort of a freak nowadays," she said.

"No. It makes you special." Grant savored the friendly smell and feel of this tiger who was curled against his chest like a lap cat. The image of her in his own arms, as evoked by her words, was alluring. In the arms of another man, even her husband, it was disturbing.

Lightning obliterated the darkness. Grant had a quick glimpse of brown eyes wide and startled, then sudden darkness, filled with the rolling crash of thunder. Chantelle shivered in his arms.

He squeezed the soft cotton pajamas covering her shoulder. "Scared?"

"Not really. My bag's a bit damp, though, so I'm chilled."

"The air will get colder now that the weather front has arrived. Come here." He pulled her toward him so that her body was stretched out the length of his. With so much cloth between them he could feel almost nothing, yet because he knew this was Chantelle he felt strength stirring in his loins.

She was quiet for several minutes, with her cheek pressed close to his heart. "It's as if we're right in the middle of the thunderclaps."

"We're six thousand feet up. That *is* in the middle of the storm."

"Does that mean I'm in heaven?" she asked in a teasing tone.

"No. But you are an angel."

"Why, Mr. Van Arden, what a sweet thing to say." She cuddled closer, then she sighed. "We made a deal, didn't we."

"You mean when we agreed to keep our hands off each other?" He moved his hand from her shoulder, then replaced it. "I guess you'll have to sue me."

"That's not what I mean. I meant our agreement to tell each other about our ex-spouses."

"This sounds like an utterly fascinating way to spend an evening alone in a tent with a young lady," he complained. "Can't you come up with a better idea than that? How about a tickle fight?"

"You're trying to back out, aren't you? Well, I won't let you. The more I tell you about Garrett, you'll be honor-bound to tell me about what's-her-name."

"What makes you think I'm a man of honor?"

"Silly, I wouldn't let you hold me like this if you weren't."

Grant wasn't totally pleased with her words, though he supposed he was glad she trusted him. She made him sound like her uncle, and he felt like anything but.

"Garrett was three years older than me," Chantelle said. "He worked at a juice-packing plant, and he wasn't really marrying me. He was marrying an idea of what a wife should be. We had absolutely nothing in common except for passion, and passion wasn't one of the things Garrett necessarily wanted in a wife. He'd have been content with cooking and sewing."

"He was a fool."

"I'm glad you understand him so well. Why, do you know that he claimed I had a temper?" Her voice rose in mock disbelief. "Me, of all people."

Grant chuckled and tightened his arm around her. "I wonder where he got that idea."

"Careful, Grant. That tone of voice borders on sarcasm." She slipped her fingers inside his sleeping bag and pressed their coldness against the bare flesh of his chest. "I punish sarcasm with icy fingers."

His chuckle grew into a laugh. The laugh quickly died when he realized just how cold her fingers were. The night promised to get colder still. He sheltered her hand with the warmth of his arm. "Did the divorce leave you with many scars?"

"No one in my family had ever gotten divorced before," Chantelle said, "but I don't think I'm the type to be scarred for life. It hurt like . . . like the devil, but I learned from my mistake."

"What did you learn?"

"Do you really want to hear this?"

"Yes."

Chantelle stirred under his arm, as if seeking a comfortable position in vain. "I learned that passion isn't enough to hold a marriage together." Her words came slowly, in a weighty voice that lent importance to their meaning. "Next time, I'll hold out for love and a long-term commitment. And also trust, understanding and a willingness to . . . to grow together." Suddenly, as if realizing how serious she sounded, her voice grew lighter. "And wild passion, of course."

"I notice," Grant said slowly, "you didn't mention money or status. That's what Linda wanted. Not that she realized it, of course. She wasn't as cold and calculating as that makes her sound."

"Tell me about her," Chantelle said softly.

"Linda? She was old money, old power. I know that in theory Canada doesn't have peers like England, but nonetheless she was from a family of aristocrats, dating back to the Loyalists who fled the American Revolution."

"She must have loved you a lot to marry the son of an immigrant."

"I guess she did, at first. But it wasn't enough. I realize now that I hadn't chosen a flesh-and-blood woman, but some ideal of what I thought a successful doctor's wife should be." He could picture her even now, alabaster shoulders rising from a strapless orchid gown, with her hair curled elaborately atop her head, greeting his new co-workers at a party soon after his move to Calgary. She had been a magnificent hostess and a strong cheerleader for his career. But that was a sorry epitaph for a marriage, that the wife was hostess and cheerleader.

"I was married to my career in those days, not Linda, and she wasn't used to being ignored," he said. "But she was strong. She built her own life in Calgary society, though I guess she missed Toronto. We had drifted pretty far apart by the end."

"Was the divorce hard? I hope you get along better with her now than I do with Garrett."

He paused. "I've been a widower for two years, Chantelle."

"Oh." Chantelle noticed his hesitation, and pondered the pain behind it. After a moment's interval, she sucked in her breath and held it. *"Ohhh."* She drew out the syllable as realization washed over her. Chantelle's heart opened to him, and to a sharp stab of pain. "I'm so sorry, Grant."

Two years. He'd left Calgary, and medicine, two years ago. He must have loved Linda a great deal, despite what he said, to have given up medicine because he'd failed to save her life. He couldn't be over her death or he'd have returned to being a doctor. After a moment Chantelle added, "Was she very beautiful?"

"Not like you, but yes."

Not like you. Grant thought she was beautiful? A shiver slithered down Chantelle's spine.

"You're cold," he said. "You'll have hypothermia again unless we do something to keep you warm." He sat up and turned on the flashlight. His face looked unreal and ghostly in the sudden shadows.

"What are you doing?"

"Unzipping my sleeping bag. I'll lay it flat, unzip yours and then zip the two together. That way we can lie next to each other and you can stay warm from my body heat."

"I'm not sure that's a good idea," she said slowly.

"I'm wearing shorts, Chantelle."

"That's not what I meant," she protested, though that was precisely what she meant. "The bags won't fit together unless by chance the teeth of the zippers are exactly the same size."

"They are." Grant began opening her sleeping bag.

"How can you be sure?" Chantelle hugged the thick material against her chest. Slowly a smile spread across her face. "Unless you've already checked to find out?"

Grant sat back on his heels and crossed his arms. What a splendid male body, she thought with another shiver, especially now as he stared back at her, wearing only his briefs. So, the thought of sharing a sleeping bag had been on his mind enough for him to have experimented with the bags. Interesting. *Very* interesting. It was so hard to figure what went on in Grant's mind that Chantelle cherished this revelation. She was enchanted, touched, secretly delighted, yet at the same time wary.

Grant looked at her with a blank expression on his face. "Tomorrow you'll need your strength for the hike. You'll be useless if you've shivered all night instead of slept. Are you going to get out of that bag, or do I have to go in after you?"

With a hesitant hand, Chantelle pushed back the cover of her sleeping bag. "I'm still not sure about this."

"Trust me, Chantelle. This is for medical reasons only."

"He wants to play doctor after all," she said as she huddled in a cold ball at the end of the tent while Grant hurried to zip the bags together. "Well, I guess I'll find out what his bedside manner is like."

"You can trust me, Chantelle." He didn't answer her teasing with a smile. His face was expressionless and hard, though perhaps a hint of fire smoldered in his eyes. She wished the light was better, so she could be sure. On second thought, maybe it was best not to know.

Crawling into the doubled sleeping bag was a delicate operation. This wasn't an unselfconscious embrace such as this morning. This was a thoroughly aware move that took her breath away yet made her feel she should apologize for brushing against him. He was warm, certainly, and stretching her body full length beside his did raise her temperature. Did it ever!

She lay there, with her breasts flattened against his chest and her thighs touching his, scarcely breathing. His arm weighed heavily on her ribs and even heavier on her mind. She waited for him to say something, to continue their probing talk. When she finally realized he wasn't going to say anything, minutes had ticked by and it seemed too late for her to speak, as well.

Chantelle was startled when he began moving the arm that was draped around her. The small circles he drew on her shoulder blades made her breath become quicker and shallower. Still he said nothing. The rain ceased, and in its place was soothing silence. Silence, and the pressure of Grant's hand on her back.

After several minutes his hand slowly dipped lower. Chantelle held her breath. He sought the hem of her pajama top, slipped his hand underneath and then skimmed along her bare skin.

This is it, she thought. *Heaven help me, this is it.*

But his hand sought its previous path, gently rubbing her back. Occasionally he moved as low as her waist or as far as her side, but no farther. After a while she realized that he was giving her a back rub, no more, that his caresses weren't building in intensity but merely repeating themselves.

So, she really could trust him. Damn.

She was angry at herself for the twinge of disappointment she felt. He was right, of course, not to pursue a physical relationship. But still . . .

Ariel's words came back to her, drowning out the sensation of Grant's touch. *You seem to be a lady. Grant won't allow himself a serious relationship, he has old-fashioned standards about toying with a lady's affections.*

This chaste touch was proof that Ariel was right. Grant was interested in neither commitment nor a woman who'd made love only to her former husband, or else they would be making love right now.

Could she unsay those words about her past? Could she convince him she wanted a good time, with no strings and no regrets? Grant's muscles were rigid, as if he was having difficulty controlling himself. With a bit of encouragement from her, a bit of writhing or moaning or rubbing against him, would he crumble in her arms? Did she have that feminine power over him? Did she just want to know the answer to that crucial question, or did she really want to make love?

She didn't know the answers to anything anymore.

Chapter Six

The next day began miserably, and slid downhill from there.

From the moment she crawled, alone, from the sleeping bag, Chantelle felt stiff, tired and cold. Everything conspired to soak her. The tent flap dropped a trickle onto her head as she emerged. When she sat on the log to drink the coffee Grant offered, her pants got soaked. Disgusted, she swayed on one leg and one crutch in the middle of camp, cradling the cup for its heat. At least nothing dripped on her.

It wasn't much of a morning for pleasantries. Grant was his usual enigmatic daytime self, and Chantelle didn't try very hard to draw him into conversation. She just felt like putting her head back under the covers.

Grant gathered the driest wood he could find and built a fire that seemed to shiver and huddle the same as Chantelle was doing. Grant explained in more forceful language than usual that they needed a fire to dry the tent because it was too heavy and he had too much to carry already. She already knew that, of course, but he repeated himself several times in rising tones. His voice grew even louder when he discovered yesterday's laundry in the lean-to was soaked. They packed up everything in silence.

They didn't break camp till noon. By then, Chantelle was already weary, cold and damp. She was soon sweating, though, because hiking with the crutches was hard.

Her dampness and weariness got worse. Every plant she brushed against smeared her with water. The constant vigilance required because of her ankle doubled the energy needed for walking. The crutches helped but they were a nuisance, too, since the damp rocks were slippery and the ground soft. Placing the tip of the crutch was sometimes like tossing dice.

Grant helped her, of course, or she wouldn't have gotten a hundred yards. With her arm around his neck, he half carried her much of the time. He let her rest often, claiming that he needed a break because of extra weight, but his breathing never matched her own gasping desperation. Whenever the footing was treacherous, as when they crossed the loose, jagged rocks of a scree slope, he carried his pack ahead, left it and came back to lift her easily in his arms. Those were the only pleasant moments in the whole afternoon.

When the sun finally came out Chantelle's spirits rose. No matter the hardships, it was good to be on the trail again. She would remember that campsite in the clearing for the rest of her life—those days seemed more vivid and important than any in her existence—but she was glad to be heading on.

They made camp early, at the edge of a stream surrounded by dense forest. Chantelle tried to help set up the tent, but Grant ordered her to sit still and, if she had to do something, she could light the camp stove.

It felt good to sit as she pumped the handle that pressurized the camp stove fuel. "How far do you think we came today?"

Grant looked up from pounding tent pegs. His shirt-sleeves were rolled up, showing corded muscles in his forearms as he worked. "Hard to say. Four or five miles."

Chantelle groaned. "Only four or five miles?" On a good day she'd hike that far in an hour and a half, at most. She wadded up the second shirt she'd tied around her waist when the sun came out, and tossed the soft bundle at him. It fluttered atop his head like a shroud. "That wasn't what I wanted to hear, Grant."

When he pulled the shirt off his head, a wide smile lit up his face. She'd seen him smile that way only a few times, with charm and virility radiating from his face. It took her breath away. Obviously he wasn't as exhausted as she was, for he began slowly advancing on his knees, like a grinning mountain lion about to pounce.

"Grant?" She narrowed her eyes, but exhaustion dropped away as if by magic. "What do you think you're doing?"

He pounced.

"Grant!" With energy she hadn't suspected, Chantelle darted away from fingers that tickled her sides. In short order he had pinned her arms over her head and sat astride her waist. He shifted her wrists so he held them both in one hand. His other hand moved to her side, as if to resume tickling.

But when his gaze caught hers, his fingers stilled. Those deep blue eyes held her as effectively as the hand on her wrists. For once his face wasn't unreadable, and what she read there sent another warm gush of energy spiraling through her. He flattened his hand against her ribs and then, with a wordless moan of surrender, moved his hand upward till it reached the swell of her breast. His breathtaking touch stopped there, encircling the bottom of her breast yet making no move to capture it in a melting embrace.

Still held motionless by his mesmerizing eyes, Chantelle moistened her bottom lip. *He's going to kiss me, and I want him to.* They lay for several heartbeats, staring at each other.

When Grant suddenly moved, it startled her. He swung his legs away from her waist. His hand abandoned her breast. Without another word he returned to putting up the tent.

Disappointment flooded her. Was she so unattractive, then? She'd had little enough experience with seduction that her confidence was quickly shaken. Why did he kindle desire and then abandon her, leaving her gasping for breath?

They spoke little at dinner. By then Chantelle felt almost grateful to Grant for turning away from her. One of them needed to show restraint, and restraint had been far from her mind. He obviously was attracted to her, at least a little, and closeness had magnified that bit of attraction all out of proportion. He was right, of course, to avoid complicating an already complicated relationship.

Except, she thought as she watched his rear protrude from the tent as he readied their sleeping bags, that her own feelings were growing deeper and more irresistible. She let out a breath with an explosive sigh. Well, there was nothing she could do about it right now. Later, in the tent, they could talk. She yawned. Even thinking was too much of an effort.

Chantelle fell asleep on the ground, without even going into the tent.

"I don't care if I never see another prepackaged, freeze-dried, lightweight meal in my life." Chantelle put her plate in her lap and rested against the pack, which was propped at the base of a car-size boulder. A cliff rose behind her so steeply that its nameless peak was hidden.

Grant went to his hands and knees to reach across to her. "I'll finish it for you."

Chantelle snatched her plate and pulled it to her chest, out of his reach. "That's different. You'll eat anything." She tried another mouthful. It was supposed to be some sort of spiced cheese omelet but she detected neither cheese nor omelet, only an unreal texture and a pervading blandness. It was, she supposed, edible.

Grant's hand was still extended toward her. She slapped at it playfully. "Can't I even complain about trail grub without you trying to steal my lunch?"

He sat back on his haunches with a dazzling smile that matched her slap for sheer playfulness. "I think the food's good. I also think you must feel better than yesterday if you're well enough to complain."

Chantelle sighed, though she couldn't quite squelch the irrational brightness that flooded her whenever he smiled like that. "Well enough to grind out another four or five miles, I suppose."

"We'll do more than that today, because we got an earlier start and you're walking better. In fact, it should be an easy walk to Trevor's cabin by dinnertime."

Her eyes grew wide as she waited to swallow a dry mouthful. "You mean we might sleep in a real bed tonight? With a real roof over our heads and real walls around us?"

"And real food," Grant said with a nod. His eyes closed in dreamy anticipation. "If I was home, I'd fix a steak about this thick." He held his fingers apart an impossible distance for a real steak.

While his eyes were closed Chantelle took the opportunity to stare at him. As they hiked they were constantly close, with his hands frequently on her, helping, guiding and occasionally even carrying, yet she couldn't sit back and drink in his beauty, as she'd done so often back at the first campsite. She missed that.

When he reopened his eyes she promptly looked down and shoved omelet around the plate with her fork. "One of the problems with this stuff," she said, "is the way it looks. Give me a garden patch and a bowl and I'll fix you the most mouth-watering beautiful salad you ever tasted."

"It's a deal."

Chantelle looked up at him quickly, then back down at her plate. "What do you mean?"

"I mean I'll let you fix me dinner when you drop me off in Clearwater. You owe me a ride home, you know."

This was the first time he'd ever mentioned any kind of a relationship after they got back to civilization. Chantelle turned the fork over and over in her hands, then darted a smile at him. "I'd like that. I'm a good cook, you know. The only problem is that most of my recipes are for a minimum of ten people. Big family, you know."

"No problem. I'll skip lunch." Grant stood up and gazed off toward the imposing bulk of Mount Robson.

Chantelle watched his back. All morning long, Robson had dominated the horizon as it rose seven thousand feet straight from Berg Lake, which glittered like a turquoise gem in the distance. But this man—not the mountain—had dominated her thoughts.

Grant silently watched the mountain for several minutes, while Chantelle forced herself to finish her lunch. When he spoke it was in a soft voice that was almost light enough to be a whisper. "How can a person feel so small and so big at the same time?"

Chantelle tried to swallow her mouthful of omelet but its dryness clung to her mouth. She looked past Grant's casual yet vigilant posture to the humbling majesty of the mountain, which invited her to lose her petty concerns in their splendor and to realize that she was part of something much bigger than herself. Layers of rock seemed as thin as cake layers, yet each was hundreds of feet thick, formed over the span of eons from mud and dissolved seashells, then thrust upward over more eons, only to be chiseled by water and ice to this dwarfing grandeur.

Chantelle's breath caught in her lungs. A shiver ran down her spine, and her spirit opened to the majesty and wonder of this spot, a feeling as magical and gently overwhelming as the first tendrils of love poking leaflets out of the barren sameness of everyday life. Moments like this, when the environment became more than mere scenery and became sunshine warming her soul, were why she hiked. Such moments came rarely and unexpectedly, and were to be stored in her soul and treasured on bleak city nights.

She felt small and yet as big as the very mountains, because she was part of it all.... Not only did she understand Grant's words, but she would have missed the invitation of this moment unless he'd drawn her attention to it.

She had to thank him. Again she tried to swallow quickly, but then decided that they were, after all, trail partners. There was no room for pretense in a backpacker's tent. This man had washed her underwear, suffered her foul tempers and helped her walk by putting her sweaty armpit over his shoulder. She could talk to him with her mouth full.

"It's magnificent," she said with only a small amount of garbling. She was quiet then, realizing the inadequacy of words. Suddenly, like a flashbulb dazzling her mind, came the realization that it wasn't just the mountain and lake that had caused this flash of exuberance. Grant's broad back and square shoulders were indelibly part of the moment.

Chantelle hauled herself to her feet, hobbled to Grant's side and leaned her head against his shoulder. Somehow she knew he wouldn't think her forward if she touched him like this. He looked at her with a gentle flame glowing in his eyes and slipped his arm around her waist. Side by side, saying nothing, they looked at the mountain and felt their kinship with it—and with each other—grow.

The rest of the afternoon was tiring but worth it. Except for the frantic babbling of overflowing streams, all trace of the rain had evaporated. It was hard to believe that the gateway to civilization lay just beyond the gray peak with its head hidden in the clouds. Of course, to get to civilization they had to hike another twenty miles around the foot of the mountain, descend three thousand feet and swat a few hundred mosquitoes. And when they got there the gateway would only be a souvenir shop, a dude ranch, a highway and a parking lot with her by now dusty car.

Chantelle used the crutches less and less. By midafternoon, in fact, she had Grant tie one onto her back, and she hobbled along on just one crutch. He still touched her often. It was always for some trail-related reason, such as branches swinging back at her on tricky footing, but his hand brushed against her more often than any trail partner she'd ever had. And, as a measure of how easily she adapted to the pace Grant set, she was light-headed and tingling all afternoon.

The sun had swung to a hand's height above the peak when they reached the frigid shore of Berg Lake. True to its name, several small icebergs floated like lonesome marshmallows in a turquoise cup. At one point Grant stopped and shielded his eyes as he gazed across the water at the glacier that ran directly into the lake. Chantelle moved to his side. She laid her hand on his shoulder and leaned against him. He glanced down at her with a smile that drew her into the warm depths of his intimate feelings, layer under layer of complexity and compassion and yearning. Chantelle held his gaze for a heartbeat before she retreated to the safety of the scenery.

The sun had just dipped behind the peak, though the sky was still thoroughly light, when Chantelle spotted the shake roof and log walls of the Park Service cabin. As they mounted the rough-hewn planks of the porch, a young man with flour dusted over his shirt and hands came out to greet them. A bandanna was tied around his forehead like a sweatband, and earphones encircled his neck.

"Yo, dudes," the cook called.

Chantelle looked at Grant and grinned. She whispered, "Does this mean we're back in civilization, Grant?"

"Such as it is, I'm afraid." Grant turned to the youth. "Trevor told us to stop by the cabin on the way down."

The young man pointed his finger at them and broke into a smile as if pleased he'd managed to figure out a puzzle. "You're the dude whose old lady broke her leg."

"Actually," Chantelle said, "It's only spr—" The cook didn't let her finish.

"Come on in," he interrupted. "Mr. T's out with the crew working on the trail near Emperor Falls, but they'll be back soon. Nobody misses dinner."

Over the next hour the park workers trickled in, and Chantelle was lost in a swirl of young people asking about her ankle and chatting merrily. The summer crew was composed of university students who wanted a dose of adventure mixed with their summer job, and working in the back of beyond was something they knew they'd never forget.

They seemed to treat the experience as a combination of summer camp and slave labor. Trevor was the slave driver. Despite their jocular high spirits, the students listened to what he said. After a dinner of real sourdough biscuits, real huckleberries and slightly less real potatoes and eggs, Trevor ordered a bath for Chantelle while he and Grant talked.

The four girls in the crew immediately organized themselves to make the injured hiker's bath a success. Baths were a major undertaking. Water had to be heated over the wood cookstove and carried outside in steaming buckets to a caulked wooden tub surrounded by a fence that, the girls explained, should have been two feet higher except that the work crews used to be all male.

The boys carried the buckets with many lively comments, while the girls tested the temperature, sent the boys for more water, and then apologized for the crudeness of the resident gorillas. With a laugh, Chantelle waved off their apologies. The boys meant well, and the high spirits reminded her of her own brothers and sisters.

When the tub was full, a girl named Cindy spread the others as guards around the fence. "Some of the boys think this is Club Med in the wilderness," Cindy explained. She rolled her eyes heavenward. "They think they're irresistible to women."

"Cindy, that's not fair," Bonnie complained. "Jason's too nice to try anything more than a juvenile practical joke—and not even that much with Trevor and that hunk Grant around."

Cindy threw up her hands. "Let's not dredge up this argument in front of company, eh?" She turned to Chantelle. "We women have to stick together. Soak for as long as you want, and don't worry about anything."

Left alone, Chantelle wondered if Grant was still studying maps with Trevor. When she stuck her foot in the water she immediately drew it back. More slowly, she lowered one leg into the water, then the other. By the time she was sitting in the tub she'd decided that heaven had rough, weather-grayed wooden walls, evergreen trees for a ceiling and, most importantly, plenty of hot water. She sighed, breathed in the soft freshness of soapy water, and closed her eyes in pleasure.

A picture of Grant immediately swam into focus. Darn. In a way, Chantelle had hoped that being among other people would dilute Grant's influence. It hadn't. He loomed large in her mind, as large and inspiring as Mount Robson, not merely because he was the only human she'd seen for days, but because of who he was and because of her sharp but confused feelings for him.

Chantelle curled up so that she was immersed to the neck. What exactly were her feelings? Was the affection she felt the beginning of love, or only hormones intensified by physical proximity? Silly question, really. She was more impressed with his mind and with the unanswered questions hovering around him than with his admittedly splendid body. That part of the attraction had nothing to do with hormones.

Okay, she liked him. A lot. But she was still confused by what those feelings meant—and even more confused by where those feelings were leading.

And they were leading somewhere, fast. Assuming they were a couple, Trevor had assigned her and Grant a shared bedroom. Chantelle had stared at Grant, and neither of them had protested. A bedroom seemed—well, not more intimate but certainly sexier than a tent. Soon, she would be going to bed with Grant. But did she want to *go to bed* with

Grant? Such things shouldn't be decided strictly by the passion of the moment. She would have to decide, and soon.

Chantelle began soaping her arms. The tingle in her skin as she washed had less to do with hot water than with thoughts of Grant. She wanted him. The very thought made her arms temporarily too weak to continue washing. Those strong biceps encircling her, pulling her breasts against the hard planes of his chest . . .

But it was so quick. Though it seemed like forever, she'd known him only a few days. His aura of mystery intrigued her, yet made her cautious. There was so much to learn about him. But she didn't know him yet, and time was running so short.

And there was Ariel. As the woman had said, and Chantelle herself had sensed, an affair with Grant would not last. How could there be a happily-ever-after with a man who couldn't even face his past enough to tell her how he really felt about leaving medicine?

But despite all that, despite all logic, she felt like a nervous teenager preparing for the prom. What should she do?

She stood up and reached for a towel. As if startled by the splashing water, a squirrel scolded her from an overhanging branch. Chantelle stuck out her tongue at the creature, which she decided must be male since it stared rudely at her. "Men," she muttered.

Grant settled into the room after Trevor wished him goodnight and went to quiet his rowdy crew. Grant glanced out the window at the near darkness, but saw no one. When last he'd seen Chantelle, the girls had been giggling and putting curlers in her hair, but they must be finished by now.

Though he and Chantelle had spent three nights jammed into quarters much smaller than this, Grant felt almost as if he'd just checked into a motel under false pretenses. Still, at dinner it had been Chantelle who'd calmly thanked Trevor for the offer of this room for the two of them. Grant sat on

the edge of the bed and bounced experimentally then
chuckled in amazement at how firm the double bed was.

He'd enjoyed talking to Trevor. The mindset of an outdoorsman was still new enough after a lifetime of medical
programming that Grant latched on to someone like Trevor
with a gleam in his eyes. On top of that, shepherding this
lively crew through a summer was similar in some ways to
teaching, and that gave Grant extra sympathy for the other
man. Hearing Trevor tell about the work involved in main-
taining trails and replacing old footbridges across the delta
of Robson River at Kinney Lake, Grant had almost wanted
to stay and help.

Grant tried a few more bounces on the bed, then lay back
with his hands behind his head. The Yellowhead Highway
was fifteen miles from here. Normally that was an easy day's
hike, especially since the trail followed the Robson River
downhill all the way. But with Chantelle's ankle, even
though she'd done much better today, he would stretch the
trip to two days.

According to Trevor, the worst section tomorrow would
be the climb out of this hanging valley to the bottom of
Robson Valley proper. In a few miles the trail dropped three
thousand feet. That was steep, and undoubtedly difficult for
someone on crutches. After that the trail flattened out,
though the river still surged downhill as only mountain riv-
ers could. The final day posed no problems like tomorrow's steep climb.

Getting home was their final goal, yet Grant found the
idea disappointing rather than exhilarating. No matter what
sort of relationship he and Chantelle developed, these days
of enforced togetherness had a magic that they would never
recapture.

She'd changed him. After two years of intense self-
examination, he was aware enough to know that he wouldn't
be the same after this trip. The mere thought of returning to
his routine, however liberated it had once seemed, now felt

vaguely stultifying. What a fascinating, powerful creature she was.

What a vulnerable creature she was, too. Relatively untried in love, she turned to him because he was there. Proximity was the love potion that glazed her eyes when she looked at him.

He didn't want only that from her. He wanted... What did he want?

Something more than that. And yet she was still his patient.

With a disgusted sigh, Grant sat up and unpacked his sleeping roll. He placed a thin foam pad on the narrow stretch of floor between the bed and wall and squatted to spread his sleeping bag on the floor. The door opened suddenly, without a knock, and banged into his hip. Thrown off balance, he landed on the sleeping bag.

He heard a feminine laugh that made his heartbeat jump a notch. "Sorry," Chantelle said.

"That's okay."

She had a row of curlers bobbing along the fringe of her hair. "No, it isn't," she said. "Now that we have doors I should remember to knock. It's just that I feel as if we skipped right over the niceties to the real people underneath. Do you know what I mean?"

"Yes." And it worried him. A relationship would have to survive in the real world; the trail was an aberration. He finished unrolling his bag.

"What are you doing?"

"Getting ready for bed."

"On the floor?"

The surprise in Chantelle's voice made Grant recognize the outlandishness of sleeping on a rough wooden floor when the first bed in weeks beckoned. He shrugged off the urge to share the bed, and more, with Chantelle, and resumed spreading his sleeping bag. "Yes, on the floor."

"Grant..."

When Chantelle didn't continue, he looked up just in time to see an expression of hurt submerge under a wrinkling of her brow. "Yes, Chantelle?"

"Nothing." She glanced away as she fiddled with a curler that had come loose. "It's just that..." Again she stopped.

The sleeping bag was in place, but Grant smoothed it a few more times regardlessly. When he was finished, Chantelle still hadn't continued and so he reluctantly turned on his knees to where she sat on the edge of the bed. She was looking down at her hands, which rubbed nervously at the knees of her jeans.

"Chantelle." When she didn't show any sign of having heard, Grant touched her jaw. He paused for a moment, fighting the urge to let his hand follow its own will, then turned her face to meet his. "What's the matter, Chantelle?"

"Well..." Her gaze darted to the wall behind his head. "Why does it bother you so much that we're considered a couple?"

"Because we aren't. You're just a woman I stopped to help along the trail."

"I see." Chantelle sat statuelike for several seconds, then abruptly jerked away. She leaned back to grab a pillow and held it out to him. "Here's a pillow. Sleep well down there."

"Let's not fight."

"How could I possibly fight with the brave and selfless hero who gave his precious time to help a damsel in distress? Here, take your pillow." When he knelt motionless, she pulled back the pillow and threw it on the floor. "Take the damn pillow!"

Grant moved so quickly toward her that she threw up her arms in self-defense. But he merely stretched out beside her on the bed and drew her against his chest. She heard his heart beating loud and strong.

"I'm not going to fight with you," he said. "I apologize, Chantelle, because this is all my fault."

His embrace blew all anger from her as if it was no more substantial than dust. "Your fault?" *Just hold me,* she thought, *and I'll forgive you anything.*

"My fault. I seem to have seduced you."

Chantelle snuggled into his weight, which pressed on her in an altogether pleasant way. "Not yet."

She felt as well as heard the depth of his sigh. "Yes, I have. Not physically, perhaps, but I have. I don't know how—" unless it was the strength of his own desire, seeping through the best of his defenses "—but it wasn't what I intended."

Did he realize, Chantelle wondered, that she could feel against her thigh his body's reaction to this embrace? Did he realize that their hearts were beating in unison, at a fast tempo? Did he realize that her muscles were turning to honey out of sheer delight in his hug? Surely not, or he couldn't apologize with a straight face for almost-but-not-quite seducing her. She turned her head, bringing their lips within inches. "Kiss and make up?"

Chantelle expected him to refuse, and was pleasantly surprised when instead he crossed those few inches. He teased her by nibbling at her opened lips, along the bottom, at the sensitive and almost-ticklish corner of her mouth, along the top, evading her attempts to deepen the kiss. When his lips finally seized hers he took her by surprise, so that her mouth opened helplessly to his onslaught.

But Grant pulled away far too soon. He stood and began fussing with his sleeping bag.

It was several seconds before Chantelle summoned the willpower to move. She sat up and spoke briskly. "Turn around, please."

Grant eyes came slowly back into focus. "Why?"

The question drove the briskness from her mind. She shrugged and tried not to look too virginal. "So I can get ready for bed." She brought her hands to her chest and un-buttoned her shirt with quick fingers that nonetheless felt like thumbs. She heard with amazement a note of coquetry in her voice. "If you'd rather not turn around, well—"

"Maybe I'd better wait outside." He turned to the door.

Her shirt fell open as she reached for him. "No, that's okay. Really, Grant."

He paused, his back to her.

Chantelle touched his elbow, and he slowly turned. Abrupt awareness smothered her, made her incapable of removing her hand from his elbow to cover herself. His gaze was riveted on her shadowed flesh. Chantelle swallowed. Her nipples pebbled, as if his gaze was actually stroking them lightly, maddeningly, sending blood pulsing through her. She licked her dry lips.

Grant closed his eyes, as if in pain.

For several seconds they remained frozen like that. Chantelle was filled with desire and a sense of expectancy that choked her lungs. Her abdomen churned.

Then Grant fumbled blindly for the doorknob. "No," he said. "I'll wait outside."

When he slipped out the door, Chantelle couldn't believe he was gone. She bit her lip till she tasted the saltiness of blood. Savagely yanking off her shirt, she threw it at the closed and unheeding door.

Sleep eluded Grant that night. The sounds of Chantelle tossing and turning on the bed, so close that he felt every movement in his soul, kept his nerves on alert. When she reached down and ran her finger along his shoulder his heart began pounding.

"Are you asleep?" Her voice was a whisper of promise drifting into his ears.

"No."

She didn't say anything. She didn't remove her hand, either.

Grant turned to look at her, but the room was darker than the tent. "Would you like to talk?"

"Sure." The pads of her fingers brushed along his shoulder, then stopped. "But I can't sleep for feeling guilty about you on that hard floor. Get into bed first."

Grant's mouth went dry. "I don't think that's a good idea."

"Because we might kiss?" When he didn't answer, Chantelle's voice grew soft. "Because we might do more than kiss?"

"Chantelle...." Grant sighed. "You're making this hard."

"I'm glad about that, at least." Then the chuckle disappeared from her voice. "It's because of what happened to Linda, isn't it?"

"No." His protest sounded weak even to his own ears, so he added, "You're my patient."

For several minutes silence filled the room. Chantelle's fingers stirred lightly. He felt the intensity of her gaze even in the dark.

"Grant, would you—" she paused "—would you tell me how Linda died?"

Grant was conscious of the effort involved in keeping himself from pacing the pitch-black room. "Linda died of cancer."

Chantelle's chest muscles were so tight that each breath was an effort. She rested her hand on his neck and moved her thumb. "Were you the one who diagnosed it?"

"No. She had her own family doctor." His voice became flat. "I didn't have time, you see, to look after her health."

"Don't do that to yourself, Grant." She felt his pain as her own. "You weren't to blame."

"Not for her illness," he agreed without emotion, "but I robbed her of her most precious days." His mouth snapped shut, as if he'd regretted his words.

Chantelle sought his hand and held it. When he responded by squeezing tightly she summoned the nerve to keep probing. "Tell me about it. Please?"

Grant sighed, the only sound in the empty air. Finally he spoke. "I won't torture you with the details, but her spinal cancer was fast growing and it was virtually too late by the time it was discovered."

He paused for a few seconds, his grip increasing to near-painful strength. "When she was in hospital, I remember being surprised at how firmly she grasped my hand, as if she needed me so much she wouldn't let go. All the guilt I should have felt earlier suddenly hit me. I remember thinking I wasn't much of a husband, but at least I was getting a second chance. Even if I couldn't give her the attention she deserved, I could make amends by giving her life. That's what I did back then—dispensed life, like some antiseptic god. Though surgery was risky, without it she only had a few months. But they were precious months."

A dark chill settled over Chantelle. She shifted to the edge of the bed, wishing she could see his face through the veil of darkness.

"Linda had rediscovered the joy of sunsets and flowers and laughter," Grant continued. "She cherished every minute, knowing she might not have many more. But I knew *I* could save her, even if my colleagues cautioned against the risks, and especially against me operating on my own wife."

"What did Linda think?"

"That's the strange thing." He eased his grip, as if realizing how hard he'd been holding her. "She looked in my eyes, squeezed my hand and said she trusted me. I remember thinking as the anesthetic took effect, as she squeezed my hand one last time, that this would be an interesting operation and few doctors could succeed. Interesting!"

Chantelle's eyes felt hot. She regretted asking him, regretted probing, regretted every harsh word she'd uttered to him.

"We were mostly through the operation," he continued in the same expressionless voice. "I was making one last incision trying to remove one last tissue, when I heard a flat buzzing sound. I couldn't figure out what it meant—I mean, I knew it was supposed to mean her heart had stopped, but I also knew that couldn't possibly be. I just stood there as the nurses and the other doctor began working frantically. They finally pushed me back from the operating table so I wasn't in their way. I stood there and held the scalpel that had stolen her sunsets, trying to comprehend what was happening."

Without letting go of his hand, Chantelle went from the bed to his side. He didn't object when she crawled into the open side of the sleeping bag and pulled a blanket over them both. He put his arm around her and held her close. His flesh was warm through the thin cotton of her pajamas. Too warm, too vibrant. Chantelle scolded herself for the thoughts and passions that swept through her, yet the sensations remained vivid. At this moment she felt something so close to love that her heart burned for wanting to comfort him with every power at a woman's command.

Instead, she stroked the light stubble on his cheek. "I'm so sorry, Grant."

"It was two years ago."

"The heart doesn't watch a calendar. Grant, you did the best you could for her, more than most men could even have dared."

"You mean the surgery? That was easy compared to opening myself to her, and even the surgery didn't work."

"But you tried." She hugged him harder, trying to reassure him with bodily contact as well as with words. "You did the very best you could at the time."

"Maybe. But when I looked in the mirror afterwards, I didn't like the person staring back at me."

Chantelle cradled his head and rocked him. She knew she would cry after unburdening such a story and didn't quite know what to do when he didn't cry. She rocked him for a long time, till his tense muscles finally lost the hardness of granite sometime during the long night.

Chapter Seven

"You're walking a lot better."

Chantelle stopped in midlimp with dinner dishes still in her hands and looked at Grant to see if he was teasing her.

"Don't look so skeptical. I mean it." Grant blew wood chips away from the repairs he was making to the footpad of her crutch. "I was worried how your ankle would hold up to that steep stretch after we left the Park Service cabin this morning."

Chantelle shrugged. "It was all downhill."

"You haven't complained once about all this hardship. Little stuff like food, maybe, but not the pain and difficulty. You've surprised me."

She answered with a smile and an even more elaborate shrug. "I guess that's a compliment."

"The descent put lateral stress on your ankle," Grant said. "If you're still walking this well after a day like today, I'd say you're nearly healed."

Chantelle balanced her dishes atop a boulder at the edge of the camp and turned back toward him, trying to keep the most blatant part of her smile on the inside because it felt silly to be so thrilled by a casual compliment. "If I'm healing," she said, "it must be because I have a good doctor."

"The best," he agreed.

Chantelle stretched her arms and legs, pleased that he'd taken this reference to last night so well. Today, the most important matter in this green, rocky world was whether Grant had recuperated from his own injuries as she was recuperating from hers. "When I get back to Kamloops I'm not even going to walk across the room for a week."

"Just one more day. Think you can make it?"

"Of course." Hiking on a sore ankle took no particular skill, just pigheaded determination and a touch of recklessness; a perfect job for her. She smiled at herself, then turned the smile on Grant. He was watching his work, though, so he missed the look. "He's modest, too."

Grant continued working for a second, his brow furrowed as if retracing the conversation to see what he'd missed. Cocking his head to one side, he looked at her. "Who's modest?"

"My doctor."

A smile lit up his face, and it was as if the sun had climbed back over the peak of Mount Robson. "I don't believe in false modesty. It's a way of getting another person to do your bragging for you, you know."

"I didn't know that. But I do know that you should smile more often." She walked to his side of the camp fire, aware of trying to make her steps as normal as possible.

Sitting on a low boulder, Chantelle watched Grant return without comment to his work. Maybe she shouldn't have said that about his smile. The way things had gone today, anything she said seemed to create awkwardness. A delightful breeze carrying a wisp of wood smoke both cooled her and chased away the mosquitoes that appeared before dusk. Today had been so hot that the already swollen river had filled to the very top of its banks with an abundance of glacial melt. The cool breeze felt good. Not as good as Grant's arm around her waist as he had guided her footsteps during the steep descent, but good nonetheless.

Chantelle sighed as she thought back over the self-conscious frustration that seemed to have marked the day's hiking. In the light of dawn, Grant seemed embarrassed by last night's revelations and more reserved than usual.

After the dishearteningly sweet agony of a sleepless night with Grant at her side, she had started out the morning totally aware of his touch as he helped her walk, totally aware of how alone she was with this man, totally aware of how much she was at his mercy. This intense awareness had led to stiff politeness. With her arm slung over Grant's broad shoulder as they walked, how many times could she apologize for bumping against him without her apologies taking on a life of their own? She'd consciously tried to stop apologizing, but then had felt aware of *not* apologizing. It had been frustrating.

How could Grant go on holding her, carrying her, helping her, sleeping beside her, without being overwhelmed by the powerful urges that had made her day a haze of awareness? Chantelle's head lowered of its own weight as she realized the answer. She had been around men before without their proximity driving her wild. Her problem was the nearness of this specific male. It was her feelings that tortured, not his body.

Her feelings... She glanced at Grant, who carved with a calm expression that inexplicably cut through to Chantelle's heart and left her trembling. The corner of his mouth curled up the tiniest bit. Her heart shattered.

Chantelle lowered her chin to her knees as realization settled over her mind. Suddenly it was obvious. She *loved* him.

Every day, she basked in the vibrancy of his smile, longed to delve under his taciturn expressions, thrilled to the power latent in his every smooth step, yearned to know all his memories and all his feelings. And when he'd bared his soul last night she'd felt her own heart shattering. It must be love. Nothing else was this powerful. The thought carried no surprise, only a sense of inevitability, as if she'd known but hadn't been aware of knowing.

Love. Wasn't love supposed to bring joy, laughter, a lighthearted sense of exhilaration? Chantelle felt inside her heart and easily found a shriek of laughter eager to escape, yet hobbled by uncertainty. A solitary love brought tears, not laughter.

Chantelle cast a guilty glance at Grant as he bent to his repairs. How did he feel? He'd controlled himself so effortlessly last night, despite having her body draped all over his on the hard cabin floor. How could he care for her and show such restraint?

On the other hand, she remembered that moment earlier today, after the growing heat had made her take off the second of three shirts she'd started the cool morning wearing. Grant had preceded her down a two-foot boulder, then reached back to help her. As she'd brushed against him his eyes had narrowed into a sharp look of awareness. On hot days Chantelle never wore a bra, and his forearm had just touched upon that fact.

Grant hadn't said anything, instead thrusting silence between them. Yet he had taken a few frozen seconds to recover and continue hiking. As the day had progressed and humid heat molded her T-shirt, he'd become just as self-consciously polite as she had started out, his eyes and arms scrupulously avoiding even peripheral contact with her chest. Yes, he had definitely waged a silent battle against his feelings, whatever they were.

How did he feel about her?

She thrust speculation aside with a strength that surprised her. Wrapping her arms around her knees, she gave in to the temptation to study him. His cheeks were shadowed by beard, the tails of his plaid shirt were loose, his hair was tousled. He looked gorgeous.

And maybe he wasn't as inscrutable anymore, because she seemed to be catching more and more insights into his feelings. Right now, for instance, she could tell his mind was far away. She didn't know where, but somewhere pleasant. *Pleasant,* for someone long on the trail, was probably home.

Chantelle licked her lips and tried to keep dreaminess out of her voice. "Are you thinking about getting home?"

Grant looked up at her with eyes more round than usual. His fleeting expression of surprise quickly mellowed into a bemused tilting of his head. Lord, he had a handsome face. No, more than handsome. It was a powerful, intriguing face that a woman wouldn't tire of. Ever.

"Yes," he said. "I was thinking about my garden. I hope the neighbor girl kept it watered."

Chantelle cupped her knee and leaned back slightly. She'd guessed correctly. She was more pleased than she cared to show.

"We made good time today," Grant said as he returned to his work. He seemed to be mostly smoothing the wood now. Maybe he was nearly finished and she could, if she dared, probe for his feelings. "My goal for the day was to get as far as the first campsite Trevor recommended. We made it to the second, instead. Here, try this."

Chantelle took the crutch from him. She tried a few steps around the clearing. "It's fine. It doesn't slip as much when I put it on a rock."

Grant brushed the carving scraps into the fire and gave her a look of such intensity that her knees went weak. She sat down quickly. He smiled, as if he could read the reason for her action.

"Trevor was right about this spot," he said. "It is a wonderful place to throw down the tent. No tourists."

"Mosquitoes, though."

"Every Eden has its flaws."

"I suppose so, but the swimming pool will make up for a lot of imperfections."

"True." Chantelle looked up at the sky. "Only another hour or two of light."

To lure her on during the miles, Grant had told her about the swimming hole Trevor had described to him. It was a pool at the bottom of a waterfall just up the creek from this clearing, deep enough to allow diving from the top of the waterfall. The pool was unusually warm because the creek was fed by rainfall rather than a glacier, and because it stood long enough to absorb the sun's warmth. After a scorcher like today the water should be warmer than normal.

Chantelle closed her eyes against a sudden image of pink flesh slicing through shimmering water. Did she dare?

She hoped so. She *had* to bare his feelings for her. Chantelle sat upright with a perkiness that suppressed the aches of the day's exertion. "Let's swim."

Chantelle insisted on walking the short distance without the crutch, so Grant put his arm around her waist to steady her. She liked the mushy sensations that spread through her, as if his arm was a warm spoon melting inexorably through a stick of butter. That was how she felt when he touched her, as if she had no shape of her own but would melt to whatever form he determined.

But that was also what she didn't like about his arm around her. She gave up control. She was mature enough to realize that love involved trusting yourself to another person, that you had to give of yourself in order to get. But her relationship with Grant wasn't like that. He gave and she took. She loved, and he...what did he feel? She wished she could just ask him, and maybe in the dark of the tent she could.

No. Actions were better than questions—actions that would encourage him to love her and thus not shatter her heart.

Grant stopped abruptly.

Chantelle tore her gaze from the fuzzy shadows highlighting his face. They'd arrived at the waterfall.

"It's beautiful," she breathed. Then she wished she hadn't spoken and admired it in the silence that was the only fitting tribute. The lacy sheen of the waterfall wasn't as grand as Mount Robson, but that monolith's grandeur was of a God-like stature; this pocket of beauty was on a human scale. Chantelle rested her cheek on Grant's shoulder and soaked up the scene.

A ten-foot cliff topped by overhanging greenery surrounded the pool on three sides, making the waterfall seem like an exotic grotto or private room. The gentle cascade hugged the rocks till suddenly jumping free and transforming into a sheet of silver. This was a spot where nature beggared the best efforts of art and produced a perfection that invaded a person's soul.

Grant looked at her. His eyes gave off a bluish glow that was echoed by the smile radiating from his face. So, Chantelle thought, he felt it, too. But then, she already knew that they saw the world through the same eyes. She felt her face soften to putty as she looked up at him.

In unison, they turned to each other. Don't be putty, she reminded herself weakly. Take charge. But her eyelids lowered without volition as her chin turned up to meet his lips.

Grant hadn't intended to kiss her. He had specifically ordered himself not to kiss her, and had spent the entire day repeating that litany of self-denial.

He kissed her anyway. It was a soft, treasuring kiss, a light kiss that tried to disavow the plundering passion he felt raging inside. Her mouth was sweet nourishment for his heart, the thrust of her tongue incitement for his passion. He pulled away before his control vanished in an explosion of lust.

When the kiss ended, Chantelle turned her back and stood breathing heavily for several seconds. She reached for the hem of her T-shirt and pulled it up. Her vertebrae and shoulder blades burned into his memory as she paused with arms raised, easing the shirt over her head. An inviting hint of roundness showed at her side, yet no one feature, not even her breast, was more erotic than the feminine totality of Chantelle—the shy yet bewitching beauty who permeated his thoughts, his emotions and his life.

She was his patient. Grant cleared his throat. "Aren't you going to swim in your shorts and T-shirt?"

With one modest arm raised to her chest, Chantelle provocatively smoothed her hair over her shoulders, hair that called out for him to caress it and lose his hands in its glorious fullness. "What do you think?" There was a question in her furrowed brow, but no hesitation. She was transformed into Eve before the apple, wanton yet pure.

When she turned back to the pool, he saw her shoulders rise, as if taking a deep breath in preparation for the next step—shy Chantelle again, rather than Eve. She bent to her shoes, keeping her back to him. When she stood and raised her hands to her belt, he looked away.

The splash of her dive came so quickly that Grant wondered if she'd regained her senses and retained her clothes. But, no, powder-blue panties lay atop jeans in a careless pile.

Her head and shoulders shot from the water. She shrieked as she pushed dark hair off her face. "It's cold! I don't care what Trevor said, it's cold!"

Grant chuckled as he sat at the edge of the water and dipped his hand. "Come on out, then."

"Not with you sitting there watching." She wiped at her eyes, then flung a spray of water his way. "You come in."

"You want someone to freeze with you. If I come in, who'll lie on top of you for body heat so you pull out of hypothermia?"

"Is that what you did? No wonder I had dreams of making love." She moved backward, waving her arms in the water to support herself. "The water isn't that bad once you get used to it. Even a real swimming pool feels cold till you're in it." She swam away from him, her body a wavering hint of brightness in the dark water. "Come on in. I won't look."

Grant shook his head, but his gaze never left the whispering glimpse of pink shimmering through the water. This wasn't smart. Not smart at all. Did she know what she was starting? And if so, was she sure? But he was already standing, with his shirt buttons undone, before he consciously decided. By then, his decision to return to camp was obsolete.

The water felt cool as he sliced into it, but not cold. Too bad, in a way. He could use a cold shower right now, and this pool wasn't having the same effect on his anatomy. But then, even a cold shower wouldn't have that effect if Chantelle was in the shower with him.

He surfaced and looked around. From here, the curtain of the waterfall dominated his vision and his hearing. The craggy cliffs seemed taller, blocking out the world and leaving him on his own planet. Adam, alone with Eve.

But Eve was nowhere to be seen. He turned as he treaded water, yet still didn't see her.

Unseen hands suddenly seized his knee, pulling him under. Water invaded his mouth. When he came back up, sputtering, Chantelle was treading water a few feet in front of him.

"You play dirty," he complained.

She arched her eyebrows. "I have six brothers and sisters. Of course I play dirty." With that, she took a deep breath and slipped underwater.

Grant dodged toward the waterfall. He ended up holding on to the cliff, waiting for her to surface. She eventually did, the heavenly curves of her chest emerging briefly into view. She looked for him in the wrong direction. Quietly he moved under the water toward her.

When his hand touched the perfect smoothness of her backside she thrashed away immediately. He surfaced, and for a moment they stared at each other as they treaded water.

"Look who complained about playing dirty," she said. "At least I kept my hands polite."

"Can't take it, eh?"

Her eyes narrowed. "So that's how it's going to be. Well, you asked for it."

She began circling him, watching him with a playful deviltry dancing in her eyes. He'd never seen this expression, never seen this side of her. A realization fueled his already rampant arousal. She'd be like this in bed, playful and active and totally, passionately involved, his every fantasy fulfilled.

Restraint dissolved as Grant abruptly threw himself toward her. Chantelle shrieked and disappeared under the water. He came up empty-handed, then felt a water-muted slap on his bum.

The game that followed was sexy and yet at the same time enjoyable and complete in itself. Chantelle flashed through the water, half emerging as she plunged back under in a blur of flesh tones that spurred his pursuit. A teasing touch rewarded her capture. Then she was gone again with surprising speed, slipping away from his light embrace. A breast jostled his back. He laughed and splashed water at her face. He pursued, she evaded; she pursued, he evaded. Yet neither of them evaded so thoroughly that they forgot they were adults, engaged in a game that would end far from innocence.

After a while Grant found a ledge of the cliff just far enough underwater to provide a bench that didn't mean surfacing into the air, though his shoulders and chest felt the coolness of evaporation. Chantelle swam on her back, a slender, seductive water nymph who eyed him warily.

He lifted his hands from the water and held them in the shape of a T. "Time out."

"Is this a trick?" Her hair was plastered to her forehead. The dimming light cast her face into soft lines of breathtaking natural beauty.

"No trick."

She swam closer, then treaded water just out of his reach.

"Don't you trust me, Chantelle?"

"I trust you with my life. Just not when we're playing."

"There's room for two here."

She waited a few seconds longer. "Okay." She edged closer, then at the last minute lunged and ended up in his arms. His hand splayed on her lower back as she rested one leg on his thighs and the other on the ledge. Each and every nerve in his body rejoiced in the long-delayed contact with her supple form.

He felt raw desire return, stronger than ever. He was about to pull her to him, but stopped to enjoy the shadowed expression in her hooded eyes. Drops caressed her neck and shoulders as they rolled down her skin. Water lapped at the curves of her chest, teasing him with what it revealed and what it hid.

But he wanted more than her body. Tenderly he brushed a strand of hair away from her forehead, daring to think that this embrace might mean what he hoped. "You're the most beautiful sight I've ever seen."

She looked into his face without raising her head. Even in the gathering shadows he saw the passion in her eyes.

He pulled her to him, crushing her breasts against his chest and her lips against his. Taste-smell-touch melded into a fierce cascade of sensation that drowned out the last whispers of restraint holding him back, and his tongue darted boldly into her mouth. She met him with an openness like never before, with an eagerness that matched her erotic play in the water, with a passion that inflamed him further. He drank greedily of the love and desire that her mouth offered, but no matter how much he drank he sought more to slake his unquenchable thirst.

When his hands began roaming her body Chantelle felt the energy flowing through her surge stronger in a quantum leap that carried her incredibly close to the pinnacle of delight. A touch, a kiss, a hug, weren't supposed to be this powerful. She opened her mouth wider, urging him to take what he wanted. He tasted so good, as if even his taste was an aphrodisiac that sent her soaring upward. His hands found her breasts, and she pushed herself up, out of the water, to offer them to his lips.

As he suckled, passion guided her fingers through his hair, holding him so he couldn't escape, couldn't withhold the indescribable pleasure that keened in her mind like the birth scream of ecstasy. His hands trailed down her back, testing the soft resiliency of her bottom with kneading motions that sent lightning bolts of fierce pleasure jolting through her abdomen.

The moan that had been building in her mind escaped once, then again. So close. Oh, already so close, so close as to be agony, so close that she was desperate.

Chantelle moved her leg off his thighs, shoveled angrily at the water when she began to float away from him, then settled on his lap with a knee on each side of his powerful thighs. She searched between them with frantic hands, found the object of her desire and closed her hand on it.

Amazement flooded through her when he closed his hand over hers, stilling her urgent movements.

"Chantelle, wait."

"No!" She struggled under his hand, realized his superior strength and settled onto his thighs with a wriggling motion that she hoped would make his desire as extreme as hers. At least he had the decency to appear tortured. "Well, not for long, okay?"

Grant closed his eyes, as if gathering strength, then opened them again wearily. "Chantelle, I have no protection for you."

"It's a safe time for me," she said emphatically. Mentally she began counting. Yes, it was a safe time.

Chantelle crushed herself against him, trying to force a culmination of the blaze inside her. She both felt and heard his sigh.

"I don't know how to ask this, Chantelle."

She snapped her head upright and looked him in the eye. Why would he want to talk at a time like this?

In the night, in the dark, words would soothe her. But now, when he could see her naked desire, her pain and humiliation, now was not the time for words. A premonition swept over her, dampening the fire inside her as thoroughly as if she'd filled her lungs with the pool. "Then don't ask."

"I have to."

Anxiety filled Chantelle's arms with tingling panic and her heart with the weight of the mountains. If Grant loved her or even cared for her he wouldn't be talking, he'd be making love. *He's an honorable man. He won't take advantage of you.* The remembered words mocked her, making her feel naked in a stranger's arms. Was he so honorable that before making love he'd make clear that he didn't love her, that she had to accept there could be no entanglements?

"I don't have any terrible disease that might contaminate you," she said, shocked by the ice and venom in her tone, when only a minute ago...

"No, you misunderstand." Grant tightened his hands on her shoulders. "You told me that you'd learned something from your first marriage."

"Yes. Men are jerks."

"You learned that passion wasn't enough." His voice was as hard as his grip. "You said you were going to wait for love."

He'd left out the part about a long-term commitment. She was tempted to throw the words in his face, but she clamped fiercely on her temper.

"Chantelle, I . . . I'm not sure this is right for you."

In other words, he didn't love her.

She pushed away, ducking underwater to escape his harsh grip. Surfacing a few yards away, she tried but failed to look at his face, staring instead at the waterfall, which bubbled as merrily as before, uncaring of her pain.

"I understand," Grant said crisply. In an explosion of water, he pushed from the ledge and began swimming furiously. Chantelle watched his arms slice expertly through the water. He swam to one rock wall, turned and swam back, as if trying to drive away all memory of her body from his mind.

At least she hadn't committed herself. She hadn't told him she loved him. At least she had that. But he'd humiliated her. He'd waited till she'd thrown herself at him shamelessly, then rejected her. The heat in her heart turned from passion to anger.

She pushed hard against the cliff to propel herself across the pool. At the edge she stopped and looked back at Grant, still splashing through the water as if chasing demons. Climbing out was going to be difficult, and not just because of her ankle. Climbing out meant exposing herself. And climbing out meant leaving Grant.

Cautiously she crawled onto land, gathered her things and slipped behind the dubious cover of some brushes before donning clothes over her wet body. Her hair dripped. Chantelle squeezed out the ends, wishing angrily that she had a towel. On sudden inspiration she returned to the edge of the pool, picked up Grant's shirt and began drying her hair with it.

The splashing stopped. She peeked out as she rubbed. Grant was watching her from the middle of the pool, his face inscrutable.

She wished he would object. She wished he would shout and come after her, argue and curse and then suddenly relent, his anger spent. She wished he would hold her in his arms and tell her he was sorry.

He just looked at her.

Chantelle lowered the shirt and jerked her hand through her hair a few times. With her gaze locked onto his, she squatted to pick up Grant's clothes and shoes. He still just looked at her, but his eyes narrowed. Without a word she turned and headed back to camp. Sounds of splashing and shouts hurried her footsteps. This, she realized, was the most thorough test she'd yet given her ankle. She hoped it would hold out.

It did. Grant was walking barefoot over rugged terrain, and so Chantelle was already seated by the warmth of the camp fire, combing her hair, when he arrived. Only his dignity was wrapped around him as he walked into the open, yet his pride was awesome, and it clothed him more arrogantly than a suit or tuxedo.

Guilt tweaked at her, but only succeeded in stoking the fire of her temper. She glowered at him, waiting for him to say something that would spark an angry answer. But he said nothing. Making no effort to cover himself or shield her feminine sensibilities, he pulled spare clothes from the backpack and dressed.

Chantelle crushed the desire she felt even now, adding its energy to her anger. He was trying to humiliate her further, dressing in front of her like that. When conscience timidly reminded her that he was naked because she had stolen his clothes, she tossed her conscience onto the fire raging inside her. She felt as if she was about to explode.

Fully dressed now, Grant calmly sat down beside the fire. She darted poisonous glances at him, but they bounced off the armor of his bland expression. He tossed another log onto the fire and then held his hands out to warm them.

Chantelle plowed the comb through her hair, ignoring him. She swore colorfully when she jerked her way through a tangle.

Grant chuckled. She glared at him through a curtain of hair, not deigning to raise her head.

"That was a nasty trick," he said with a dash of silky humor in his voice.

Chantelle shot to her feet. "Nasty? Look who's talking!" She pulled back her arm and then, because his grin merely widened, she threw the comb at him.

He caught the comb, shook his head and sighed. "Don't start throwing things again. One of these days I'm going to have to teach you to control that temper of yours."

Again, she slapped down her irksome conscience. "Is that a threat?"

Grant opened his mouth to speak, then closed it with a shake of his head. He stood up, looming over her but still saying nothing. He dropped the comb in her lap, walked to the dirty dishes from dinner, picked them up and disappeared in the direction of the creek. Chantelle was left to simmer beside the fire, alone. She hugged her knees and stared into the savage flames.

"Keep your hands off me!"

Grant mentally cursed the bulky backpack that kept him from catching Chantelle in a few quick strides. Today, the final day of the hike, her ankle seemed fine. She wasn't even using the crutch.

"Chantelle, we have to talk. You aren't still angry about last night, are you?"

She stopped abruptly and turned to face him with her hands planted on her hips. Her narrowed eyes flashed.

"Okay," he acknowledged, "you are still angry. At least tell me why."

"Why? You know why." She let out a derisive bark of anger, then turned and charged down the bush-lined trail.

Grant was about to open his mouth to protest, then closed it so hard that his teeth ground together. With a grim heart, he followed in her tracks. Yes, he did know why. She'd tried to seduce him, and instead of following his heart he had chosen the safe, cowardly route of forcing her to declare her feelings first. He hadn't planned to be a coward—considering her lack of experience it had seemed noble at the time to make certain she knew what she was doing—but his nobility had been an excuse.

He watched the sway of her hips as she walked ahead of him. Heat had darkened the back of her shirt with a patch of perspiration. Her slender arms caught the sunlight as they swung back and forth in a hypnotic rhythm that made him wish this hike would go on forever, rather than ending in a few short hours.

He decided to let her anger dissipate till lunchtime, then try to win her over. How, he wasn't quite sure. His guts told him kisses would be best, but his scientifically trained mind demanded a more logical solution.

He glanced at the angle of the sun. He'd give it another half hour till he stopped. He could tell by the widening of the valley that they must be almost to Kinney Lake, where they had to cross the Robson River on a series of footbridges spanning the delta. As soon as they were across he'd halt.

A short time later, he saw her stop and plant one hand on her hip and pointed to the wide, fierce river. She muttered something he couldn't hear.

When he reached her side, he saw a footbridge dangling steeply from the riverbank. The far end of the narrow, logs-and-planks structure bobbed loosely in the current. Only a submerged clump of bushes marked the island where it was supposed to end.

Grant hitched the pack higher on the small of his back and shook his head. "I guess Trevor will have to wait for the river to go down to replace the bridges."

Chantelle glared at him. "Is that all you can think about?" She shook her clenched fist against her thigh as she scanned the waters.

On the far side of the submerged island, the next footbridge was half underwater and turned on its side. Skeletal roots of driftwood trees were piled upon it. The river seemed to laugh at them as it rushed past.

Grant sat down, eased the pack off his shoulders and watched Chantelle pace. "I wonder where's a good place to pitch the tent."

Chantelle went rigid. "What do you mean?"

"Just what I said. We have to wait till the river goes down." He began removing his heavy boots.

"How long will that take?"

Grant shrugged, not really wanting to hazard a guess. "If it doesn't rain anymore and if this heat eases, maybe a day or two."

"No! I mean, we're so close now." She looked toward the open space of the five-mile-long lake, straining toward the far end where casual tourists in thongs and Bermuda shorts must be snapping pictures of Robson's reflection in the water. Only a stroll beyond them was the highway and her car. "There must be some way we can cross."

Grant sighed and began retying his boot.

"There is, isn't there? You know another way across."

He looked up at her, shaking his head. "The river is awfully high."

She sat down beside him. "You mean there's a spot where we can ford the river? Did Trevor tell you something?"

"Forget it."

"No! I want out of the wilderness. I want a real tub filled with bubble bath, and perfume so I can smell like a woman. I want my own mattress, doors that lock, and food that tastes like food." Her arm stretched hesitantly toward him. "Please, Grant. Let's at least check out the ford."

Her furrowed brow and trembling lip tugged at his emotions. He was right to wait for the flood waters to recede, wasn't he? Or did he just want to be with Chantelle as long as he possibly could? He listened to the voice of the river as he looked inside himself. Almost certainly they could cross, since Trevor had said that the half-mile wide mouth of the delta was only calf-deep. The current would be dangerous if Chantelle fell, but that was unlikely with his help. If it was just himself, he wouldn't hesitate.

"We'll check out the ford. But after lunch, mind you."

Chantelle hurried through her meal. This was the last trail food she'd have to stomach for a long time. A very long time, since she suspected hiking would always retrieve memories better avoided. She glanced at Grant as he ate. This would be the last meal she would share with him, as well. Considering how the humiliation and rejection of last night kept rushing back to her in shockingly vivid images, she couldn't imagine fixing dinner for him as he'd once asked. Grant lived in the past, not the present. Her ankle had healed better than his heart. What a fool she'd been, totally misreading his interest in her. What a stupid fool.

Stupid. How she hated that word. Back in school she'd shouldered the reputations of her two older brothers. They weren't good students; Bert had a hearing loss that hampered his learning, while Martin had been scathingly uninterested in school. Quiet, shy Chantelle, who loved to read but couldn't add two plus two and who froze when teachers asked a question, had believed her peers' assessment that she was unintelligent. Though she'd gotten over the misconception she'd never gotten over the hurt. Even now, the worst thing she could call herself was stupid.

And with Grant, she'd been stupid.

She hurried through the meal and then badgered Grant into eating quickly. She couldn't wait to get home.

At first, the crossing was easy. Though the water was frigid, it came only to her knees. She had time to look to her right at the expanse of the lake, and then at the river. The channels of the delta had merged into a broad, frothy sheet that overran the shrubby islands in between.

They reached the first "island," where the water was only shin-deep. Grant took her hand. "Are you okay?"

Chantelle couldn't bring herself to look at him. Being wet reminded her of last night. "I'm fine. Let's keep going."

The next channel was deeper and faster, so that each step was a slow-motion struggle. She began using the crutch. Grant waited for her and tried to put his arm around her waist, but she pulled away from him and surged ahead to the shallows of the next island. The river had washed a small pebble into her boot, but there was nowhere to stop to shake it out. She kept going, her eyes doggedly fixed on the riverbank.

As they caught their breath on the shallows of another island, Grant touched her arm and spoke in a voice as impassive as his face. "How's your ankle?"

"It's fine, I tell you."

Chantelle turned to resume walking, but Grant tightened his grip on her arm. A muscle in his cheek twitched. "I don't like this, Chantelle. Those are rapids over there. I'll carry you across on my back."

"Oh, sure. Just put me on top of the backpack like old luggage."

"Wait here while I take the pack across," he urged in a tone that was too calm, too controlled. "I'll be back in a few minutes."

The impersonal politeness of his voice did nothing to dim the sense of expectancy, of imminence, that grew within Chantelle as she watched the white waters race past. One more channel, only one, the widest and fastest of all. The last major barrier between her and normal life. Life without Grant.

"No!" She pulled from his grasp. "Let's get this over."

Soon Chantelle was in water above her waist. She slowed, fighting the current while carefully keeping her balance. Despite the handicap of his pack, Grant caught up to her. Again he put his hand on her, and again she tried to pull away.

He jabbed his finger in the direction of the lake, a few hundred yards downstream. "Do you see that?"

"Of course." She tried to walk away, but her elbow was firmly in his grasp.

"If the river sweeps you into that lake you won't last five minutes."

Again she tugged at her arm, and this time he let go. She felt silly standing in water past her navel, arguing. Besides, he should have the sense not to argue with her here, reminding her that last night they'd argued in the water, too. A quick flush of heat drove away the water's chill.

With a curt shake of her head, Chantelle took a wary backward step. "I'll just have to be careful."

"Chantelle, don't endanger yourself just because you're angry at me. I should never have let last night happen. I should never have let things go that far. It's my fault."

Renewed memories banished the river's cold. Chantelle's hand tightened into a fist. "You did an excellent job of protecting my morals. I suppose you expect me to thank you?"

"You're a marriage-and-forever woman, Chantelle, and I can't offer you that."

"So, you rejected me for my own good, is that it?"

"Yes!"

"You know what's wrong with you, Grant? You're afraid. Something happened to you two years ago, something bad, and you're afraid to start living again. But don't try to make excuses about how you rejected me for my own good."

"Chantelle, I—"

"I'm a big girl now," she interrupted, "and unlike you, I can live with my mistakes." She raised her fist out of the water. "But making love would have been the biggest mistake possible!"

"Chantelle, you're overreacting."

"Overreacting! I'm glad you noticed. I've been overreacting since the first moment I saw you. You don't think I'm usually like this, do you?"

Grant raised one eyebrow and opened his mouth, but she held up her hand to stop him. She spoke in a quiet, dispirited voice. "Well, I'm not. With all your fancy degrees, can't you figure out why I overreact?"

Not waiting for an answer, she turned toward the riverbank. Immediately the water slowed her angry stomp to a crawl.

Again Grant caught her elbow. The worry etched deeply on his face almost made her relent. He shook his head, and his rugged jaw knotted into a harsh square. This was the first time, she realized with surprise that immediately turned to resentment, that she'd ever seen him really angry. "Chantelle, let me help you. Don't be stupid."

"Stupid!" She jerked her arm from his grasp. "Leave me alone, Dr. Van Arden."

"At least let me tie us together."

But she was already forcing her legs against the molasses caress of the river. Out of the corner of her eye she saw Grant reach for her. Quickly, too quickly, she jerked away. One foot lost touch with the river bottom. She swayed on her bad leg, but to her relief the painful ankle held.

Then his hand brushed her arm. Not much, but just enough to throw her off balance. Straightening up should have been easy. It would have been, too, without the irresistible current. But her weight was too far back, and she couldn't quite straighten against the thrust of the water. She took a step away from him, adding momentum to her fall.

"Chantelle!"

Not again, she thought. Do all falls feel as though they happen in slow motion? She had a second to feel stupid, then regretful. She turned to see Grant's panicked face and the impossibly distant hand he extended toward her.

His face was the last thing she saw before the water closed over her head.

Chapter Eight

When Chantelle slipped under the water, Grant's self-control snapped. He took huge, current-aided steps toward where she'd been. His frantic eyes searched the rushing river.

There! A few feet downstream, her hand speared out of the water, then her head. But she was tossing and floundering at the whim of the current. Grant dove toward her, trying to reach her with one desperate lunge.

His outstretched hand touched nothing.

He tried to regain his footing, but the packsack acted like a sail and the river like the wind, blowing him toward the frigid lake. His head bobbed to the surface. Air refreshed his lungs and none too soon, for the sack was filling with water, dragging him to the smooth rocks of the river bottom. He rolled over the rocks till he feared he could hold his breath no longer.

A plant rasped at his arm. Grant tried to grab it but failed. The water was shallower here; a submerged island. He managed a quick breath, then opened his eyes to the cold, murky water and tried to watch for another shrub. He reached, grasped, but the small plant pulled from the soft mud without even slowing his roll.

And then he came to a sudden stop as an unseen bush grabbed him from behind with rough tentacles. Water rushed cold and tasteless into his mouth as he struggled toward the leafy air.

While he filled his lungs, Grant darted his head from side to side, searching for Chantelle. All he saw were a few man-size shrubs marking this sandbar and, just beyond the island, the wide abyss of the lake. He stared toward the shore, hoping against hope for some glimpse of a stubbornly independent, dark-haired woman.

Nothing.

Grant tried to tell himself Chantelle was fine, but an overpowering fear was invading his chest. She was in danger. Mortal danger. He suppressed panic, trying to think of some way to find Chantelle, some way to rescue her, some way to do something other than lie here helplessly. He took several deep breaths, keeping the frenzy trapped inside though it screamed madly for release.

Grant wiped hair from his forehead and tried to sit up, but the leaden weight of the backpack felt like a mountain tethered to his shoulders. He grunted as he pulled his arms from the straps. He cared little for the pack, though rope and matches might be useful. He fished around till he found the waterproof matchbox and a slender coil of yellow plastic, then let the water drown his possessions and carry the carcass away.

Away to a cold, deep grave.

Away, he was afraid, to join the only woman whose smile shone brightly enough to light even the darkest corners of his soul with fiery warmth. He felt overcome with mortal pain as he stood, yet he wasn't injured.

He was in a dangerous spot, so close to the lake that unless he forced his way directly across the current he would run into deeper and deeper water as the bottom dropped off into the lake. It scarcely mattered, of course, unless Chantelle was safe.

Grant doubled over with a pain in his chest that wasn't physical, an all-consuming burning that was reducing his heart to ashes.

Aside from the small scrape on her forearm from climbing the riverbank, she seemed to be all right. The current hadn't carried her far before she'd started thrashing toward the shore. Once under control she'd crawled across a shallow stretch till she reached safety.

Chantelle hugged her elbows and silently gave thanks. This could have been disastrous. As it was, though, the only damage was that she'd gotten completely soaked instead of half-soaked. She hoped Grant wouldn't laugh too hard at her bedraggled state.

Laugh? She chuckled ruefully. Grant wouldn't laugh. He'd be upset with her, instead. Well, she deserved his anger. Her temper had really done it this time. Her temper and her stubborn, silly self-sufficiency. When would she ever learn?

Right now, she vowed. She pushed herself to a sitting position. There was nothing like a little danger to provide perspective.

True, Grant had rejected her last night. There would be other nights and other chances, unless she let her juvenile anger ruin the relationship. She would do everything in her power to make Grant love her. Maybe she couldn't make him love her for the rest of her life, but she clung to the thought that he must care enough to sustain a short relationship, at least. He *must*. She would risk the pain of losing him, if only she could have him for a while.

Where was Grant? By now he should have reached the bank and begun searching for her. She shaded her eyes as she peered upstream through the thick brush, but saw only leaves.

"Grant? Where are you?"

Forcing her way through the trees and shrubs lining the bank, Chantelle again called his name above the roar of the river.

"Grant?"

Something made her turn around. Maybe it was a sound, a voice that somehow pierced the white noise of the water; maybe something more, something beyond mere perception. When she turned downstream she immediately saw a distant figure huddled by a drowning bush.

She surged toward Grant, only to be entangled in a welter of shrubbery. Paying no attention to scrapes from twigs, she pushed inland from the dense bank so she could run faster. Though her ankle protested, she kept running.

The riverbank opposite Grant was lower and mostly clear of trees and bushes, so that when she began waving he could see her easily. Even from sixty feet, she saw the life return to his posture and expression. The sun on her back didn't warm her nearly as much as the sight of him.

Grant shouted something that was washed to murky incomprehensibility by the river. He waved his arms in a gesture of disgust with the noise. He tied the rope around his waist and waved the loose end high in the air. Yes, she realized, he would need her help to get off the sandbar. Nodding her head was probably useless, but she did it anyway.

Then she waited with her arms outstretched as he threw the rope. It splashed far short of the bank and floated quickly downstream. By the time Grant began reeling it in for a second try it had stretched like a yellow snake atop the deep water of the lake.

The rope wasn't long enough for her to stand safely on the bank. She guessed it would barely reach when taut, and slack was inevitable during a throw. As Grant readied for another throw, Chantelle took a deep breath and slid down the steep bank into water that shoved against her knees and then, after a few steps, her thighs.

Grant reared back and threw. The rope again fell short.

If she dared a bit farther...

"Go back. Chantelle, go back."

She was just close enough to decipher Grant's shout, but she ignored both his muffled words and his frantic waving. She stepped forward. With cold wetness lapping at her belt, she braced for the next toss, thanking God that the current was weaker this close to the lake. Grant stared at her. She feared he wouldn't throw unless she retreated, but after a moment he drew back his arm.

Grant paused in throwing position and stared at her. His mouth moved. The words were aimed at her, but their meaning was washed away by the relentless water.

Chantelle swallowed hard and tried to piece those garbled sounds into the words she wanted to hear. "I love you, too."

Too quiet, she realized. He couldn't have heard. She opened her mouth....

Then he threw. The rope landed upstream, giving her a chance to react. She willed it closer, but the current was curving the rope so that it would pass beyond her grasp. She stepped forward, the bottom deepening rapidly beneath her.

"Go back, Chantelle!"

Water surged against her chest as she reached out, her full weight on the tender ankle. A wave slipped into her mouth, forcing her to realize that another step would be her last. She suppressed her sputtering and froze, willing her body not to start floating. The rope drifted toward her.

Two fingers grazed the rope, then scissored around it in an awkward, tenuous grasp. She stood there for several heartbeats, fighting the swirling water for fragile control over her body, before she inched the rope into her palm. Only when she grasped it firmly did she realize she'd been holding her breath.

Feeling like a tightrope walker fighting a hurricane, Chantelle edged toward the shallows. Water splashed into her eyes, turning the world into a distorted sheen of confusing colors, yet she dared neither wipe her face nor even shake the water away.

Please, she thought, *let my ankle hold. Not for me. For Grant. I may deserve this, but he doesn't.*

She didn't stumble until the water was knee-deep. She crawled to the slope of the bank, still dragging the rope behind her, and leaned against tangled roots while filling her lungs.

When she stood, she was ready for action. Climbing the bank took long, painful seconds, but she never rested till she waved at Grant. Though she strained her ears to hear what he shouted, the river blotted out the sound. So close to rescue, now. Surely he would make it. . . .

Chantelle looped the rope around the trunk of an evergreen leaning from the bank and stretched it as tight as she could. Grant, meanwhile, had tied the rope around his arm. She waved to him, a lump filling her throat as she saw him blow her a kiss. He stepped into the current, and she began pulling.

It was a ticklish task. If she pulled too much she might yank him off his feet, yet if she allowed too much slack he might be swept into the lake. Perspiration, from concentration rather than physical strain, beaded her brow. When Grant had taken a few steps she wrapped the loose end of the rope around her waist and continued pulling. In midstream the water was up to his neck, but Chantelle knew that even if he lost footing the rope—and her determination—would help him survive. It seemed like hours, yet when she finally helped him onto dry land she knew they'd never been more tightly joined than by that rope.

Greedily gulping air, Grant flopped onto his back and pulled Chantelle half atop him. His water-darkened hair was plastered close to his head, his shirt was torn, his eyes were closed so tightly that his temples were wrinkled. But he was alive.

Chantelle felt a crazy grin twist her features as her body began to glow, to shout, to revel in life and rejoice in what the future held. Chantelle rested her cheek on his chest and savored the labored sound of his breathing. To her, he had never looked better, never felt better, never sounded better.

When his hand sought her cheek she raised herself to look at him. His voice came in gasps. "I wouldn't be alive if it wasn't for you."

Chantelle shut her eyes against emotions that threatened to overflow. "You wouldn't have been out there if it wasn't for me."

"You saved my life," he insisted.

"And you saved mine. We're even."

"Chantelle..."

She kept trembling eyelids closed, but responded by pressing her hand against his shoulder. Grant pulled her fully atop his chest and drew her knees to either side of one of his. Chantelle's heart began to pound and her abdomen to glow with warmth. The contact heated more than her body, though. Grant's closeness warmed her heart till it melted, leaking raw and uncensored emotions into her veins and nourishing every cell in her body with the tingling, dazzling energy of love.

"We'd better get out of these clammy things." She'd never heard her own voice sound this way, so deep and sultry.

No words had been necessary. Nothing could stop the urgent need that she felt and that she saw mirrored in Grant's face. His eyes were dark with desire, half closed and yet compelling in their masculine power. He moved his hand to the top button of her shirt, then paused, unmoving yet promising delight.

Chantelle swallowed and squeezed her eyes shut. Scarcely breathing, she nodded.

Grant seized her shoulders and pulled her to his mouth. The kiss kindled fiery sensations in Chantelle's body, ardent midnight sensations that built with astonishing intensity till they obliterated all awareness of coarse grass, cold wetness and hot sun. Everything vanished except the man holding her. She opened her mouth, welcoming and inciting his passion with lustful probes of her tongue.

As his fingers opened the buttons of her shirt she did the same for him. Only when she pulled back to slip her shirt off did their lips separate.

"Chantelle—" he began.

She stopped him with a finger across his mouth. A shiver rippled along her spine as he seized her finger between his lips. "Grant, just love me."

He did, with a fervor that was frantic in its celebration of life. His hands sped over her body, exploring with a reckless need that inflamed the urgency of her desire. As the last of their clothes disappeared, she looked into his eyes and her breath caught inside her. This was *Grant*. It seemed like a miracle.

His mouth sought her breast, and the miracle grew sharper. She wanted him. Now. The wonder of him drove her to a boldness that vaguely amazed her. She tore at his clothes and, refusing further delay, urged him into her. When he filled her, she heard a cry that was a mingling of desire and fulfillment, of rising passion and also of ultimate contentment. Her own voice? His? Or both, indistinguishable?

Though her passion was still rising, being joined with him was a satisfaction in itself, a completeness that robbed her of the capacity to do anything but move in the frenzied rhythm they effortlessly discovered. Urgency gave no time to savor slow caresses or words or anything but desire. No time, and yet a lifetime. They were Adam and Eve, consecrating their lives in primordial, mythic desire. Together they rejoiced with a frenzied passion that made Chantelle cry to the heavens.

Grant joined her at the peak, moving against her and in her as if they were one, forever bonded, forever inseparable, forever transfigured in the image of the other. Sensation exploded, and the world was pleasure.

After an eternity, Chantelle opened her eyes. It was over. Yet it had just begun. Together they settled to earth, floating on breezes that made their bodies pause, stir sensually, then pause again. Each intimate movement was a mutual declaration of satisfaction and awe. Not needing to speak, unable to speak, Chantelle wrapped her legs around his and strained to hold him inside her as long as possible.

So sharp, so sudden, so total. She'd never known anything could consume her like this. She'd never suspected anything quite this perfect could really happen.

Chantelle studied Grant's face as he stared down at her with a hint of a crooked smile playing at one corner of his mouth. Yes, it was the same face she'd lived with for the past week. Incredible. Did she look the same, too? Was it possible to experience this ecstasy, and not be totally changed?

No.

She opened her mouth, then closed it. She shook her head almost imperceptibly. She swallowed. Finally she managed to breathe a drawn-out syllable.

"Wow."

Grant's smile broadened till it took over his whole face. "Wow, indeed."

He nuzzled into the hollow of her shoulder and began shaking with laughter. His joy was infectious, and Chantelle joined him in laughter. Since meeting Grant, life had felt so vivid, so *important,* as if destiny had finally arrived. Making love had given so much more than she'd known she could experience. She wished she could forget tomorrow and replay the half hour since their quarrel, endlessly and forever.

She shook her head at her own foolishness. No. She was eager to see what tomorrow held for her.

For *them.*

Grant stretched, exhausted now that their long journey was virtually over. Road vibration and the mesmerizing flash of yellow center lines, only occasionally broken by the headlights of another car, had him two-thirds asleep. He was glad he wasn't driving.

To wake himself, he reached across the cool vinyl of Chantelle's seat and curled his fingers into the cascade of her hair. It was too dark to see color, but his mind supplied the right shade of auburn, complete with fiery flashes of sunlight.

"That feels nice." Chantelle glanced at him. The faint green glow from the dashboard cast her face in another new expression, one of soft mystery and stark beauty. But then, she was beautiful in any light, or no light at all. "Everything you do feels nice."

Words rose to his throat to warn her that wasn't true, that he could hurt, probably would hurt, if she stayed with him long enough. He said nothing.

"How much farther to your house, Grant?"

"Once we pass Clearwater, about four miles."

The events of the day replayed yet again in his mind. No day had ever been as full of intense emotions, vivid events and startling transformations of his life. The implications of this day would filter through the rest of his days.

After making love he had gathered firewood to dry their clothes. Chantelle had insisted with impish stubbornness on stacking the kindling herself, saying something about having studied his technique. When the flames had hesitated, she'd gone on her hands and knees to fan the infant flames rather than light a second match.

Grant had watched Chantelle's determined antics with a combination of desire and pride. Desire had won out. When he couldn't keep his hands off her any longer, he'd swatted her backside.

She had squealed indignantly, then arched her eyebrows and asked if he was ticklish. His hand remembered the feel of her, and the sensuality of her frisky retaliations. With the smell of wood smoke perfuming the air, they had made love again. The second time had been gentler and less frenzied, but no less magical for either of them.

Grant smiled and ran his fingers along her neck. She stretched against his hand, a breathless expression softening her features.

"Are you tired?" She spoke without looking at him, her bedtime gaze watching on the road yet obviously recalling other things.

"I certainly should be." But, as if by magic, her throaty tone banished his exhaustion. "The walk to the highway seemed awfully far in wet boots. I can't wait to get out of these things."

Her eyes darted toward him. "Me, too." Perhaps her eyes twinkled, though he couldn't tell for certain in this light. But her voice definitely held a wink and a twinkle.

"And take a real bath," he added.

Her voice floated lightly through the car. "How big is your tub?"

"Not big enough for what you have in mind. With two people, there'd only be room for you to sit with my arms around you."

"I can live with that."

He glided his fingertips along her neck and up the soft smoothness of her cheek. "And then," he continued, "I want to climb into a real bed."

"Mmm. Getting better and better all the time."

"And go to sleep on my own pillow."

Chantelle sat up straight and feigned disgust. "Totally unimaginative. Can't you think of anything better to do?"

"Better than sleep?" He rubbed his chin. "What's better than sleep?"

"I take that as a challenge. I'll have to show you."

"I'm looking forward to that." He chuckled again, then leaned across and kissed her cheek.

As they drove through the small village of Clearwater, he pointed out an occasional building, but was mostly silent.

"Grant?"

"Yes?"

"Are you all right?"

"Sure. I'm just tired."

"You've been so quiet in the three hours we've been driving. Even at the restaurant in Blue River you hardly said anything." Chantelle flexed her hands on the steering wheel. She faced resolutely toward the highway. "I . . . I just want you to know that . . . well, we've only known each other a week."

Grant leaned forward in his seat, wondering what she was getting at, but prepared to let her tell him in her own way. "It seems like all my life."

A smile flitted across her mouth. "To you, too?" The smile disappeared. "Still, it's just a week. What I'm trying to say is that despite what happened and despite your offer to let me stay at your house for a while, I think we should take this relationship day by day. You know, not look too far ahead. No strings."

Grant felt his muscles tighten as he leaned back. "Is that what you want?"

"Absolutely."

Had she hesitated? Maybe not. Grant said nothing. Chantelle had just put into words what he'd thought he wanted; time to see if the relationship would thrive now that they were stepping from a dream into reality. But her words hurt, and he realized they would have hurt Chantelle if he'd said them. There were so many ways to hurt her, without even trying. . . .

"Four miles, Grant."

He jerked his head toward her. "Pardon me?"

"Four miles past town. How do we get to your house?"

"Take a right at the intersection. The first white fence is mine."

Grant shook his head, but was unable to shake a sense of unreality. Here in the real, mundane world, would they be able to maintain the aura of magic that had surrounded them in the wilderness when they were the only people for miles? Did people who were stranded together on desert islands form relationships that weathered the countless weary erosions of everyday existence?

If he had anything to say about it, yes. But he no longer had unquestioning confidence in his own arrogant infallibility. For the first time in two years, he wished he did.

Grant ran both hands through his hair. He thought he'd come to terms with the uncertainty that had swamped his life when the machine registering Linda's heartbeat had started screaming. He hadn't; Chantelle made him face the truth. He'd dealt with uncertainty by merely avoiding matters of prime importance.

Medicine.

And love.

When he got out of the car Grant tried to banish dark thoughts by whirling Chantelle off the ground. Her laughter mingled with the crunch of gravel under his feet. When he stopped, he held her at his eye level. The look that passed between them was as powerful as high-tension wires. Still holding her, he eased his lips to hers for a feathery kiss.

"I guess I should put you down," he said.

"I wouldn't touch the ground even if you did."

Chantelle kept glancing at Grant as they walked to the porch of his log house. He seemed so glad to be with her, yet he'd readily accepted her suggestion that their relationship have no strings. At least he could have argued.

Not that she hadn't meant it. She would forget the future and suck the last drops of happiness from each moment as it happened.

Chantelle thrust her thoughts aside as she stepped into Grant's impressive house. It had a masculine beauty that came more from the design rather than from decorating, but she hadn't expected anything this stunning. The walls were logs, turned on a lathe to rounded perfection. The ceiling had the rich, colorful grain of cedar. Against the far wall of the huge living room was a freestanding wood stove that appeared capable of defeating a Canadian winter even in this size of house. On either side of the stove were large openings that gave shadowed glimpses of spacious kitchen and stairway leading to the second floor.

"I love it, Grant." As she turned around in the center of the living room the thought came unbidden that a house like this cried out for a wife and children. She thrust the thought aside. "I thought you called it a cabin, though."

He shrugged, but his gaze moved around affectionately. "Back in Toronto anything made of logs is called a cabin, even if it's huge."

Chantelle ran a finger through several weeks worth of dust on an end table, tracing a heart pierced by an arrow. She turned to him, but kept her eyes on the green carpet. "Where's your bedroom?"

His hands gripped her shoulders. "Upstairs."

"And this bathtub you promised me?"

He turned her around and encircled her with his arms. His lips felt warm and alive on her forehead. "Downstairs. The upstairs has only a shower."

She looked at him, trying to assume an expression of disapproval. "You mean we have to hike after our bath?" She shook her head sharply, but the effect was somewhat spoiled by the smile she felt creeping around the corners of her mouth. "Grant, this won't do. I've had my fill of hiking, so maybe I should just go home right now."

When she turned as if to leave, Grant jerked her back into his arms. "Come here, you silly fireball."

He stifled her laughter with a long, loving kiss. Chantelle snaked her arms around his waist and strained to feel the beating of his heart against her own.

"Well," she whispered, "maybe I can manage one flight of stairs."

Grant kissed her again. They left a trail of clothes from the living room to the tub.

Late-morning sunshine sparkled off the most fascinating variety of home canning Chantelle had seen since leaving the farm. The amazing thing was that Grant did none of it himself. Friends and neighbors kept him stocked with this embarrassment of produce, and Chantelle knew from long, sweaty experience that this much canning wouldn't be given to just anyone. What had Ariel said—that Grant was the best-loved man in Clearwater?

The ratchety sound of Grant turning the washing machine knob reminded her of why they'd come into his utility-storage room. Chantelle re-rolled the sleeve of his shirt that she was wearing, then put her hand on his shoulder and leaned. "Just what am I supposed to wear while my clothes are in the wash?"

"What you have on right now looks fine to me."

She glanced down at her mostly-bare thighs, then shook her head with mock severity. "Men."

"As a matter of fact," Grant said, "I consider you totally overdressed."

"Grant, there's nothing under this shirt. I'm hardly overdressed."

"For my purposes you are. And there definitely are things under that shirt. See?"

"Grant," she said with a giggle as she slapped at his hands, "didn't we just do this?"

"Practice makes perfect."

"It was perfect last time, and the time before." She craned her neck to give his marauding lips better access to her neck, and closed her eyes in delight. "Oh, what the heck. If you insist on practicing . . ."

She put her arms around his neck and jumped up so that her face was on a level with his. Hooking her feet around the back of his knees to hold her position, she dusted quick kisses on his face while he began walking out of the utility room, with her still twined around him like a vine.

An hour and a half later, Chantelle slipped on her own clothes, still toasty warm from the dryer. After checking her freshly set hair, she went into the kitchen where Grant reclined in a ladder-back chair. She put one hand on her hip and twirled. "How do I look?"

"Spectacular, of course."

"You were supposed to say something like 'clean' or 'civilized.' I could even believe 'winsome.' But 'spectacular'? Nobody calls someone like me spectacular."

"That's their problem, not mine . You're cute—"

"Okay," she interrupted, "I can accept cute."

"Your figure is absolutely perfect—"

"No," she interrupted again.

"And best of all, you have intriguing expressions that I'll never get tired of watching." Grant cocked his head to one side and grinned. "What, no interruption?"

Chantelle twitched her shoulders and managed a small smile. *I'll* never *get tired.* His choice of words, whether intentional or not, took her breath away.

A devilish light danced in Grant's eyes as he surveyed her from head to foot. "Still, I can't say the jeans are any improvement over the way you looked in my shirt."

Chantelle felt warmth rise to her neck, but it wasn't from embarrassment. In fact, she found it surprising how quickly she had sprinted from modesty to shameless desire, but her shamelessness had limits. "There's a time and a place for everything. And the time for pants is when we go outside for you to show me your ten acres of land."

Grant's eyebrows rose and his mouth curved upward as he held out his arms to her. "We could postpone the guided tour."

"The man's insatiable." With a laugh, she darted past his outstretched arms into the living room. "We only postpone it till I finish phoning my sister, okay? I've got to see if she's had problems with the store. She expected me back days ago."

He made a sound low in his throat as he smiled at her. "You're too responsible, you know that? Go ahead, use the phone. I'll be seeing how the garden fared while I was gone." He pointed an accusing finger at her. "And no phoning your sister collect, you hear?"

Chantelle phoned collect regardless. In a way she felt strange doing it, because she'd shared his bed but felt uncomfortable making him pay for a phone call. They hadn't shared many niceties of civilization like telephones. Furthermore, she intended to pay for half the groceries for as long as she stayed here.

The phone began ringing in her ear. How long would she stay with Grant? They'd never talked about it, and she had no idea where this relationship was headed. The thought of explaining where she was to a member of her family, even her kid sister, spread uneasiness through her. *I'm having an affair.* The unprecedented phrase sounded so clinical compared to the magical reality.

She wrapped the cord around and around her fingers while the phone continued to ring. "Come on, Ricki," she muttered.

By God, she *was* having an affair—not that she would blurt it out to Ricki that way. A smile curled across her mouth as warm new connotations attached themselves to the word *affair*.

Ricki finally answered. Chantelle told her sister as little as possible, not even mentioning Grant. Yes, her ankle was fine. The trip had been enjoyable. She'd be back in a few days. Yes, she was certain that she was all right.

After hanging up, Chantelle went outside. She stood on the veranda that extended across the front of the house, looking around. The house was at the back of the lot, away from the road, with a pasture in front and a few acres of pines behind. Grant had visible neighbors, but distant ones, so that the view from the porch was dominated not by the works of man but by the round, forested mountains and occasional sharp peaks that rimmed this narrow valley. All in all, the scenery was halfway between the majesty of the Rockies and Kamloops' picturesque landscapes. She took a deep breath as she headed toward the garden. A person could live here without being intimidated, yet still be inspired.

Chantelle found Grant vigorously digging clumps of weeds from around a row of raspberries. His shirt was unbuttoned, and that was the finishing touch on the picture of Grant as man of the soil. She marveled again at the realization that this rugged man had been a doctor, of all things.

He smiled at her and leaned against the shovel handle in a way that made him appear a gentleman, rather than a farmer. "How are things at your store?"

"Pretty good. Ricki was getting worried, though. Ariel had phoned last week, but didn't say much. I told Ricki an abbreviated version of what happened." She didn't bother to mention just how abbreviated that version was. "My cousin Paulette stopped by the store on her way to Vancouver but didn't buy anything. My sister-in-law Ruth and her three children came in, but they didn't buy anything, either." Chantelle shrugged and sat on a half buried log that marked the boundaries of the garden. "Aside from that, Ricki was worried about an eye doctor's appointment the day after tomorrow. She wondered if she should close up, but I told her I'd come down and watch the store."

"Leaving so soon?"

She wished she could read his expression, but suddenly he was a stone face once more. "Grant, I have one set of underwear, jeans and a battered blouse. My socks deserve to be taken into the woods and shot."

"I'd like you to come back, if you can. I want you to stay as long as possible."

Chantelle grinned. "Nobody buys books when the weather's nice, anyway. But it depends a lot on my sister. If she can handle the store and isn't about to collapse from overwork, then sure, I'll come back."

Grant resumed digging, but his face was back to normal. "I am going to be so nice to this sister of yours tomorrow—"

"You'll come, too?"

"I want to see the bookstore again and where you live. I want to know everything about you."

Chantelle hugged her knees, absorbed the peace and serenity of the moment, and was content.

The rest of the day passed in a haze of love and satisfaction. They went to the grocery store, and Chantelle was impressed by how many people said hello to Grant or waved as they drove. Even in a town the size of Kamloops this kind of easy recognition had been lost. She enjoyed it, though she had no doubt that those friendly people would speculate about her.

Yes, they would say, *Grant Van Arden's back from his holiday. Had someone with him, too. A cute young thing with freckles, though her clothes looked as if she'd spent half her life in them. No, I don't know who she is.* Rather to her surprise, Chantelle found she relished the role of the mystery woman in Grant's life.

She and Grant spent most of the day and evening in his house, reacquainting themselves with modern conveniences such as refrigerators, televisions, stereos and, of course, furniture with soft, comfortable cushions. Grant liked the opportunities to study Chantelle in new lights and new situations.

He put down his accumulated mail and turned his full attention on her. The yellowish glow of a lamp drew intriguing shadows on her face as she leafed through a book about a nearby provincial park. She noticed that he was staring at her. She smiled and then returned to her reading.

Grant stepped outside for a moment. When he returned with an armful of wood, Chantelle asked what he was doing.

"Making a fire," he said as he opened the front of the wood stove so that it was in fireplace mode.

"I guess it is a little chilly now that the sun's gone down." Chantelle put down her book and came to sit cross-legged on the carpet beside him. As the wood crackled to life, she hugged her arms. "This reminds me of the camping trip."

"Is that bad?"

"Not at all. It was the best trip I ever took."

Her gaze caught his, and Grant felt his lungs accelerate. "Shall we camp out right here?"

She was already up and gathering cushions from the couch. "You read my mind."

Grant spread a spare sleeping bag atop the couch cushions in front of the wood stove, while Chantelle gathered all the pillows she could find and spread them in padded luxury around their impromptu camp fire. When he turned off all the lights, he felt that the flickering reddish glow did indeed recapture some of the magic that had swallowed his heart whole.

They made popcorn over the fire, arguing amiably about when to move the popper so the corn wouldn't burn, then laughing when despite their efforts half of it was blackened. Grant leaned against the pillows with his arm around Chantelle, neither of them feeling the need for words. Words could add nothing to a time like this.

By mutual, unspoken agreement they turned their lips to each other at the same moment. Grant wasn't surprised at their silent communication. He was surprised only at the strength of his feelings and the power of her response.

With restrained haste, they took turns removing each other's clothes. Firelight lapped at Chantelle's soft curves, obliterating shadows with a flowing, lingering tenderness that Grant tried to match with his caresses. Her texture burned indelibly into his hands and into his heart. Soft, warm, silky, moist; she was as variable as the wind and as difficult to capture. Yet still he tried to capture her and tie her to him, not with a rope, but with soft kisses. Her tastes teased his palate as his lips slid from her face to the hard nubs of her breasts, lingering there as she murmured soft noises of encouragement. Her tastes defied description, yet branded themselves forever in his memory. The soft sounds she made as he suckled alternately soothed his ears and encouraged him to shift his kisses lower to the shaded mystery of her femininity. Her moans grew more insistent.

When she pulled him up and into her with urgent hands, the myriad sensations that were Chantelle combined with a flash of desire into an all-consuming conflagration that drove him to move with her in ever-increasing rhythm. Molten passion softened his edges, till he lost track of where he ended and she began. When she cried out wordlessly, the sound of her passion melted the last of his self-control. He gave a final thrust, his arms tightening around her as if to merge their bodies totally. His heart sank effortlessly, endlessly into hers, and they were one.

Afterward he held her, still enjoying the light that danced over her wondrous body, but enjoying it in a softer, less urgent way. As passion ebbed into smug contentment, he shook his head in wonder that she was his.

"I love you, Grant."

He squeezed her shoulders in answer. He'd been wrong, and he was glad. The last day and a half here had been idyllic. He'd been wrong to worry about whether they could maintain the magic here in the real world.

The next morning they lounged on the chalet-style balcony off his upstairs bedroom. A cedar wall three and a half feet high blocked out pasture and houses and all but the highest mountain. Only the birds could look down at them.

Chantelle again wore only Grant's shirt as she stretched on a lounge chair. She filled her lungs with the clean smell of country air, then looked over at Grant's terry-cloth robe that teased her with glimpses of thigh as he read the newspaper. The top of his head was visible over the paper, his hair showing the same sinful disarray as hers. The only sounds breaking the quiet were the soft rustling of the newspaper and the murmur of a creek that ran behind the house. Chantelle closed her eyes and imagined that she was in heaven.

It was easy to do.

After a while, the sound of an automobile crunching on gravel approached. Chantelle opened her eyes. "You have company."

Grant went to the balcony railing. Chantelle figured she'd best stay where she was, considering how she was dressed. Mystery women needn't be blatant, after all.

A car door slammed, and Grant waved. "Hi," he said.

"Hello, Grant," came a female voice that positively gushed with happiness. "I was hoping you'd be back. I can't tell you how I've missed you and how much news I have for you and...well, how good it is to see you again. And I have something for you."

The voice was familiar. Against her better judgment, and with a sour feeling growing in her stomach, Chantelle went to the railing.

Smiling broadly, brandishing an envelope and leaning against the gate with girlish abandon, was Ariel Johnson.

Chapter Nine

Ariel's face froze. She slowly straightened till she stood beside the gate like another fence post.

Grant ran his hand through his hair, glanced apologetically at Chantelle, and then nodded to Ariel. "The door's open. I'll be down in a minute."

Chantelle followed him through the sliding glass door into the bedroom. As he pulled on his pants, she did the same.

"You don't have to come down if you don't want to," he said.

"Are you kidding?" She crossed her arms and looked at him as if he was a naive lad. "I wouldn't stay up here for anything."

"I didn't realize you'd be so glad to see Ariel."

Chantelle gave him a how-dumb-can-you-get shake of her head as she tucked her shirt into her jeans. "I like Ariel, Grant, but I'm not quite sure how she feels after seeing us together like that. She loves you."

"No, she doesn't." When Chantelle still appeared skeptical, Grant put his hands on her shoulders. "I know Ariel better than you do. We're just friends."

Chantelle's face softened. "Sure, Grant. Just friends."

Ariel was sitting on a wooden rocking chair when they came downstairs. She looked up at Grant and Chantelle with a smile.

There was an awkward pause that Ariel politely struggled to fill. "So, what happened while you were out in the wilderness?" Her cheeks colored, and she quickly glanced out the window. "Forget I asked."

Grant sat on the edge of the couch and glanced from one woman to the other. Chantelle sat with her hair uncombed and a frozen expression, saying nothing. Ariel was the kind of person who smoothed out awkward moments like this, yet she sat stiffly with her hands clenched in her lap.

Tension floated thickly in the air, like a curtain of camp fire smoke on a shifting breeze. He couldn't ignore this unpleasantness, because it was important that these two be friends. He liked Ariel. He liked and loved Chantelle. "How is your summer-school class, Ariel?"

"Fine."

"Ariel's taking a class in whole-language reading instruction in Kelowna," he told Chantelle. He turned to Ariel. "Chantelle grew up on an orchard near Kelowna."

Ariel just nodded. Her eyes were shiny and her lower lip trembled. When he saw the tear glisten at the corner of her eye, he knew.

What an ignorant fool he'd been. He'd thought he knew Ariel, thought they were just friends. How blind was he to other things that were obvious to someone like Chantelle? He gave Chantelle an apologetic nod, then realized that he didn't know what to say, either.

Strung taut between the two women, he felt on the one hand as if his happiness tortured a helpless puppy, and on the other as if friendship threatened Chantelle. Ariel sat with her hands in her lap, clenching an envelope as she looked out the window. Chantelle kept glancing from her knees to the woman in the rocker. Grant's sigh seemed loud in the heavy silence.

"The backpack got washed away," Chantelle said finally, in a friendly tone that seemed all the warmer for the chill in the air. "The only clothes I have are on my back. Do you have the rest of my things that you carried out with you earlier?"

Ariel wiped her cheek with the back of her hand. "Uh, no, sorry. I dropped them off with your sister on my way to summer school."

"It's kind of you to go out of your way to help a stranger like me. I appreciate it." Chantelle got up and crossed the chasm between her and Ariel, holding out her hand.

Ariel smiled as she shook Chantelle's hand. "You're welcome."

"You said you had something for me?" Grant said.

"Two tickets for the play next weekend." Ariel hit the back of her hand repeatedly with the now-crumpled envelope, then thrust it toward Grant. "Here." Then she left, with scarcely another word.

Grant was alone with Chantelle. Her face relaxed into a look of bemused sadness.

"Chantelle, till just now I had no idea she was in love with me." He shook his head. "I never knew." Chantelle took his hand. He hadn't realized how much he needed human contact till he felt her cool fingers slip into his.

"You value her friendship," she said.

"Very much." He leaned against the back of the couch and stared at the cedar ceiling.

After a few seconds, Chantelle spoke softly. "She seems like a lady, the way she talks and carries herself. Tell me about her."

"You're really curious about Ariel, aren't you?"

"You call her your best friend. Do you blame me?"

"No, I guess not." Grant stroked her hair, enjoying the way his fingers disappeared under that luxurious silkiness.

"When I first came to Clearwater I was more or less a hermit. I didn't know anyone, and I wouldn't make the effort to meet anyone. Ariel was my one contact, since she went out of her way to see how I was doing. I guess I was one of the strays who collect around Ariel. She introduced me to people in town and urged me to apply for the science teaching job, then spent hours helping me prepare for class. The last two Christmases she's had me over, along with other lonely souls with no family."

Chantelle put her hand around his waist and pressed her cheek against him. "I can tell it bothers you that she was hurt."

"Yes. Besides, I feel stupid. I should have seen this coming."

"I get the impression you aren't always aware of how people react to you."

"I'm getting better, really I am. I used to be such an insensitive clod that you couldn't have stood being around me."

"I doubt that." Chantelle put her arms around his neck and raised her face, inviting a kiss. "But if so you're an honorable clod, and I'm very much in love with you."

"You say the sweetest things."

After lunch Chantelle picked vegetables from the garden, while Grant dug out clumps of grass invading the asparagus. As she picked peas, her gaze kept lighting on his virile form. Slipping into the routine of his life would be so easy. She could picture them still gardening together forty years from now. There would be more weeds because bending would be harder, but love would make their garden fertile, forever.

Dangerous thoughts, or at least premature. But fun.

Opening a pod and eating the peas like candy, Chantelle stopped picking and just watched Grant. A leisurely glow spread through her mind. Even when gardening he exuded an aura of nobility that singled him out.

He was a nice man. *Nice* was an overused word, yet in its unsullied sense it captured the decency and compassion that was Grant. The medical profession had lost a true star, and the thought made her sad.

She absorbed the play of light over the muscles of his arms as he dug and occasionally reached to pull away a clump of grass. On top of being noble and intelligent and nice, he was sexy, too.

"Grant, would you do me a favor?"

"Sure."

"Take off your shirt."

Grant looked at her with one eyebrow raised, but he removed the shirt and draped it across a raspberry bush. He pushed the shovel into the ground, then leaned his forearm on the end of the handle. "Your turn."

"What do you mean?"

"To take off your shirt."

Chantelle stuck out her tongue at him.

"Being disrespectful, eh?" Grant's face twisted into a playful frown and he started toward her purposefully.

She laughed and ran through the garden, down one row and up another. She dodged a raspberry cane, then pulled it back like a catapult and turned to face him. "I'll let you have it if you don't stop chasing me."

Grant shook his head and snapped his fingers. "Foiled by my own raspberry plant." He stood for a moment, allowing her to catch her breath. Abruptly he leaped over the cauliflower and came at her from the right. Laughing, Chantelle darted out of the garden and sprinted toward the open pasture that fronted the road.

Grant was faster yet he allowed her to stay ahead, enjoying the chase and the dire threats he called to her. Capture was inevitable, though, and even desirable, so when Chantelle was cornered between a bushy clump of cottonwoods and a barbed wire fence she surrendered meekly.

"Now I've got you," he growled.

Chantelle turned her head at an angle and, with arms at her side, edged toward him with a sultry look in her eyes. "And just what are you going to do with me now that you've got me?" She stopped within inches of his chest.

"I'm sure I'll think of something." He put his arms around her waist and kissed her on the forehead.

"Is that the best you can think of?"

"No. But when we're so near the neighbors' trailer it's the best I can *do*."

"You're forgiven, then." Chantelle rested her head against his shoulder and savored the smooth texture of his skin on her cheek.

She'd been here less than a day, yet his place already felt special to her. His land was comfortable, the kind of spot that cried out for love and children and dogs because it was a *home*, not just a place to live. Partly it was gardening sights and smells, and partly it was the nearby rise of the mountains, all reminding her of her childhood. But mostly it was Grant. She felt as if she belonged at his side forever.

They walked along the edge of his property, hand in hand. "The fence needs some work," Grant commented in a lazy tone that said he'd get to it some other day.

Chantelle scouted the hillside, wondering where was a good Thinking Place. It was mere idle speculation, really, because right now she wished not distance from life but involvement, not analysis but emotion.

"Grant! You're back!"

Chantelle shaded her eyes and looked for the source of that high-pitched shout. A boy of four or five waved frantically from astride a pine on a logging truck parked in the neighbors' yard. The boy clambered down with a speed that would have killed an adult.

"That's Robby," Grant told her as the boy charged toward them. "I'm his hero because I bandage his scrapes."

Chantelle winced as Robby ducked through the barbed wire without slowing. "I bet he has a lot of scrapes," she said.

"That he does." Grant sat on his haunches as the boy skidded to a stop with a yell just like squealing air brakes of a logging truck.

Robby held up his elbow to display a small bandage. "See," he proclaimed proudly. "I fell through the roof of the chicken coop."

Grant examined the minor injury, a serious expression shading his face. "You're lucky that's all that happened to you. When are you going to listen to your mom about playing carefully?"

Robby ignored these words. Except for one quick glance, he ignored Chantelle, too, in the way of young children. "Mom doesn't have striped bandages like you do. Hers don't make it feel as good."

Chantelle looked up at a sound from the neighbor's yard. A pregnant young woman wiped her hands on a dish towel and patted ineffectually at stringy brown hair as she walked from the trailer. The woman's gaze flicked ever so quickly over Grant's bare torso before she looked Chantelle squarely in the eye.

Grant stood and extended his hand over the fence. "Hello, Marcy."

"Hi, Grant." Marcy shook hands, then offered her hand to Chantelle. "I'm Marcy McDonall, the little monster's mother."

"I'm not a little monster."

Though she appeared totally unconvinced, Marcy smiled at Robby fondly. "What are you, then?"

"I'm a big monster!" To prove it, he roared.

"I apologize if he's being a pest," Marcy said with a laugh. "He just loves you, Grant. He can't decide whether to teach or drive a logging truck when he grows up. After you went away he pouted for two days."

"Robby wasn't bothering us," Chantelle said. So, Grant was good with children—another desirable characteristic.

Marcy looked at Chantelle with frank curiosity. "Angie mentioned that Grant went shopping with a friend."

"I'm forgetting my manners." Grant gestured from one to the other. "Marcy, this is Chantelle DuMaurier, from Kamloops. Chantelle, Marcy. Chantelle and I met near Mount Robson after she sprained her ankle."

"So you're the one," Marcy said. "Ariel mentioned to Jane that Grant had stayed to help someone. I'm not surprised he was a hero."

"He's my hero, all right," Chantelle said. His hand grasped hers. She glanced up at his strong features, but not before she'd noticed Marcy's gaze flick to their hands.

The pregnant woman nodded, a smile turning her plain features into a pleasant picture. "I'd ask you over for dinner tonight, but I suspect you'll want to rest." Her eyes lifted briefly to Chantelle's, and the smile widened. "When you get the chance, though, stop by. Jeff and I—that's my husband," she added for Chantelle's benefit, "we picked your strawberries and raspberries while you were gone and froze them for you. There's some rhubarb and asparagus, too."

Marcy urged Robby to her side, then turned toward the trailer. She glanced back at their joined hands. Another smile spread across her face. "Nice to have met you, Chantelle."

"You too, Marcy."

Chantelle put her arm around Grant's waist as they headed back to his house. The Clearwater rumor mill had just gotten a load of new grist, but . . . well, this was Grant she was with. She didn't care what people said.

Kamloops, Chantelle thought as they drove into her hometown, was big enough to afford some privacy from gossip. Her sister, Ricki, would be another matter.

As they waited at a traffic light, Chantelle smiled at Grant, sitting in the passenger seat of her car. "Am I ever going to be glad to change clothes."

"Does this mean I have to take my shirt back? It never looked as good on me as it did on you, you know."

"Cheer up, Grant. Remember that you've never seen me in a real dress, or anything else feminine."

"Hmm. That is something to look forward to."

It was good to be home. The familiar mountains, though lower than the Rockies, had a stark beauty of their own. Bare of trees except near the top because of dryness, every wrinkle and gully changed texture with the progress of the sun.

Her bookstore, Second Thoughts, was on the flats of the north shore of the Thompson River. Located on a business street with lots of car and foot traffic, Second Thoughts was nonetheless empty when they arrived.

Chantelle had never noticed how dark the store seemed. She wondered how hard a skylight would be to install, so she could grow weeping figs and other greenery. If she could sweet-talk a few of her brothers into visiting one weekend...

Grant looked around with interest. He'd been in the shop that one time, but now the bookstore held a new meaning. All these books, mostly hardcovers, were part of Chantelle's life and thus intriguing. She had a good eye for decoration and display, he noticed. Second Thoughts was modest yet full of pride of ownership. He'd known intellectually that she liked books, but seeing the careful arrangements of old hardcovers made it an emotional reality. A shelf of poetry. A shelf of Canadian literature. Several shelves of back-to-the-land advice.

Footsteps sounded from the back room. Ricki burst through the curtain, chewing frantically, a smudge of ketchup at the corner of her mouth. Though she was the same size as Chantelle, they looked unlike sisters except for similar dark auburn hair. Ricki's hair, however, was short and in the latest fashion.

When he looked at her, Grant thought of the word perky. Ricki was perky and lively and, at the moment, laughing happily at the sight of her big sister. He surveyed the shelves while the sisters exchanged greetings and hugs.

Ricki noticed him then. "I'm sorry, Chani, I didn't realize we had a customer while I was stuffing my face with
lunch. May I help you, sir?"

"Yes," he said while Chantelle sat on a stool. "You can
tell me all about your charming sister, especially the juicy
little stories from childhood that embarrass her."

Ricki glanced from Grant to Chantelle. "You two are together, right?" She put her hand on her hip as her expression transformed into a frown of playful indignation.
"Chani, why didn't you tell me?"

"Ricki, this is Grant Van Arden, who helped me after I
sprained my ankle. Grant, my sister Erica. Everyone calls
her Ricki."

"You never said anything about anyone helping you."
Ricki eyed Grant with a look that was friendly and yet
speculative. "And now he's here in Kamloops with you."

"Yes." Chantelle's response seemed a bit clipped. "Ricki,
I want to go home to change. I've worn these clothes for
days, ever since my things got washed away in the river when
the bridges were down."

"I thought you said you fell into a pond or something?"

"That was nearly two weeks ago. The river was three days
ago."

Ricki went over to her sister and put her hand on her hip
again. She sniffed. "You don't smell as though you've worn
these things for three days."

Grant joined them at the counter. "We washed her clothes
at my place."

"Your place." Ricki again darted a glance from him to
Chantelle. She broke into a laugh. "Big sister, I think you
left a few things out of your telephone call."

Chantelle slid off the stool and drummed her thumb on
the edge of the counter. Grant suspected she was uncomfortable acknowledging their relationship. He wanted to
reach across and cover her hand with his, but this wasn't the
best time. Tonight, in the dark, they'd talk about it. They
did their best talking in the dark.

"Well, I won't tell you anything until I've changed." Chantelle glanced at Grant, then hesitated.

With Ricki here she must be reluctant to invite him into her house while she undressed. "I'll wait here," he said. "The books look interesting."

Chantelle acknowledged his understanding with a grateful nod. "I won't be long."

Ricki waited till the door had closed before motioning Grant to the stool. An eager expression lit her face. "You've been here before, haven't you?"

"Once."

"I thought so. I'm thrilled to see my sister look so happy. Chani hasn't seen any man more than twice in the year I've stayed with her, and she deserves all the love in the world even if she still is a bit shy."

"Don't forget her temper."

"Oh, that." Ricki dismissed Grant's words with a wave. "She's pretty good at controlling herself."

"Hmm."

Ricki's eyes grew wide. "Did she lose her temper?"

Grant rubbed his jaw and nodded.

"More than once?"

"I couldn't count the times." Grant felt a genuine smile growing from the edges of his mouth. Chantelle in full rage, her eyes flashing and her features overflowing with vitality and spirit . . .

"That's wonderful! I mean, not wonderful for you—well, yes, it is, though it might not seem like it. You must really get to her. Oh, this is happening even faster than I could have hoped."

"I'm glad someone's happy that she throws things at me."

"She *threw* things?" Ricki appeared about to die from ecstasy. Then, catching the expression on Grant's face, she sobered. "Chantelle is a generous, intelligent person, and she's very easy to live with. Do you know that she's the only one in the family who treats me as if I'm an adult?"

"She's incredible."

Ricki nodded emphatically. As if Grant's good opinion of her sister was enough to mend all differences, she smiled. Her face radiated conspiratorial glee as she rested her chin on her hands. "And now tell me everything, Grant. I mean *everything*."

Though Chantelle tried to hurry—she suspected the grilling Grant was undergoing—many little things needed doing. The tartan skirt needed ironing, the houseplants Ricki had forgotten to water were within minutes of death, and she had to search Ricki's closet for her white silk blouse. Makeup felt unfamiliar in her hands. She ended up scrubbing her face and starting all over.

And then before Chantelle left, she straightened up the living room and washed the dishes. Ricki wasn't a terrible housekeeper, but she was only nineteen and an almost spoiled youngest child who'd never had quite as many chores as the rest of the family.

By the time she got back to Second Thoughts, Ricki was alone with a few customers. Grant was gone.

"He had some shopping to do while he was in town," Ricki explained. "He said you knew about it, and that he might as well get it out of the way now."

"Yes, I knew." Still, Chantelle was disappointed. This was the longest they'd been separated since she'd met him.

Ricki rang up a customer's purchase. Chantelle's spirits rose as she watched Ricki work. For two weeks she hadn't seen her baby sister.

Besides, she valued Ricki's opinions, especially in social situations. She was eager to hear Ricki's estimation of Grant, but she wasn't about to start discussing her private life in front of strangers. She waited till the store was empty before pulling Ricki behind the counter for a girl-to-girl chat.

"Well?"

Ricki shrugged her shoulders casually. "Well, a friend of mine from Cariboo College who's studying library science fell in love with the store and volunteered some time while you were away. Nancy said you have the best collection of hard-to-find books in the southern Interior, and one day she'd love to own a place just like it. She had all sorts of ideas for how you could market the place in the Okanagan and even Prince George and draw people who don't want to bother with a trip to Vancouver. I have her phone number if you want to hear her ideas."

Surprise kept Chantelle from changing the subject immediately. "Someone your age is interested in a bookstore?"

"No, silly. Nancy is old, in her thirties at least."

"How ancient?"

"Well, late thirties." Ricki stuck the tip of her index finger in her mouth and squinted in thought. "Let's see, what else happened while you were gone?"

"Ricki," Chantelle said in a warning tone of voice.

The younger woman turned on Chantelle with wide eyes. "Yes?"

"Stop teasing. What did you think of him?"

Ricki sat straight. Her face went still. "Chani, I don't know how to tell you this." She pursed her lips. "About Grant, I mean."

"Do I have to strangle you to get it out of you? What about Grant?"

Ricki burst into a giggle. "If he wasn't taken I'd go after him myself. Chani, he's so handsome. He's wonderful."

Chantelle joined in her sister's laughter. It was important that Ricki like him. She couldn't imagine any possible reason why Ricki wouldn't like him, but she was relieved nonetheless.

"Tell me everything about him," Ricki urged.

"Unless I'm mistaken, you've already been pumping him."

"Well, sure." Ricki didn't look the least embarrassed. "But he's so darned discreet, and besides it was all from his point of view. I want to hear it from you."

Chantelle did, warming to the topic so that it took a long time to tell. She edited it a little—this was, after all, her youngest sister whose morals were in her care—but she was sure that love radiated from her words, her expression, her tone of voice.

Besides, Ricki was no longer a little kid. She looked at Chantelle with a dreamy, romantic expression as she said, "It must have been pretty cozy, sharing a tent."

Suddenly Chantelle didn't know what to say. She shrugged.

Ricki studied Chantelle's face for a few seconds with a gleam in her eyes, causing Chantelle to drum her fingers with impatience. Suddenly Ricki broke into a smile. "It *wasn't* innocent!"

"Well, no, but..." Chantelle owed her sister honesty, though she would rather have avoided the question. After growing up almost strangers because of their age difference, in the last year Ricki had learned to read Chantelle with an accuracy that was sometimes uncomfortable. Like now.

Ricki gave her a hug. "I'm so glad for you."

"Just don't go getting any ideas, young lady."

"I'm careful, don't worry."

Chantelle's big-sister-ears pricked up at Ricki's phrasing. She pulled back from the hug and held her sister at arm's length while staring into her eyes. "You don't even have a boyfriend. What do you mean, *you're* careful?"

"Oh, nothing. Say, can I tell our parents or do you want to?"

"What? Stop changing the subject."

"They'll be delighted to hear about Grant," Ricki said with an innocent expression. "You and I are the only ones who haven't given them grandchildren, and you know how Dad worries about you growing old alone."

"I'm not old yet, young lady. And don't you even consider producing grandchildren till you're married."

"Me?" Ricki smiled angelically. "We're talking about you, not me."

"Just be careful, honey. Very careful. Promise me?"

"I already said I was careful. Maybe I should have you promise the same thing."

Chantelle sat back on the stool and looked around the store that was such a big part of her life, then at her baby sister. Ricki always traveled in a pack, seeing no one boy more than another. *Had* she found a special boyfriend? Her brow furrowed nonetheless.

Chantelle caught sight of Grant approaching the store from across the street. She swallowed hard, both because of love and because of something else.

Ricki rushed over to Grant when he entered the store. Chantelle sat still. It wasn't as if she was cheating on a husband. Nothing had changed between them just because she'd talked with her sister. Grant was still as handsome, as well educated and capable as ever. Her heart still began to pound when the corner of his mouth crooked up.

But did he belong here, in her life? Coming to Kamloops made her realize how different their lives and their backgrounds were. They lived seventy-five miles apart. This wasn't just an affair, it was a long-distance affair with the cards stacked against it. How long before it dissolved into an occasional weekend when Grant had shopping to do in town?

She'd once told him she'd learned from her divorce that she needed a long-term commitment. Had she cheated herself out of something precious, or had she found something precious? Was she making the same mistake as before, mistaking sex for love?

Grant came over to her and put his hands on her waist. "Are you okay, Chantelle?"

"I'm fine."

"Sure?"

"I'm sure."

Ricki leaned against a row of Shakespeare and stared at the two of them dreamily. Chantelle moved to the far side of the counter to put space between her and Grant.

"While I was out," Grant said, "I was thinking that we ought to take Ricki out to dinner with us."

"I accept," the girl said instantly.

"All right then," Grant said. "You two plan where you want to go. After dinner we'll head back to Clearwater."

Chantelle moistened her lips. "Grant, I was thinking that maybe I'd stay here."

His face grew still. "Is something the matter?"

"No." She shrugged, then took his hand in hers and looked into his warm blue eyes. "I've been away a lot longer than I'd planned, though, and I need to keep my life going. You know that play next weekend that Ariel gave you tickets for?"

"Yes."

"I'll drive up for the play. That's only three days away."

"It's too long for me. But if you need the time..."

"I do."

His face stilled to an unreadable mask. "You'll spend the weekend?"

"Saturday and Sunday nights, at least. And I'll bring real women's clothes. Grant, I..." With a glance at her sister, Chantelle leaned forward and lowered her voice. "I love you."

Grant rubbed his nose against hers. He brushed his lips along her forehead.

Chantelle sat back, both happy and perturbed. Why didn't he say that he loved her?

Chantelle didn't want to uncurl her hand from around Grant's biceps, but she did it anyway. The enthusiasm of the actors deserved her applause, even if the "snake" crawling into the heroine's bedroom had fallen with a rubbery thump, and the villain's top hat had slipped off when he was most villainous.

The lights in the school gymnasium came on, and the scraping of chairs replaced applause. Chantelle glanced around at the horde of unfamiliar faces. There must be two hundred people at this amateur production, nearly a tenth of the population. Some things about small towns hadn't changed.

Chantelle took Grant's hand in a grip of need and love as they filed toward the aisle. The second thoughts about Grant she'd had back at the store had been buried under regret that she wasn't with him. When the phone had rung she pounced, hoping it was Grant. That first night they were separated he'd phoned at midnight, and she'd never been more glad to talk to anyone in her whole life. She had phoned back at one.

In a way, going to the play had felt like a waste of time, though of course any time spent with Grant wasn't wasted. She would prefer to be in his arms. After that she wanted to be in his mind, talking with him about the way she felt and about his being a doctor again and about Ricki's reaction to him and about how to treat Ariel so as to soothe her hurt and about the best varieties of tomatoes and about the Lion's chances for the Grey Cup and about ... well, about everything.

A short woman with dark hair reached across a row of chairs to tap Grant on the shoulder. "Coming to the reception?"

Grant glanced down at Chantelle. "Are you interested in homemade goodies and a chance to meet the actors? It's just out in the hallway."

Chantelle enjoyed a moment's silence as she basked in Grant's gaze. They had a lot of love to make up after three days' separation, but if he could wait then so could she. "Is this the Clearwater equivalent of going to Sardis?"

The woman with dark hair laughed. "Sort of. By the way, I'm Peg." She pointed to the man beside her. "This is my husband, Dale."

"Pleased to meet you." This was the first of many introductions to come, Chantelle knew. She decided to use a technique she remembered from a high-school era book on shyness. She would try to memorize the names of the first four people she met, not worry about other names until she felt ready—and above all, she'd stay close to Grant's side.

Her plan didn't work out. For one thing, Grant was pulled away by a man. The woman Chantelle was with mentioned that the man was a doctor. She ached to listen to their conversation, but a group of women who'd heard of her through the grapevine crowded around. No one was nosy or rude, though.

When the group thinned and the remaining women became engrossed in talking to each other, Chantelle looked around for Grant. Grant was partly behind someone she'd undoubtedly met, over by a water fountain. He was still talking to the doctor.

Chantelle slowly headed toward him, trying to be inconspicuous and chewing on a brownie that gave her an excuse not to talk. As she studied the school's trophy case, she glanced occasionally from a basketball award to Grant's strong profile, or strained for a glimpse of him in the reflection off the glass. Her heart felt as if it was swelling. Her entire posture straightened as she reveled in the miracle that this handsome creature who outshone everyone else was *hers*.

She glanced over at him again, and he met her gaze. He motioned with his eyes toward the exit, then raised his eyebrows questioningly.

Chantelle nodded. Yes, it was time to go home.

As the car bumped over Grant's long driveway, Chantelle's mind buzzed with unanswered questions and unfulfilled desires. She wanted to reach inside Grant's head and drag out answers and soothe away pain, performing surgery on the surgeon. So simple, that way. Just reach in, snip away the bad parts and blow a kiss of love just before closing.

Chantelle shook her head. No matter how technical, surgery would be simple compared to the complexities of building a relationship. She reached across and stroked his temple lightly.

Grant darted his eyes in her direction. "You must like me in a tie."

"With a tie or without, I like you."

He'd been one of two or three men at the play wearing ties. Chantelle was glad she'd dragged Ricki out to help choose a new dress. She smoothed the tight pink cotton over her thighs and smiled to herself.

As they stepped into the dark hush of his house, Chantelle took a deep breath and put a hand on his arm "Grant, who was that man you talked to tonight?"

"Bob Isaacs."

That told her nothing. "Someone told me he was a doctor."

"That's right."

"Do people here know you used to be a doctor?"

"A few. Ariel does, of course, and so does Bob."

Grant reached for the light switch, and again Chantelle stopped him with her hand. "What did you two talk about?"

"What Bob and I usually talk about." Grant took her hand in his and held it gently at first, then with increasing pressure. "Bob wants me to practice medicine again." With his other hand, Grant turned on the light.

Chantelle blinked in the sudden brightness. "Well?"

A smile curled across Grant's face. He held out his arms and embraced her. "Well, your dress is beautiful but not nearly as beautiful as you." He placed several kisses on her cheeks, the type of kisses that didn't end, but led to more kisses.

"That's not what I meant, Grant." But she was glad he'd noticed, since the dress was especially for him. She leaned into his kisses.

His breath was warm on her cheek. "What did you mean, then?"

"Are you returning to medicine?"

Grant stepped back a couple of feet, holding her hands in his. The smile was still in place, and his head was cocked to one side. He began to pull her toward the stairs. "In four weeks I go back to teaching science at the high school."

"They could replace you."

"Not on such short notice. I'd be letting the school down." He pulled her to his side as they mounted the stairs. "Besides, I was a surgeon. The hospital here is too small to have an operating room."

"The hospital in Kamloops does."

"Hush." He stopped at the top of the stairs and placed a kiss on her forehead.

Chantelle leaned into his kiss despite herself. "But this is important, Grant. We need to talk."

They were in his bedroom now, but he didn't turn on the lights. "We will talk." He took out matches and lit a candle atop the dresser.

A warm glow, suited to the one springing to life inside her, bathed Chantelle's skin. Each flicker seemed to caress her like the touch of a feather. Grant lit more candles. There were candles everywhere, waiting for him to bring them to life. Would he need matches, or would his magical touch be enough to light a candle as it did her heart?

She took a deep breath and kept her voice calm. "When will we talk?"

He bent to light a stick of incense. "Afterward."

"Don't you think we should talk about it now?"

"No."

The fresh aroma of balsam forest filtered into Chantelle's senses. She swallowed as she stood in the middle of the room and watched Grant move from candle to candle.

The click of a tape recorder sounded loud in the stillness. Soft strings and winds joined the candles and incense in permeating the air with romance.

Grant faced her, desire so plain in his eyes that even without candles she would have felt it. He pulled the bedspread back and ran his fingers along the sheets. "Silk."

Chantelle squeezed her eyes shut as she felt a sweet trembling begin to promise her heaven itself. When she opened her eyes Grant was inches from her, gazing into her face. She put her arms around his waist and, with lips parted, raised her chin.

He kissed her. The feel of his lips on hers still had the wizardry of that first time he'd kissed her in a dream, but with the added aura of hope, intimacy and the depth that came of sharing life-and-death experiences. Chantelle surrendered to the probing desire of his tongue. Power surged through her and obliterated all thoughts.

The dress fell easily from her shoulders, without their lips parting. Grant moved his hands over her body with ever-increasing familiarity and urgency, his expert touch sending sensations sliding along her nerves with gathering speed. Her trembling grew to a shiver that slalomed down her spine with an exuberance that made her weak. Even the effort to maintain the kiss became too much. She gasped.

"I missed you this week," Grant whispered into her ear.

"I love you, Grant."

He looked into her eyes and smiled. Taking her hand, he led her to bed.

She wondered briefly, just before emotion and sensation overwhelmed her, when they would ever talk.

Chapter Ten

The following week seemed endless to Chantelle. Though it was now nearly time to see Grant, impatience made her pace from one end of her store to the other. Two boxes of books needed shelving, but Chantelle stepped over them and plopped down on the stool instead.

It was late Saturday afternoon. In an hour she could close the store, shower, change and then drive the hour and a half to Clearwater at slightly over the posted speed. She kept one eye on the customers, urging them to leave. The world wouldn't end if she closed a bit early, would it?

This weekend would be wonderful again, as would next weekend, though perhaps not as wonderful as three weeks from now. This weekend she was taking favorite recipes to cook and bake. In a few weeks, Grant and a couple of acquaintances were showing her Wells Gray Park, the huge wilderness area north of Clearwater.

But three weeks from now... Chantelle popped off the stool impatiently, then forced herself to sit back down and fold her hands demurely. Ricki had insisted that, before her classes resumed for the fall, Chantelle take a week off. With a note of guilt that had been quickly lost in a symphony of eagerness, Chantelle had accepted.

A whole week of being together....

Chantelle abruptly noticed that while dreaming of the future she'd drawn hearts in the margins of a chemistry text. She shut the book with a soft thud, then drummed her thumbs on the counter. Realizing that she was frowning in the direction of her two customers, she eased her face to a neutral smile. Weren't they done browsing yet?

Chantelle's imagination returned to her favorite topic, Grant.

They would live in Clearwater, she decided. The downstairs bedroom with its sturdy log walls would be for their firstborn son. For their daughter, Chantelle would hang flowery, feminine wallpaper in the upstairs back bedroom. She imagined no more than two children, or Grant's house would run out of bedrooms and she couldn't envisage living anywhere else. Two children would do just fine.

Chantelle brushed away the possibility that this image of domestic bliss had problems. Her store, for example, was far from Clearwater, as was the closest hospital with an operating room. Grant had never breathed a word about marriage, and seemed to be holding to her words about a relationship with no strings.

But minor problems evaporated as she rested her chin on her palm and dreamed.

The brass bell above the door tinkled as a woman left without buying anything. One down, one to go. *Soon, Grant. I'll be with you soon.*

Grant had halfheartedly proposed traveling during their week together, perhaps to Vancouver for a cruise to Alaska and back. She had stilled his words with a finger to his lips. His house was fine. She didn't need distractions or entertainment when he was with her.

A tremor of anticipation traveled down her spine.

The other customer carried an armful of books toward the counter. Not even the sizable amount of the man's purchase made Chantelle feel as good as the simple fact that he was leaving.

Sweet fragrances assaulted her when Grant, dapper in trim blue slacks and knit shirt, opened the door of his house. Vases of flowers were everywhere, filling the air with a riot of perfumes that brought the outdoors inside.

"I missed you."

"I missed you, too."

Chantelle looked from one side of the living room to the other, amazed and a bit perplexed at his preparations for her visit. Besides the flowers and a scattering of candles, he'd set up a yellow tent in front of the wood stove. The lonely cry of a loon sounded from a tape of environmental sounds.

Leaving her overnight case and bag of cooking supplies on a chair, Chantelle put her hand to her mouth and turned in place to get the full effect of the room. She cocked her head to one side and looked at Grant. "Did you rob a florist shop?"

"Too much?"

"It's beautiful." The familiar glow she felt in his presence kindled in her heart, making her feel special and beautiful and...loved. "Grant, I'm touched that you'd go to all this bother for me. I'm amazed." She lifted the tent flap and noted silk sheets atop thick foam pads. A bottle of wine nestled in an ice bucket. "This is where we're spending the weekend?"

"In honor of the anniversary of our meeting."

"It hasn't been a year. Maybe," she said with a teasing smile, "it just seems that way to you."

He sat cross-legged on the rug with that supple grace that never failed to capture her mind. "It's been exactly one month come Wednesday."

Chantelle sat on the foam pad and peeked out at him through the tent flap. She lifted the chilled bottle, then snorted. "This wine isn't even made from Canadian grapes. Is it one of those cheap French imitations of our Okanagan champagnes?"

"Cheap?" He feigned insult, though not very well. "Even when I was a doctor, Dom Perignon didn't seem cheap. For our two-month anniversary, woman, you'll be lucky to get Baby Duck."

Another month of such bliss? The world seemed too good to her. She put the bottle back in the ice and looked at him with a hint of shyness. She hesitated to bring it up—though in another way she couldn't wait to tell him—but during her lonely week in Kamloops she'd had a brainstorm. She had realized that if he went into general practice rather than surgery he could stay here in Clearwater.

"About you being a doctor, Grant." She paused. It was dark outside but the room was lit, and so confidences came harder.

"Hmm," he said noncommittally. As if sensing her reservations about the artificial lighting he rose, lit a solitary candle and then flicked out the electric lights.

The tent glowed with a wan light that was so achingly familiar it took away her breath. Was she developing a tent fetish?

Grant sat on his haunches, a dark shadow at the entrance of the tent. "You were going to say something, Chantelle?"

"Yes." She licked at lips that felt dry. She *had* been going to say something. What? "Don't ever lose your imagination for creating romantic settings. You're a true genius."

"I work at it." His chuckle was deep and predatory as he began to creep toward her. "Besides, you inspire me."

"Grant," she breathed in a voice whose husky intonation was beyond her control, "the inspiration is mutual." In the face of his irresistible advance she lay back on the thick foam, though she registered a mild protest. "But we haven't even eaten yet."

He kept coming at her, till he filled her mind with his warm, musky animal presence as he loomed over her. "We'll start with dessert."

She didn't do much cooking that weekend after all.

The fluttering of wings jerked Chantelle's attention to the shadows guarding the loft of the abandoned log cabin. Birds had taken over this place where once people had dreamed and hoped and loved. The thought blended with the drift of her emotions into a bittersweet enjoyment of the impermanence of life.

She thought back over the time since her return from the Rockies. This was the fourth weekend in a row she'd spent with Grant. The joy of those weeks felt huge enough to last all her remaining days. But would it?

Chantelle walked out of the old cabin and shielded her eyes from the sun as she scanned the rolling fields, gone to weeds and seedlings. She saw neither Grant nor his friends who were showing her Wells Gray Provincial Park. He must be close, however.

They were at the Ray Farm, where a family had eked out a wilderness existence sixty years ago. Chantelle had enough of the recluse in herself to comprehend the urge that had driven John Ray past the end of the road and into isolation. This entire homestead was his Thinking Place. In a way she hoped the Park Service never restored the farm, because its lonely slide back into wilderness presented a more powerful scene than would artificial permanence. But then in twenty years nothing would remain. It was transient.

Transient. Grant came down to see her during the week, of course. This week, they'd had dinner Tuesday night, and on Wednesday he surprised her by showing up at the store at closing time. He had ended up spending the night.

Chantelle felt more reserved in Kamloops than she did at his house, though. They couldn't exactly pitch a tent in the middle of the living room, or cook dinner at midnight wearing nothing but aprons. Sharing a two-bedroom house with her kid sister made intimacy difficult. She wondered how parents managed to keep passion alive.

Ever since that conversation in the shop, Chantelle was aware of being a role model for the younger woman. She told herself that Ricki would be helped by seeing a relationship based on love and caring, but her conscience responded with niggling little whispers about wedding rings.

Chantelle heard voices from behind the cabin, then saw Grant peer around the corner and smile. "Jack and Jo are heading to a spring half a mile from here where the carbonated water has the best taste. Want to go?"

"If you do. I'd rather stay here and think."

His face softened. In the past few weeks the tight muscles of Grant's face seemed to have regained their power of expression. When he showed his poker face she knew something was wrong, especially when he seemed lost in thought and in the past. One night when they weren't lost in passion—if there were any—she'd have to ask where his mind went at those moments.

Grant wondered at the soft, pensive look on her face. He turned and waved to his friends behind the cabin. "We'll wait for you here. Bring us a bottle of water." The couple had filled the trunk of their car with gallon bottles and a wheelbarrow to carry them, claiming that plastic ruined the taste of the spring water.

Grant joined Chantelle sitting in the rectangle where a window had once been. The clinking of bottles soon faded, leaving them alone with the murmur of the wind as it poured lazy waves through the tall grass of the field.

Grant put his arm around her, resting his hand on the proud swell of her hip. The bridge of her nose was so perfectly shaped that he wanted to run his fingertip along it. If he did, her cheeks would scrunch up in the cute welcoming smile that lit her face when he broke into her silent reveries. The smile would melt into her usual contented grin if he continued to stare at her, and finally her face muscles would loosen into an expectant tranquillity that showed how seriously she took the emotions she felt. If he still stared, her lips would part ever so slightly, and he would know she wanted to be kissed.

He'd learned many of her expressions. He wanted to learn more. Would there always be something to fascinate him about this woman?

"You're quiet around other people," he said.

"Sorry. I guess it's a leftover from my shyness. I like your friends, though."

He lifted a leg through the window and sat astride the log, facing Chantelle. "Why did you buy a retail store, then?"

She half turned, her pensiveness gone and her contented smile warming his stomach. "I like books. Besides, I think I handle meeting people fairly well now."

Grant felt a chuckle stir up the warmth in his belly.

"Why are you laughing?"

"I'm remembering how you acted when you met me. You swore, insulted me, threw things and generally were a pain. Yeah, I'd say you've mastered the art of making friends."

Her face softened. "It worked didn't it?"

"Yes." He stopped chuckling and watched her slightly parted lips. "It certainly did. I almost miss your tantrums." He leaned forward and touched her with only his lips. The gentle fragrance of her perfume seemed to lift him to other times, in the dark. He kept his hands off her with difficulty. "I wish we were alone," he whispered.

"We are."

"Jack and Jo could come back anytime, and we're in full view of the road if anyone passes by."

Her eyes grew wide, pretending shock. "Why, Grant Van Arden," she protested, "just what did you have in mind?"

"The same thing you did."

Chantelle's face held exactly the right amount of desire and frustration to stroke his ego and his libido, while her words had held exactly the right amount of humor to make the situation bearable. He shook his head, his voice momentarily silenced by a lump in his throat. She said the right things so often that it was scary. "Thank you, Chantelle."

She arched her eyebrows. "For what?"

"For teaching me how to laugh. For reminding me not to take myself so seriously."

She put her hands around his neck, brushing his sensitive nape with her thumbs. "And thank you, Grant, for teaching me about romance and love."

He looked out across the restless, whispering field. The wind seemed to tell him what he already knew, that he'd never imagined loving more than he loved Chantelle right now. The moment seemed perfect, complete in itself.

Yet a shadow lurked at the periphery of his mind's vision. When Chantelle used the word *love* she seemed to promise eternity and make him yearn for even more. To him, what did the word *love* mean? Chantelle had made him realize that he'd never before known what love was. Yet even now, as his heart swelled with emotion, an arrogant remnant of his former self readied a scalpel to hack at the tender growth of intimacy. Grant wanted to answer Chantelle in kind, to promise something beyond this perfect moment, something for the future. He wanted that very much.

The words clung to his palate.

He cleared his throat. He had to say something. "Anything in particular you want to do during our week together?"

"Yes," she answered promptly. Then she paused, studying his face before continuing. "Do you remember those nights in the tent?"

"Do you think I'll ever forget them?"

A smile touched her mouth, but her eyes were pensive. "They were wonderful," she agreed. "Lying there in the dark, talking, exploring each other's minds, getting closer and closer...."

"The good old days."

"They were, weren't they?" She paused again, studying him closely as she cupped his cheek with her palm. "Grant...let's devote a night to talking. Just crawl into bed, turn out the lights and talk. It seems as if we never just communicate. We talk, but pretty soon I reach for you or you reach for me and we make love instead of talking."

Grant cupped her cheek as she was cupping his. "I think," he whispered, "that a night without sex, without touching you, is a high price to pay for communication." He smiled reassuringly as Chantelle lowered her eyes. "But worth every minute. It's the time away from you completely that's wasted."

Her face melted into a smile.

Grant winked at her. "We'll make love in the morning instead."

Chantelle met his wink without changing her expression. "What do you mean, instead? Don't you mean *also*?"

Grant's chuckle grew into a laugh, as it did more and more often when he was around her. It felt good.

Two weeks later, Grant rested one arm on the balcony railing and the other on Chantelle's shoulders. She was gazing intently at the pasture and the ridge that marked the other side of the narrow valley. Here in the shadows her hair didn't dance with fire, yet its dark promise portended a mystery just as intriguing. He leaned into the soft fullness of her hair and inhaled its clean, desirable aroma.

"I'm so glad we have this whole week together," he whispered.

Chantelle rubbed her head against his chin. "I broke every speed limit in the book getting up here."

"It still wasn't soon enough for me. I wish you would let me stay with you in Kamloops."

Chantelle straightened. "Not with Ricki there."

"I understand. I just wish things were different."

"Me, too."

Grant feathered his lips over her temple and gloried in the way she bent her head into his kiss. She twisted so their lips met. He nibbled at the corner of her mouth, one of her many sensitive places that he'd learned.

A faint, high-pitched yell momentarily distracted him. "Grant!"

Together, they turned to look toward the barbed-wire fence. The young neighbor boy, Robby, jumped and waved at them. Grant waved back.

"I think," he whispered into Chantelle's ear, "we'd better sit down before continuing."

She stepped back toward a lounger and pulled at his hand. "Sounds like a good idea to me."

Chantelle sat, then reached underneath her to pull out a small, roughly whittled cube of white pine. She studied it for a moment. "What are you making?"

Sitting beside her, he took the block and pointed to a carved area. "A ball in a cage."

"Like the one you gave Robby last weekend?" She turned the cube over in her hands. "How do you get the ball inside the bars, anyway?"

"That, my dear lady, is a professional secret."

"It's more like magic. Come on, you can tell me." She snuggled against him suggestively. "Pretty please?"

"Hmm. If I refuse, how hard will you try to change my mind?"

Chantelle rested a finger against his chin, then turned her head to one side and pouted. "Please, honey bunch?"

"I'm putty in your hands. You carve the ball out of the wood between the bars, making sure it's too big to slip out."

She sat up straight and reached for his knife on the balcony railing. "Show me how to do it."

Resting his cheek against hers, Grant took her hand and guided the knife repeatedly into the soft wood. "This is fun," he commented.

"With you around, everything's fun."

He turned from the soft vow in her eyes when he heard bumping noises, as if something was knocking against the house. Chantelle screeched when a shock of brown hair appeared over the railing, followed by the rest of Robby's face.

"Robby!" Grant reached for the brave but foolish lad.

The boy waved, seeming to hang by one finger. "Hi, Grant."

Grant snatched the youngster to the safety of the balcony. "How did you get up here," he demanded sternly, "and why?"

"Up the plant thing."

"And why did you do such a dangerous thing, Robby?"

"I wanted to see you." Robby glanced over at Chantelle, then smiled up at Grant. "You ran away when I called to you. You're always busy with *her*."

Grant and Chantelle exchanged looks. She leaned forward and took the boy's hand. *"And you'd do anything to get Grant's attention, wouldn't you?"* she said quietly.

Robby looked down at his runners. "I cut my finger on the barbed wire. He needs to bandage it."

"It just so happens," Grant said, "that I have a box of bandages inside, on the dresser. I'll be right back."

He was gone only seconds. Chantelle still held the boy's hand.

"Robby," she said, "Grant was showing me how to make a ball in a cage, like the one he gave to you first." She emphasized the last word slightly. "Would you like to help me?"

The boy glanced back at Grant and, his loyalties easily switched, plopped down on her lap. "Sure."

Grant leaned against the railing and enjoyed the sight of Chantelle holding a child. Something deep and powerful stirred inside of him. "Whatever you do," he warned her, "watch this wild man with that knife."

Both of them smiled up at him. His protective urge grew still stronger.

He and Chantelle needed to talk, as she'd insisted when they were at Wells Gray Park. Not tonight, perhaps, because they'd been apart too long. Tomorrow night.

"Remember," Chantelle called from behind the closed door of the washroom. "This is our night for talking."

"I remember, I remember." Grant pulled the covers down and lay atop the bed. Since Chantelle had insisted he wear pajamas, he didn't think he'd need even a sheet.

"I'll be out in a minute."

Grant laced his fingers behind his head and smiled as he thought back over the first two days of their week together. They had already shared quite a bit. Much of it was quiet sharing, but that kind counted, too, even if they hadn't tackled the weighty matters. Grant reached over and turned out all but the bedside lamp, waiting for her.

When the door opened, Chantelle breezed into the middle of the room and posed with her hand on her hip. Her hair bristled with an overabundance of curlers, the housecoat she wore over baggy cotton pajamas was splattered with paint, and a thick, greenish mud pack covered her face.

Grant looked at her as she posed. "Is it Halloween already?"

"No making love," she reminded him again.

"No making love," he agreed with a laugh. "I'm not even sure I'll let you into my bed."

She glared at him. At least he thought she glared, though it was hard to tell through the mud pack.

"Hmmph." Chantelle stuck her nose in the air and sat on the edge of the bed. "I guess I'm safe from your advances, then."

Grant's chuckle slowly subsided, till he was simply looking into her eyes. They were still her eyes, dancing with life. Her lips were still her lips. Underneath the bag-lady clothes, her smooth and supple body was still her body. Most importantly, underneath it all was still the same wonderful person. "To me, you're beautiful regardless."

"Grant Van Arden, you're impossible." She flung herself back on the bed and folded her arms over her chest. She didn't seem displeased, however. "I never thought you were capable of such bad taste."

"Neither did I," he admitted.

"Watch what you say, buster." She reached for the edge of the mud pack and began peeling it off. Grant leaned close. "Haven't you ever seen a lady take off a mud pack before?"

"No." He watched in fascination as she stretched her face muscles once the pack was off.

"Your wife never used mud packs, then?"

"Not that she ever let me see. But then, she had the good taste of a lady."

She didn't respond to his teasing with a smile. Here it comes, he thought, the serious stuff, and he guessed the topic would be his former wife. Chantelle sat up to pull the old housecoat over her head, turned out the light and lay down facing him. She was a palpable presence beside him in the dark.

"Grant...." She paused, then sighed loudly. "Now that we're here it's hard to start."

When she remained quiet for another minute, Grant spoke into the silence. "I saw Ariel's car last week. She must be back from summer school."

"Oh?" Chantelle felt her face grow warm.

"If I know Ariel, she's lain awake nights trying to figure out some graceful way to explain the awkwardness of that scene after we got back from Mount Robson."

Chantelle shifted position so her cheek rested on Grant's chest. The rhythm of his heart seeped into her mind and calmed her.

Ariel wasn't her rival. Linda's ghost was.

"Grant," Chantelle whispered, "what do you think Linda would think of you teaching rather than practicing?"

"I think she'd consider it beneath me." He chuckled briefly. "Or more precisely, she'd consider it beneath her to be married to a high school teacher."

"Would she want you to avoid medicine because of what happened?"

"Chantelle...." He left her name hanging in the air. She felt him move, and could imagine him running his hand roughly through his hair. "You don't understand."

"I'm only too aware of that." She snuggled against his chest, as if trying to burrow inside his skin and experience his feelings for herself. "But I want to understand."

"It isn't Linda. It's me."

Grant paused. His pulse pounded faster against Chantelle's ear.

"Linda wasn't the first patient I ever lost," he said, "but I'd always been shielded from the harsh realities of medicine by this unthinking certainty that I would save a greater percentage of my patients than other doctors. I improved the odds, and I figured that was enough."

Chantelle lifted her head to look toward where the darkness hid all but the vague outline of his face.

"But medicine isn't about odds. It's about people, and about caring. Before Linda's operation I didn't care, not deep in my heart, about the hopes and dreams and loves of my patients. They were bundles of symptoms, not people.

After Linda's operation, I cared too much to risk stealing anyone else's sunsets.''

He took a deep breath, then continued. "When I was a little boy, I used to climb this one particular tree. The limbs were sturdy enough that I could sit as high as the second story, if I dared. But at night I'd sometimes jerk awake in terror from a dream of falling from that tree. Now, I jerk awake in terror from a dream of holding a scalpel.''

Chantelle put her arm around his waist and hugged him tightly. "But did you stop climbing the tree?''

Grant let out a long breath. "No. I was afraid, but I didn't stop climbing.''

"You have stopped being a doctor, though.''

There was no accusation in her tone, only a question, yet she felt his muscles stiffen. He began stroking her hair, and slowly his muscles loosened and his breathing slowed.

"I've done a lot of thinking lately." Grant's voice was a velvety whisper through the darkness. "One of the conclusions I've reached is that, well...." He hugged Chantelle tightly. "You know, despite all my aloofness, I loved Linda.''

Chantelle returned his hug, filling a long silence with the reassuring expression of touch. After a while Grant's chest moved more slowly and evenly under her chin, in the cadence of sleep.

Chantelle, however, remained awake. In a way she was glad he'd admitted his emotions about the past, both to himself and to her. But in another way...well, he could now acknowledge having loved Linda; but he'd acknowledged nothing of his feelings for *her*. Chantelle's eyes burned. Grant loved her, she knew he did. But she needed to hear the words, needed to live them for the rest of her life.

In the middle of the night Chantelle suddenly jerked to a sitting position and tried to remember what had torn her from sleep. It had been a premonition of Grant, years from now, holding another woman in the hush of night and finally admitting that, once upon a time, he'd loved a woman named Chantelle DuMaurier.

The next morning, clouds of steam swirled around Chantelle as she turned slowly in the shower. The details of Grant's tragedy were burned into her mind, as clear in the morning light as the pulsing of water on her skin.

Not so clear was what she should do about it. Underneath his rugged, capable exterior he'd developed sensitivity and compassion; she marvelled when she recalled her initial assessment of him as a thick-skinned Tarzan. But was he done reacting and ready to continue his life? Maybe, just maybe, his relationship with her was a major step in that direction.

But if that was the case, why couldn't he tell her that he loved her?

Chantelle turned off the water and reached for a towel. So many questions, she thought as she shivered in the sudden cold, and so few answers, at least so far. Give her time, and she'd do everything she could to help him heal.

Time. Would she have enough time? She'd thought she could forget the future and enjoy an affair while it lasted, but she'd been kidding herself. She wanted Grant for the rest of her life, and she'd settle for not an hour less.

Chantelle heard a knock. She wrapped the towel around her, more for the cold than for modesty, and opened the door.

Grant put his head in. A soft smile captured his face when he saw her. Last night's revelations seemed the farthest things from his mind. "You have company," he said.

"Company? Here?"

"Well, not right here. Downstairs. I thought you might object if I brought them in here. If you want, though, I can run down and—"

"Very funny. Who is it?"

"Ricki and a friend."

"Oh God, something's happened to the store." Chantelle wrapped another towel around her hair, turban fashion, then reached for her clothes without drying.

"Relax. Nothing's wrong, she's just visiting. And the friend is a young male." Grant winked at her, then shut the door.

"Who's watching the store?" she said to the closed door, which didn't answer. Relax, indeed. Easy for him to say. It wasn't his store sitting closed in the middle of the week. Chantelle dressed, then hurried downstairs without bothering to remove the turban from her hair.

Grant was standing at the open fridge, getting cream for tea. Ricki sat on the living-room couch, looking very young in a denim skirt and low-cut blouse, much too young for the way her "friend" draped his arm around her shoulder, his hand resting with breezy overfamiliarity on her cleavage. His thinly mustached lips nuzzled her ear.

Ricki's giggle had a husky, grown-up quality. "Behave yourself. My sister could be down any minute."

Chantelle took the last three steps slowly. So, this was the boy Ricki was *careful* with. She'd seen him before, but only as a face in a crowd of friends. Dan something. He'd tutored Ricki in math and then come to a few parties—but not as a *date*. When had things gotten serious?

And why? What did Ricki see in him? Chantelle felt like a mother as she surveyed the lanky youth's casual clothes and decided he wasn't good enough for her sister. She took a deep breath, coughed discreetly and tried to push the hasty judgment aside.

"Chantelle!" Ricki bounded from the couch as if it was an ejection seat, and her face colored. She tugged her blouse together, laced her fingers primly and nodded toward the boy on the couch. "I'd like you to meet my boyfriend, Dan Arlinson."

Dan's manners, at least, were impeccable. He shook her hand, mouthed a few easy words of small talk and ignored the towel turban on her head.

Chantelle sat on Grant's rocking chair and kept her voice milder than if Dan wasn't present. "What's going on at the store?"

"Nancy—the librarian friend from Cariboo College I told you about before—is working there today," Ricki said. "It's okay. She's totally honest, once owned a store of her own and knows Second Thoughts from when she helped me earlier this summer. She was delighted to do it, I think because she's serious about wanting to buy it. It will be all right."

Her store was left in the clutches of someone who wanted to take it from her. Great. Chantelle was going to say something, then remembered that Ricki had volunteered to give her this week off. Ricki's judgment and maturity were beyond her years. Maybe it would be all right.

Chantelle decided to say nothing, though the incident pointed out that she needed to spend more time at her business and less up here.

"Anyway," Ricki said, "I thought it was time for you to meet Dan. A bunch of us were at a pizza place just before school got out, when I suddenly realized the only reason I wanted to go out with the gang anymore was to be near Dan. It turned out he felt the same way." Her gaze lingered meltingly on her boyfriend.

If this . . . romance was recent, that helped to explain why Chantelle didn't know about it. But that didn't explain why Ricki had been secretive, or why she'd driven to Clearwater all of a sudden. Then again, Chantelle had been gone at the beginning of the summer, and since then she'd been so involved with Grant that she hadn't seen much of Ricki.

She smiled at the young man, determined to be a supportive sister rather than a disapproving parent. "So, Dan, as I recall you're nearly finished with school?"

"Yes. This is my final year."

Grant came in from the kitchen carrying a tea tray. Conversation moved to neutral topics such as Grant's garden and what courses the two young people were going to take. Dan suggested they double-date some weekend, causing Chantelle to smile. She'd be more of a chaperon than a double date.

The visit passed quickly. Chantelle slowly tempered her opinion of the young man. Someone like Ricki deserved the very best, and if this youth fell short of that ideal he was nonetheless pleasant and forthright. Chantelle trusted Ricki's judgment in other ways, and if she'd been less emotional she would have known to trust her about Dan, too.

Before the young people left Grant and Dan went outside to look at Dan's car, leaving Chantelle and Ricki alone. Ricki's face dissolved into a mass of smile lines as soon as the door closed. "Isn't he wonderful, Chani?"

"He seems very nice."

"He is. I like him a lot." Ricki sat on the couch and looked at Chantelle, her dreamy expression fading to a look of concern. "He's asked me to live with him this year."

"Oh?" Chantelle hadn't the faintest idea what else to say. "What do you think?"

What did she think? She thought Ricki was her little sister in pigtails who'd gotten her first training bra just yesterday. She thought her mother would blame her for letting this happen. Mostly she thought the house would be empty and lonely without Ricki.

Still, if Ricki loved Dan the way she loved Grant, that was everything. "My opinion isn't as important as yours, Ricki. You have to look into your heart for the answer."

Ricki scrunched up one cheek and spread her palm wide. "Come on, Chani, I need your help. I mean, you lived with Garrett. You're the only one in the family who might understand. Should I move in with Dan or not?"

"Living with Garrett didn't exactly turn out well. I'm no authority." At Ricki's disappointed expression, Chantelle sighed. "Look, I don't know how you feel about Dan. If you love him—really love him—then go for it."

Ricki set her face aglow with a smile. "I love him, Chani."

"Really love him?" Chantelle couldn't help posing the question. When she'd been Ricki's age she had no idea what love was. "Does your skin feel as if it comes alive when he walks into the room? When you're working, do you forget where you are, thinking about him? Does your face get all flushed remembering the way he stirs his tea?"

Chantelle leaned back on the couch, and her unfocused eyes drifted to the window. She hugged her elbows. "Has he changed your existence so thoroughly you have trouble imagining the world still turning without him? Do you feel as if all your life you've been only a bud, yet now you've opened your petals to the sunshine?" Her voice drifted away to nothing.

"Wow," Ricki said in a hushed voice. For a moment she said nothing. "You feel that way about Grant?"

Chantelle nodded.

"You're lucky, Chani."

"It's taken me twenty-eight years to find Grant. You're young, Ricki. Don't be in a hurry, unless you're sure."

"Grant must be quite a man."

"Yes, he is." Putting her feelings into words made Chantelle realize even more what Grant meant to her, and how determined she was to help him face his past so they could face the future together.

Ricki looked solemn. "I'm fairly sure about Dan, Chani. But I'll think hard about everything you've said before I decide. I promise."

Chantelle pulled her sister into a hug. "You think about it, and whatever you decide you have my full support."

"Even with our parents?"

So that was the true purpose of this little visit—family politicking and alliance building. With a rueful smile on her face, Chantelle sighed. "Even with our parents."

"Ouch!"

With pursed lips, Chantelle held the barber scissors poised in midair. "Grant, I haven't even touched you yet."

He grinned crookedly, then hung his shirt from a fence pole to keep hair from getting inside and settled back onto the bar stool they'd put in the woods back of his house. Chantelle was beautiful as always, and as always he enjoyed the sight of her as if for the first time. Dappled sunlight filtered through the trees to spread new and fascinating shadows across her face and neck. The scissors glinted in a shaft of light, sparking him to tease her again.

"Are you sure you know how to cut hair?"

"I used to cut my brothers' hair, and Garrett's hair. Of course," she added with a wicked smile, "I didn't always do a very good job on Garrett."

"That's reassuring."

"Grant," she barked in a voice that recalled the temper she'd shown the first few days on the trail, "sit!"

Grant smiled at memories as he sat down.

"That's better," she said. "Now sit still, and if you do as you're told you'll be presentable for the first day of school next week."

"And if I don't sit still?"

"Then you'll look like Garrett."

He squirmed on the stool. "I've never had a barber threaten me before."

Chantelle ran a comb through the hair at the side of his head and began snipping. "Threats were the only way to get my older brothers to sit still. They knew that if I got angry I'd carry out my threats."

"What about your younger brothers?"

"They were easier. A lollipop worked miracles on their attention spans."

Grant turned his head to face her. "I react much better to lollipops than threats."

Chantelle rested one hand on his bare shoulder and the other on her hip. "Sorry. I thought this was going to be an adult holiday and I didn't bring lollipops."

"Shows how wrong you were." When he was around her he felt like a youth again, transported to a carefree time of first love without the painful insecurities of the teen years. Chantelle gave him the best of all worlds. He speared out and caught her cheek in a quick kiss. "Adult, indeed."

A smile played around the corners of her mouth. "Yes, adult. This is hardly a Disney version of *Bambi* or *Cinderella* we've got going between us. It's R-rated, at a minimum." She straightened up and became businesslike. "How short do you want it?"

They spent a few minutes discussing the style and length of his hair. Her scent, the sight of her jeans-clad hip, the occasional touch of her body against his bare back, were already combining to make this a memorable haircut. Everything about Chantelle triggered something primitive and possessive deep inside him.

Chantelle was cutting in a fast, steady rhythm that proclaimed her experience. "Tell me," he said, "have you thought any more about what Nancy said?" Ricki's friend who'd minded the store the other day had phoned this morning, sounding Chantelle out about whether she might indeed be moving to Clearwater. Chantelle had been noticeably guarded about moving. Disturbingly so, as far as Grant was concerned.

The rhythmic snipping of the scissors slowed a bit. "Yes. I know the store isn't doing well, and I know I need to do something. Marketing and bookkeeping are my two weak points."

"Hire a bookkeeper to set up a format for your records," Grant said. "After your record keeping is in shape I can help you. I have a good head for numbers."

"I'd appreciate any help I can get." Chantelle moved in front of him and combed his bangs across his forehead. She smiled without taking her eyes off his hair as she trimmed the front. "Can you help me with marketing, too?"

"Maybe. For starters, how committed are you to the type of books you carry?"

"That's the kind of books there were when I bought the place."

Grant wriggled his nose, then wiped some tickling hairs off his cheekbone. "I don't know about Kamloops, but here in Clearwater you'd do better with lighter books. We don't have a bookstore," he said with a casualness that he didn't feel, "so people go to Kamloops. I bet if someone promoted a Clearwater bookstore by going around the schools, by advertising in the paper and by putting handbills in the shopping center, she could drum up business quickly."

For several seconds the scissors were silent. Finally Chantelle resumed cutting, but more slowly than before. "Maybe," she said. "Maybe."

Grant found that his heart was beating more rapidly. They were skirting territory new to them.

Chantelle paused again, standing behind him. She put her arms lightly around his neck. Her chin pressed against the top of his head with a weight that felt marvelous. "Summer's nearly over." Her voice was quiet and tentative. "Sometimes I wish time would stand still. Everything's going to change."

"No, it won't."

He felt her head shake in disagreement. "Ricki's going back to school and I'll have to work fifty-hour weeks again. She may even move out, and if she does I'll be even busier. You'll be working and won't be able to come down during the week. We'll see each other on Sundays, at best."

"It won't be like that unless we let it be."

"Maybe." She sounded doubtful. "Grant . . ."

When she stopped, he twisted around in the chair to face her.

Chantelle swallowed, then continued in a level voice. "Grant, if you were going to consider returning to medicine, now would be the time, before you've committed yourself to a year of teaching."

He shook his head ruefully. He'd thought she was going to say something quite different, and his voice was harsher than he meant it to be. "I was a surgeon, Chantelle, and you know there's no operating room here."

"Then work as a general practitioner." When he opened his mouth to say something she plunged on quickly. "Grant, you'd be perfect as a G.P. You'd need all the attributes you've worked to develop—empathy, caring, nurturing. It's perfect for you."

"They need me at the high school."

Chantelle raised her fists to the level of her head, then with a burst of breath forced them to her sides. "You're not irreplaceable, damn it. There are other teachers, a lot more teachers than doctors. Tell the school board you'll work till they find a replacement."

Grant saw the fire in her eyes and felt an answering heat rise in his own. "Chantelle, going back to medicine is my decision. One way or another, it's my decision."

"And it affects me, too, if I'm to be part of your life."

"Wait a minute, here. I never signed over control of my life to you."

"No, and you aren't going to share, really share, until you've made yourself return to medicine."

Grant rose from the chair and towered over her. "That's the stupidest thing I've heard you say."

"Don't call me stupid!" Her narrowed eyes flashed still brighter. "What do you want to be doing two years from now?"

"What are you talking about?"

"I'm talking about the future. When you were a doctor I'm sure you planned ahead. Now you just live day-to-day. In two years, do you still want to be in Clearwater? Do I have a place in your future? Or have you even given it a thought?"

The sound of tires on gravel registered on the periphery of Grant's attention, but he never looked away from the flaming beauty in front of him. "Yes," he said quietly, "I think you have a place in my future."

Chantelle's fierce expression immediately softened. She went into his outstretched arms, her warm body a salve to the inflamed emotions of only moments before. "Oh, Grant," she breathed.

An approaching pickup truck stopped in front of the house with a squeal of tired brakes. A gray-haired man and woman got out. Chantelle stood straight and tugged at the bottom of her blouse. "Great," she muttered. "Just great. Fantastic timing."

"Do you know them?"

Chantelle sighed and waved to the newcomers. "It's my parents."

Chapter Eleven

Chantelle folded her arms across her chest and walked slowly toward her parents. Grant plucked his shirt from the fence post and put it on as he walked. From his smile, Chantelle realized that he was more pleased to see her parents than she was. But he had reason to be glad for an interruption. He'd just been about to tell her where she fit into his future, and her parents' arrival had saved him.

Chantelle stopped a dozen feet from her parents. "What are you doing here?"

Grant spoke at almost the same time. "Welcome. I'm glad to meet you both."

Chantelle glanced over at him as she tapped the back of her leg with her fingers. A few seconds ago they'd been in the middle of their first fight since the hiking trip. She still felt riled up, yet Grant seemed completely calm as he extended his hand. "I'm Grant Van Arden."

Her father, a short, wiry man with surprising strength, gave Grant a handshake that made him wince momentarily before he returned it in kind.

"Frank DuMaurier. This is my wife, Libby."

Grant turned to her mother and kissed the back of her hand. Libby was the more forceful parent, in a subtle, outwardly submissive way. But under Grant's gallant attention she lowered her eyes like a timid schoolgirl. "We were in the area," she said lamely.

Chantelle drummed her fingers harder against the back of her thigh. In the area, indeed. "Did the orchard burn down?"

"Of course not, dear," said Libby. "Why would you even ask such a thing?"

"Just wondering how you managed to get away during apple harvest."

"Well," her father said, "we wanted to a take a bit of a drive."

"Two hundred miles, at the busiest time of year?"

Frank began walking toward the pickup. For a second Chantelle regretted her brusqueness, fearing he was leaving, but instead he gestured to the bed of the truck. "We thought you might like some fruit."

Grant took Chantelle's stiff hand and guided her to the truck. The memory-laden aroma of ripe peaches surrounded her, yet did nothing to soothe her.

"There's a couple boxes of Tydemann's—sorry, but the Red Delicious and MacIntosh are just coming in now—some pears, plums and a few peaches."

"Dad," Chantelle said gently, "you sent me a load two weeks ago. There must be two hundreds pounds of fruit here. It'll just spoil."

"This is for your friend, dear," Libby said.

Chantelle blinked. "Oh."

Her father turned to Grant. "This looks like the kind of place that has a root cellar."

"Yes, sir," Grant said.

"What say you and I carry this stuff down, eh?"

Grant tried unsuccessfully to protest Frank's generosity, but the older man already had a huge box of apples balanced on his shoulder. A ready smile on his face, Grant picked up a box and led the way to the back of the house.

Chantelle led her mother to the bench swing on the front porch. Libby looked around with unabashed interest at the pasture and the distant peaks. "Your young man has a nice piece of property. Nice, solid house, too."

Chantelle wasn't in the mood for small talk. Her parents were here because of Dan and Grant, the new men in their daughters' lives, but Chantelle didn't feel like being grilled or fighting her mother's overconcern about Ricki. She braced herself.

"How did you know I was here?" she asked. "No, don't bother to answer. Ricki told you." No wonder Ricki had enlisted Chantelle's help. She must have known this was coming.

"Your sister could never keep a secret from me. You were the only one of my children who ever managed to do that, and not very often, either. Tell me, have you taken Grant to Williams Lake to meet Bert?"

"No." Her oldest brother Bert, had grown up to be human, to Chantelle's amazement. His wife and children were sweet and lovable. But if Chantelle introduced Grant to all her relatives they'd never have time alone.

"You should drive over some afternoon since you're so close."

"Bert lives over two hundred miles from here, Mother."

"Still, he's family."

Suddenly this whole thing seemed funny. Her parents dropping by when they were "in the area," the overdone gift of fruit, the admonition to visit her distant brother. Chantelle felt a smile tug at her lips. "Yes, Mom."

Another thought drove away all vestiges of enjoyment of her parents' visit. How would Grant react to all this? Would nosy parents turn him off and make him wonder what he was getting himself into?

Now that her parents had visited, word would spread throughout the family. *Gee, it's Sunday,* she could hear her brothers and cousins and aunts and uncles say, *let's pack a picnic and visit Chantelle and her boyfriend in Clearwater.* Soon they'd come with their children and dogs, expecting to spend the night. This could be the vanguard of an invasion.

And for all Chantelle knew, she was just a summer romance to Grant.

"Your young man seems polite." Libby's eyes twinkled. "From what I saw before he put on his shirt, quite a he-man, too. Not as handsome as your father, of course, but a good catch."

"He's not a fish, Mom." Her next words seemed to lacerate Chantelle's throat. "And I haven't caught him, either."

Libby took some crocheting from her handbag and began the soothing rhythms that were so typical of her. "Do you want to catch him?"

Chantelle watched the flickering movements of her mother's hands as she considered her answer. Of course she wanted to marry Grant. But talk of catching him made the whole relationship sound calculated and impersonal, distorting the depth of her feelings. "I love him."

Libby smiled, but never missed a stroke. "Does he love you?"

"I think so." She *knew* so. Why had she hedged? Maybe, she thought, because a positive answer would have had her mother addressing wedding invitations on the drive home. Or worse, because he never said so.

Libby's fingers stilled. The sympathy in her eyes indicated that she understood a great deal more than Chantelle had said in words. "You're not sure where you stand, are you?"

Chantelle licked her lips and watched Grant and her father walk toward the garden to inspect the fruit trees. They'd likely respect each other, because they'd see the quality in each other despite their differences. Grant would be by far the best in-law in the entire DuMaurier clan, if only...

"No," she admitted, "I'm not sure where I stand."

"And that bothers you, doesn't it?" Click, click. "You don't have to pretend. I know things are different these days. No matter what you do, you're still my daughter."

Chantelle gave a push that set the swing in motion. "Yes, Mom, it bothers me that I don't know what Grant wants."

"Maybe your young man isn't so nice after all. You want me to tell Frank to pound a proposal out of him?"

"I hope you're kidding."

Libby covered Chantelle's hand with her own. "I guess there's nothing we can do to help."

"No, I guess there isn't."

They didn't say anything for several minutes. Finally Chantelle roused herself and smiled at her mother. "What are you making?"

"Christmas stockings for this year's two new grandchildren." Libby glanced at her daughter with eyebrows ever so slightly raised.

"No, Mom, you don't have to make an extra stocking on account of me."

"Good." Libby's hands worked relentlessly at the yarn. "What about Ricki?"

Here it comes, Chantelle thought. "No stockings on account of Ricki, either."

"She has a beau, I hear. We're going to meet them on the way back, but we wanted to talk to you first. Have you met the boy?"

"Yes." Chantelle gave the swing another hard shove. "Don't you dare intimidate him with a heavy interrogation. Grant and I can take it, but Ricki and Dan are young. You might scare him off."

"We weren't planning on causing trouble, but I'll keep what you say in mind. So, the boy's name is Dan. What's he like?"

"He has excellent manners. He's in his fourth year at Cariboo College, and he seems to want to make something of himself." Chantelle proceeded to trot out everything positive she could remember about the youth who loved Ricki. Sisters had to stick together, especially sisters in love.

Libby kept crocheting through it all. When Chantelle ran out of Dan's good points, Libby said firmly, "This Dan fellow has an apartment, I hear."

"Oh?"

"Yes. He wants my baby to live in sin with him." Libby looked up at Chantelle accusingly. "Chantelle Marie DuMaurier, are you pretending you didn't know?"

"I knew."

"And what do you think?"

"I think I'll miss her if she decides to move out."

"We trusted Ricki to you."

"And now you have to trust Ricki, period." Chantelle turned on the swing to face her mother. "She's an adult. I don't think she'll make a mistake, but if she does then she's the one who has to live with it. She's mature enough to judge whether a relationship has a future and is good for her."

"It's not that we blame you, dear, but—"

Chantelle interrupted. "You can't *blame* me for Ricki falling in love. Love doesn't call for blame, even if it doesn't turn out as well as for you and Dad." And I'm the family expert on love that doesn't turn out, Chantelle thought wearily. "Trust Ricki. If Dan isn't right for her, she'll know it. She's only nineteen, but she's wiser than I am."

"I don't know about that, dear." Libby shook her head and smiled. "I've always thought that you were the smartest of my children. I never told you that, did I?"

"No."

"Well, it's true. Ricki's smart, too, but she's impetuous. When we sent her off to Cariboo College, we hoped that you would rub off on her so she'd stop and think things through."

Chantelle recalled her sister's promise to think carefully before deciding to move in with Dan; exactly the sort of thing her mother was talking about. "I think you've gotten your wish, Mom. Please, trust Ricki's judgment."

Libby put down her crocheting and fanned herself with her hand. "You're probably right." She laughed, and it was the fresh sound of a teenager's laugh. "But you're not a mother—yet—so maybe you don't understand how I worry about her. About all of you children."

"You're wrong, Mom. I worry about Ricki, too."

The rest of the afternoon passed quickly. Her father spent most of his time with Grant. The two men seemed to get along, with Grant asking for help pruning and grafting his young fruit trees. Frank was in his element, wielding pruning shears and tree paint.

Libby helped fix tea, openly admiring Grant's teapot, which she explained to Chantelle in a whisper, was very expensive. Libby served Grant his tea with respect. Her parents weren't quite obvious enough to give Grant a report card, but if they did she knew that he would pass, magna cum laude.

Frank invited Grant to visit the orchard, and drew a map on an envelope. Her parents declined Grant's offer of dinner, explaining that they would eat in Kamloops with Ricki.

Poor Ricki, Chantelle thought. She must phone to warn her.

Chantelle was exhausted when the white pickup finally headed down the driveway in a cloud of dust. She put one arm around Grant's waist and waved with her other hand. When the dust ended at the highway, they watched from the porch till the truck disappeared, then walked side by side into the house.

Chantelle perched on the arm of the chair Grant sat in. "What did you think of my parents?"

"Your father should write a book about fruit trees. He not only knows them, but he loves them, too."

"That's Dad, all right. What else?"

Grant looked at her with amusement in his eyes. He pulled her around so that she sat in the warm haven of his lap. "I'm not sure what else you want to know. They're delightful people."

"Maybe." Her parents were certainly pleasant and friendly, with a fundamental goodness that won people over in the end. "But you can't expect me to believe that you and Dad spent all afternoon talking about nothing but trees. He came here to learn what kind of man I'm involved with, and he isn't noted for subtlety."

"You mean like when he asked about my work, how much I owe on the house, what I'm planning for my retirement and how much money I have saved. That sort of thing?"

"Oh God. Did he really ask all that?"

"And more."

"What did you tell him?"

"I stopped short of showing him my bank statement, but he knows I own the house outright."

Chantelle buried her face in the niche between Grant's shoulder and his neck as she groaned. "I don't know how to apologize enough, Grant."

He waved away her apology. "It was kind of fun, actually."

"Fun?" She looked askance at him, but he seemed serious. "You're as crazy as they are."

Grant laughed and hugged her. "Don't worry, I can handle a few questions from someone whose only concern is your welfare. Don't you know that it's part of a father's job to be nosy about the man in their daughter's life?"

"Nosy is the correct word, all right."

"Relax. I like your parents. They're everything mine aren't—warm, caring, outgoing."

Chantelle snuggled against Grant's solid body and thought how impossible it was to stay upset while he held her. She slipped her fingers between the buttons of his shirt. "They are good people."

"Do you know your father even asked me what my intentions are toward you? I thought that question was only asked in old movies."

"He asked you that?" Chantelle's laugh was somewhat hollow. Though she waited, he didn't elaborate. She wanted to grab Grant's ears and shake till he told her what he'd answered, but she restrained herself. She took a deep breath, trying to prepare to ask for herself: What are your intentions toward me?

But then he might tell her, and she might not like the answer. Maybe it was better to wait and give herself more time to win over his heart. Or was that cowardice? Though she'd known Grant less than two months, that time—and especially the first week—shone brightly in her memory as when she'd been most aware, most susceptible, most alive. She loved Grant, and she wanted to marry him. She couldn't forget tomorrow, and she didn't know if he could forget the past.

By pressing him now, wouldn't she be acting as overbearing as her parents? Taking another deep breath, Chantelle made herself sit upright and smile into his bottomless blue eyes. "Poor Ricki and Dan," she said. "They're in for the same grilling we got."

Grant studied her face intently, then stroked her cheekbones lightly. "You're upset. I'm sorry that your parents' visit upset you."

She felt her face go slack. *It's not them,* she wanted to shout, *it's you. Will you marry me?* She said nothing.

"Tell you what," Grant said. "Let's go out to eat. I'll show you the best the town has to offer."

Chantelle nestled her head against his shoulder to give herself time to compose herself. "Well, we didn't get to the grocery store this afternoon because of my parents' visit."

"Is that a yes?"

Dinner with Grant, every woman in the restaurant eyeing her enviously? Candles on the table highlighting the smooth muscles of Grant's face as he ate? The two of them alone, yet in public like...well, like pretend husband and wife? "That sounds nice."

Yet the thought didn't give her as much pleasure as it once would have. She didn't want to pretend. She wanted the real thing.

Chantelle looked through the meat department of the grocery store. None of the steaks was as thick as the one Grant had imagined out on the trail, so long ago. She picked up the thickest and pushed her cart into the next aisle.

Her mind wasn't really on food. As usual, Grant filled her thoughts to overflowing.

Last night she had awakened around two, feeling uneasy and apprehensive. Maybe it was the wind that woke her, rustling through the woods behind the house with fuzzy words that tickled at her sleepy comprehension. Maybe it was a dream that had filled her with dissatisfying premonitions. Maybe it was just last night's chicken cacciatore.

In any case, after unsuccessfully trying to sleep she'd carefully extricated herself from Grant's embrace and tiptoed downstairs to find something to read.

She'd found a photograph album on the bookshelf, with a yellowing inscription on the inside: *To our son on graduation from medical school.* Chantelle had clutched the treasured find to her bosom and padded out to the couch.

The album had nearly as many clippings as photographs. *Science Fair Winners. Debating Team Sweeps Clean. Van Arden Wins Scholarship.* Some of the clippings were in Dutch, chronicling a local family's success in the New World.

Chantelle backed up the shopping cart because she'd absentmindedly passed the dairy section. She picked up cheese and put it in her shopping cart, her eyes still focused on memories.

The pictures had been even more interesting than the clippings. As a youngster, Grant had been gangly and inward-looking. A skinny, blond-haired boy had stood self-consciously in swim trunks at a beach, then sat at a desk with huge stacks of books on either side of him. Somewhere in adolescence, though, the pictures had begun to capture a growing strength and confidence.

It struck her that the pictures were almost always of Grant by himself. Chantelle had a few childhood pictures of herself alone, but most were with family or friends. Not Grant. What would it have been like to grow up alone like that?

The cold down draft from the freezer section seeped into Chantelle's bare arms, but she paid less attention to the cold than to the remembered photograph album.

In the final pictures Grant hadn't been alone. He was with a stunning brunette whose curvaceous figure was showcased by elegantly tasteful clothes. Linda had been a princess. Chantelle felt herself to be a peasant by comparison.

This section of the freezer was filled with frozen entrées for one person. Grant would buy things from here, she thought. So might she, once school resumed next week and she saw him less. The thought of eating alone was depressing.

Being alone was hard. But it was just as hard to lower one's barriers and let someone else into all the nooks and crannies of one's life. She couldn't force herself into Grant's future, or he might resent it as much as she resented her parents' interference.

"Hello, Chantelle."

She jumped and turned away from the frozen foods. Ariel Johnson stood nearby with both hands gripping the handle of her shopping cart.

Chantelle didn't quite know what to say. Though the other woman smiled, her posture was defensive. For several seconds Chantelle stood, her back chilled by the freezer and her mind frozen to inaction.

"You run into everyone at the grocery store eventually," Ariel said. "It's the town meeting place. Is Grant here with you?"

"Uh, no. He's at home preparing lesson plans."

Chantelle moved her cart to let a shopper pass. Ariel moved to her side, as if intending to continue the conversation. With a glance of curiosity Chantelle moved slowly down the aisle. Ariel's face was clear and unperturbed—yet she didn't even glance at the food shelves.

"You and Grant must be pretty serious about each other."

Chantelle put a couple ice cream bars into her cart. "Why do you say that?"

"You're still seeing each other for one thing, and the fact that you're shopping for him says a lot about how well you know and trust each other."

Chantelle felt a tendril of a smile reach her lips. Looking the other woman full in the face, she saw only friendship and polite curiosity. Chantelle's smile bloomed. Could she have misjudged this woman's love for Grant?

Ariel smiled back. "Have you got a few minutes to talk?"

"Where?"

"Why don't we pay for the groceries and go over to the park at Dutch Lake?"

"That sounds fine."

A few minutes later the chatter and splashing of children filled Chantelle's ears, and a cool breeze ruffled her hair as she walked across the beach with Ariel. The hills on the far side of the small lake were densely forested, with few homes to deny the mirage that they were in the wilderness rather than in the middle of town.

Ariel led the way to a picnic table shaded by cotton-woods, away from other ears. Even eating the drippy ice cream bar Chantelle had given her, Ariel nonetheless appeared as fastidious as if having tea at the Empress Hotel. For a few minutes they both ate in speculative silence.

"So," Ariel said at last, "you and Grant are still together."

Chantelle didn't know what to say, so she merely nodded.

"If you don't mind my asking...well, Grant's a dear friend of mine. I was wondering what your intentions are."

Chantelle burst into laughter, smearing ice cream along her chin. First her father, now Ariel. Chantelle wiped her chin and she smiled wholeheartedly at the brunette, who watched with a quizzical expression. "It's an inside joke," Chantelle said. And then, realizing how she hated it when other people shut her out with words such as those, she stilled her laughter. "It's just that I've wondered about that myself. Not about my own intentions, but about Grant's."

Ariel nodded slowly. "I think I know what you mean. Grant has some sort of hang-ups from his past—but then, maybe you know more of the details than I do?"

Chantelle nodded.

Ariel raised one eyebrow, waited for a several seconds and then smiled. "You know, but you aren't going to tell me. I like someone who can keep another person's secrets, Chantelle." Ariel swallowed the last bite of her ice cream and daintily wiped her fingers together, though not a single smudge was visible. Her features took on a handsome cast as they settled into firm lines of decision.

"We've got to get that man to make a commitment," Ariel declared. "For his own good. And yours, too, if that's what you want."

"That's what I want. God, that's what I want."

Ariel laughed delicately, and Chantelle suddenly felt like a teenager scheming with a girlfriend about how to get a date with the captain of the local hockey team. She didn't have to remind herself that this was much more serious than that, of course.

"All right, then." Ariel leaned toward Chantelle and spoke softly. "I'm not sure, but I suspect Grant might not be ready to marry until he can face practicing medicine again. What do you think?"

Chantelle nodded. "He has to make a commitment to his own future before he can make a commitment to me."

"Good. At least we agree on the problem." Ariel's voice grew even softer, and her conspiratorial smile grew more intense. "Now, last week I just happened to visit Clinton Darrow, the science teacher with back problems whose classes Grant assumed."

Chantelle felt her heart flutter as she began to hope that Ariel might be of real assistance. "I've never met the man, but I truly hope his health has improved."

"I'll pass along your most sincere best wishes," Ariel said with another soft laugh. "That's exactly why I dropped in on him, to see how his surgery and therapy have progressed."

"And?"

"And the doctor says Clinton won't be eligible for a permanent disability pension after all."

"That's good news. For Clinton, I mean."

"That's what I thought," Ariel concurred, "but poor Clinton didn't totally agree. You see, he made the mistake of giving up his job permanently and now he's faced with the prospect of selling his house and moving to find another job.''

Chantelle lifted her face to the brisk lake breeze and filled her lungs with some of the freshest air she'd smelled since leaving Mount Robson Provincial Park. ''He wouldn't have to move,'' she said, ''if the current science teacher would be willing to find a different job and help out poor Clinton.''

''True.'' Ariel's lips twitched, but she kept a straight face. ''Helping poor Clinton is the humanitarian thing to do.''

''Poor Clinton,'' Chantelle agreed.

When Ariel broke into laughter Chantelle also abandoned control and laughed heartily. The two women embraced.

''Ariel, would you be willing to tell Grant about Clinton?''

''Well . . . sure.''

''Great. Come to dinner. Grant would love—'' Chantelle paused as an almost-imperceptible pain flicked across Ariel's sunny features. Some of Chantelle's joy evaporated, and she continued soberly. ''Grant would be glad to see you.''

''I'll bring dessert.''

''Ariel, I . . . I want you to know how much I appreciate your help. This is more than any woman should ever have to do for another.''

''I'm sure I don't know what you mean.''

Chantelle looked into the brunette's face, till Ariel dropped her eyes to her hands. ''Yes, you do. And Ariel, I think you're a saint.''

''Hardly.'' Ariel uttered a wry laugh. ''More like a nun, I'm afraid.''

''Well. . . .'' Chantelle took her hand and squeezed. ''Tonight around six thirty?''

''I'll be there.''

* * *

Chantelle worked hard that afternoon to make the dinner special. The whole evening was so ripe with potential that it *had* to be special. Grant had to leap at this opportunity to get out of his teaching contract. He had to.

Even beyond that, entertaining in Grant's house made her feel even more a part of his life. This was her chance to prove that even if she wasn't a born lady like Ariel she was nonetheless a passable hostess.

She dug up fresh potatoes and carrots to go with a pot roast, made buns from scratch, cut flowers for a centerpiece, and at the last minute picked strawberries for a family recipe juice drink.

"This table has never looked so good," Grant said as Chantelle fussed with the bow around a napkin.

She put her hands on her hips and surveyed the table critically. "It would look better with a decent set of china."

"We lonely widowers aren't into things like china. You're worrying too much. Ariel's eaten here straight from a can without complaining."

"That's different." Chantelle shook her head, still looking at the table. "This tablecloth isn't right. Would you help me change it?"

Grant put his hands on her shoulders and turned her to face him. "The tablecloth is perfect. The flowers are perfect. The food is perfect. Relax."

That was easy for him to say. He didn't realize yet how important this evening was. Chantelle looked at him stubbornly.

"I appreciate you inviting Ariel for dinner," Grant said. "I understand that you're trying to be friendly for my sake—but you're going to drive me insane if you fuss one more time with the table. Okay?"

Chantelle absorbed the warmth of his hands and hoped he'd be this understanding when he realized she'd invited

Ariel in order tó convince him to give up teaching in favor of medicine. "Okay, Grant."

A knock sounded from the living room. When Grant went to answer it, Chantelle hurriedly adjusted the silverware a fraction of an inch, then followed him to greet their guest.

She reminded herself that everything would be all right. Her friendship with Ariel would be cemented. Grant would agree to let Clinton have his job so he could return to medicine. And he'd be so thankful to Chantelle that he'd ask her to marry him. Chantelle hugged her arms as she smiled brightly at Ariel. After this evening, everything would be all right.

She hoped.

The time passed quickly. Ariel and Grant obviously shared a special relationship and were willing to invite Chantelle into that relationship. Just as obviously, Ariel's self-control was magnificent. At no time during the dinner and dessert did the smallest shadow of pain cross her face.

After dinner they went onto the front porch. Ariel sat on the porch railing and swung her feet with a girlish abandon at odds with her usual patrician reserve. She was a moving silhouette against the darkening sky and its streaks of blood-red clouds.

Chantelle and Grant settled onto the swing, with his arm lightly around her shoulders. Lulled by the easy-going camaraderie, she leaned her head against his.

"It looks like I'm going to be in the way soon." Though Ariel's words teased, her voice was strained.

Chantelle jerked her head upright, silently cursing herself for unintentionally taunting her friend. Grant looked at her sharply, then over at Ariel.

"Have you heard about Clinton?" Ariel asked him.

"The science teacher?" Grant ran his hand along his chin. "What about him?"

Chantelle took a deep breath and held it.

"His back's better," Ariel said.

"Oh?"

Chantelle kept the breath in her lungs and forced herself to silence.

"Yes," Ariel said. "The surgery did him more good than expected. They fused a couple vertebrae, or something."

"Oh?"

Chantelle couldn't stand Grant's noncommittal grunts. "That means he isn't eligible for a disability pension, Grant. He could take over your job at any time if you wanted to return to medicine."

The swing creaked and moved as he turned to face her. "You knew about this?"

"I think I mentioned it to her in passing," Ariel said quickly.

The silence that followed was broken only by the restless, lonely honking of Canada geese, heralding change by flying south. "I'm surprised you didn't say something, Chantelle. That seems the kind of news you wouldn't be able to wait to tell me."

Chantelle stiffened at the implied criticism in his voice, as if he suspected her of plotting. "I thought you might take the news better from Ariel than from me," she said honestly.

"And that's the real reason for inviting Ariel here tonight, isn't it?"

"Grant," Ariel said softly, "I wanted to come."

He shook his head and sighed. "So you two are in on this together?"

Chantelle took a deep breath, disappointed at his reaction but determined to tell him the truth. "Yes."

Grant's voice took on an arrogant note. "Did it ever occur to you that I might prefer to make my own decisions without your conniving, Chantelle?"

Ariel stood. "Don't take it out on her, Grant. I was in on this, too."

He removed his arm from Chantelle's shoulder and stood rigidly. "Would you leave us alone, please, Ariel?"

"Grant, I . . ."

"It's okay, Ariel," Chantelle assured her. "This is between Grant and me."

"All right. Thank you for having me over, Chantelle. Grant, I . . . I hope you wake up soon."

After Ariel left, Chantelle put off discussion by going to the kitchen to wash the dinner dishes. Grant followed her and leaned back against the counter, his arms folded. He watched her in silence for several minutes. The dishwater was so hot it burned, but no more than did his gaze.

With the pots still dirty, Chantelle dried her hands and faced Grant. "I'm not going to apologize," she said. "You belong in medicine."

"It's my decision, Chantelle."

"It affects me, too." She ran her hand through her hair. "Look, Grant, teaching is a noble profession, but you drifted into it at a time when you were lost. Now's the time to steer your own course. Going back to the high school is a mistake."

"A mistake?" A surge of energy drove Grant to pace to the living room, then return. "A mistake?" Maybe she was right, but he felt his eyes narrowing dangerously regardless.

"The fact that Clinton wants his job back is an omen." Chantelle was almost pleading. "Can't you see that?"

"I no longer know what I can see and what I can't." Grant's body suddenly felt heavy, too heavy to hold upright without slumping. Wearily, he wandered to the living room couch and turned off the light.

Almost without a sound, Chantelle came and sat at the opposite end of the couch. She said something that he couldn't catch.

He turned to look at her profile, backlit by the glow from the kitchen. "Pardon me?"

"I said, it isn't working anymore."

"Don't be crazy."

"No, I mean it," she insisted. The quiet intensity of her voice chilled him. "As soon as school starts everything changes, whether you admit it or not. We both know that, and we can't handle it."

Grant exhaled loudly. "Don't do this, Chantelle. If I was out of line when I got upset, then get angry at me. Swear. Throw something."

"No." Her voice was lifeless, as were her hands that rested limp in her lap. He was surprised when she jerked her head toward him suddenly, fervently. "Grant, lets get—" She chopped off her words as with an ax and stared straight ahead. "I just thought," she said listlessly, "that if you could return to medicine it would mean that you're ready for a lasting relationship."

Grant rubbed his palms on his slacks. "We have a good relationship right now."

"The best I've ever had. But..."

But. The word seemed to echo through his head with painful volume.

What did he want? He opened his mouth to ask her to move in with him, but he stopped in time. He'd be asking her to make all the sacrifices—her store, her home, her sister—with no assurances. And he suddenly realized that assurances were what she needed most right now. Assurances, and a wedding ring.

Marriage. The word reverberated even louder. He might hurt her even more, with the best will in the world. Grant remembered his thoughts on the trail, that Chantelle was a forever girl and that he had no forevers to offer. He should have listened to himself better and saved her this pain.

Chantelle stood abruptly. While he'd been deep in thought she'd been thinking, too, but her face was as expressionless as his.

"I think," she whispered past the pain that was growing in her throat, "I'd better go back to Kamloops."

Grant bolted to his feet. "No." He surrounded her in an embrace that was gentle and treasuring. "There are two days of our week left."

"I need to think, Grant. I need time to figure out where we're going."

When she tried to move, Grant didn't loosen his gossamer grip. She looked into his eyes, then blinked against tears that splintered his handsomeness into shards, just as her heart was splintered.

"Think about it overnight before you go home. Please, Chantelle. We owe each other that much."

Chantelle lowered her chin against his chest. If she didn't get away from his embrace soon she wouldn't be able to hide the sobs that threatened to break loose at any moment.

"Till morning," she whispered. "But then I'm leaving." And with a certainty that made her physically ill, she knew that once she left she might never return.

Chapter Twelve

A sharp ringing sound pierced Chantelle's troubled sleep.
She slapped out in the direction of her alarm clock, but hit
the empty table instead.

Then she remembered where she was. Grant's bedroom,
alone.

The telephone rang again. She forced her eyes open and
dragged her head off the pillow.

Grant had slept in the downstairs bedroom, after Chantelle had said she'd sleep there. Why didn't he answer the
phone?

It rang again. Chantelle pulled the receiver to her ear.
"Van Arden residence."

"Hi, Chani. I hope I didn't wake you."

"Ricki?" Her sister usually sounded so mature on the
phone, but now she sounded young and flighty. Chantelle
forced herself to sit up. "Is something the matter?"

The young woman giggled. "Hardly. But I had to tell someone what happened last night, before I burst. I waited as long as I could this morning."

"You had me scared." Chantelle let out a long breath, then fluffed the pillows behind her. She needed some good news about now. "Don't keep me in suspense. I can't imagine what's made you overjoyed so soon after our parents' inquisition."

"Oh, that's what started everything. After talking to you, and then Mom, I told Dan that I couldn't move in with him. No matter what people do these days, living together doesn't feel right to me and if two people love each other then living together isn't enough. He started crying! And then . . . you'll never guess what happened next."

Chantelle's heart seemed to catch in her throat. "He asked you to marry him."

"Chani," Ricki said with a disappointed groan. "I wanted to surprise you." Her voice immediately perked up. "I said yes, but I also told him it might be a long engagement if we don't have enough money for him to finish school this year, because I'm not giving up school to support us. Do you think I said the right thing?"

"I think," Chantelle said with pride and love glowing in her voice, "that you said exactly the right thing."

"Oh, Chani, I'm so happy."

"I'm happy for you."

Ricki bubbled on for several minutes, elated. Chantelle was glad for her sister, she truly was, but the contrast between Ricki's evening and her own was almost too much to bear. Her eyes were brimming by the time Ricki said goodbye.

Grant appeared at the bedroom door as Chantelle hung up the phone. "Who was it?"

Chantelle laid her head against the wall and stared up at the ceiling. "Ricki."

"Is anything wrong?"

Chantelle clenched her teeth and fought for control of her tear ducts. After a minute she finally faced Grant. "She's getting married."

"That's great news. Tell me more."

"No."

"No?" Grant's voice became wary. "I should think you'd be eager to talk about your sister's marriage."

"Later." Chantelle hugged her elbows and took a deep breath that did nothing to calm her. "It's just that I can't wait to get away from here."

Grant put his hands on his hips and stood as if to block her exit. "Now, Chantelle—"

"Grant Van Arden, if you're smart you'll get out of here right now."

"I'm not going anywhere till we've talked, and neither are you!"

She grabbed a pillow from behind her and threw it at him.

"Chantelle, don't start this." He dodged a second pillow, then lunged to catch the radio it knocked over. While he was off balance she grabbed the first pillow and hit him over the head with it, hard enough that a seam tore and feathers sprinkled the air as she reared back again.

"Ow," he said as he sat heavily on the floor.

"Get out! I need to think things over." Her next hit with the pillow did little more than send a cloud of feathers swirling through the air. "Go away, Grant. Please."

Grant stood and walked to the door with as much dignity as a man with a feather on his nose could. She noticed for the first time the dark pads under his eyes. He looked as if he'd slept as little as she had. "Chantelle, this is my house."

"Then I'll leave." She tossed the vanishing pillow at him as he pulled the bedroom door closed behind him.

Grant leaned against the closed door and shook his head. Maybe by the time she got dressed and came downstairs she'd be calm enough to talk to. He doubted it, but went downstairs to wait anyway.

"You're serious about leaving?" Grant clenched his fist as he sprawled in an easy chair in the living room, watching Chantelle fasten the top button of her sweater.

Morning light spilled in the front door as she opened it. Circles and a hint of puffiness were the most obvious signs of misery on her face, yet the set of her jaw was unflinching. She stood there with her hand on the doorknob, silently looking him in the face, then reached for her suitcase.

He sighed and spread his arms. "Don't go."

"Has anything changed?"

A cold lump of anger grew in his belly. She would actually let her temper ruin everything between them! Well, he'd be damned if he'd surrender to every rush of temper that buffeted her. With a grunt, he pushed himself out of the chair and went to help her with the suitcase.

When his fingers touched hers Chantelle jerked the suitcase away from him. "Don't try to stop me," she warned.

Grant held his palms up in a brusque gesture, but the lump grew a bit harder, a bit colder. "I was just going to carry it for you."

"Oh. Well, I guess you can."

Did her eyes seem relieved or disappointed? He couldn't tell, because it was as if she'd drawn a curtain over her emotions.

He reached for the suitcase. At the last second, however, she snatched it away and hurried out the door. "I'll carry it myself," she declared.

Grant shook his head and followed her outside. The sky was too bright and blue, the spirited song of the meadowlark too strong, for this to be happening. It should be dark and stormy, like that night on the trail.

The neighbor boy, Robby, yelled to Grant from his perch atop his father's loaded logging truck. When would that child learn to be careful?

Grant turned his attention back to Chantelle's retreating form. How long would she keep him dangling with her fit of pique? A day? Two?

He would check the paper to see when that theater company from Calgary was coming to Kamloops. He'd meet Chantelle at the store, rent the fanciest suite on the top floor of the Stockman's Inn, and romance her to a warm reconciliation. Anticipation and planning would give him something to hold on to besides anger.

Grant rested his elbow on the roof of her car as she put the suitcase in the rear of her hatchback. "I'll stop by the store in a couple days."

Chantelle glanced up at him. His shoulders were so broad, so rigidly square and arrogant. The utter unreadability of his countenance stabbed at her heart. She now understood this fascinating, wonderful man and the pain he hid so well. Yet there was nothing she could do to help him.

Despair buffeted her. She tried to seal away the emotion behind the same wall of blankness that had stolen the rest of her heart. "I don't think that's a good idea."

His face showed nothing. He must be quite angry.

Robby called to her, but she only glanced in his direction. She slammed the door on the suitcase, then paused with her hand still on the cool metal. One last try, she told herself. One last try, before she abandoned all hope except for a chance self-awakening. "You still don't understand, do you? We want different things. I want strings. You don't. I look to the future. You're stuck in the past. I thought that wouldn't matter, that we'd grow closer together, but it didn't happen." Chantelle took a deep breath. "Grant, this is it."

A muscle twitched at the side of his jaw. He seemed frozen in position, as if he hadn't heard her, as if he hadn't heard the finality of the trunk slamming. She pressed her car keys painfully into her palm as she waited for him to say something.

What sound did despair make? A soft crunch of gravel, a hinge squeak, a whoosh of upholstery, a muffled sigh?

She was leaving, Grant realized abruptly. She really was.

Something shattered inside him. His fist slammed against the hood, sending starbursts of pain hurtling along his arm. He hadn't even been aware of raising his fist.

Chantelle shot out of the car seat and looked at him with a stricken expression. When her glance darted to the hood he wondered briefly if he'd dented her car. He never took his eyes off her face long enough to see.

Suddenly Chantelle's face glazed over, as if she was no longer looking at him. Her mouth opened wide, her forehead wrinkled in the middle and her cheeks twisted into a grimace of horror. My God, how much damage had he done to her car?

When he heard the frantic cry of pain he thought it came from her. But of course not; the sound was behind him. He followed the direction of Chantelle's pointing finger just in time to see a blur in blue jeans and T-shirt fall headfirst off the logging truck.

Together they ran toward Robby. Chantelle ducked through the barbed wire with practiced ease, but Grant caught his shirt. He yanked savagely, and the material tore.

Robby was sitting up and moaning. He was bleeding, and resting most of his weight on one arm.

From his posture, there was probably no neck or back injury, Grant thought. But there was blood everywhere, on his face and running into his eyes and dyeing his T-shirt red. His free arm hung limply, at an odd angle. Broken. Grant's frazzled nerves skittered haphazardly inside him.

Marcy McDonall reached the boy at the same time Chantelle did, with Grant only slightly behind. Marcy cried out, put her arms around the lad and jerked him against her in a panicked embrace that set Robby howling in pain. His cries made her hold him still harder. There was a wild look in her eyes. Robby's screams grew louder.

"Marcy, let go of him," Grant ordered gently.

"My baby. My baby." She looked at Grant as if not understanding what he said, rocking the boy in her arms. He cried out with each movement.

Grant tried to pry Marcy's fingers off Robby's broken arm. The boy screeched, and the shrill cry sent Grant's already worn nerves over some internal edge of desperation. He had to get the arm away from Marcy's grasp, yet his efforts were making the pain worse. The boy's agony was as real to Grant as if he felt it himself. "Chantelle, help me."

Chantelle raised her shoulders as if she didn't know what to do. She turned to Marcy. "Robby will be okay, Mrs. McDonall," she said as she placed gentle hands on the woman's shoulders. "I'm not sure that you know Grant used to be a doctor."

"A doctor?"

"Yes," Chantelle said. "Robby's in good hands." She eased the mother's hands off the boy.

Marcy looked at Grant. A timid smile of apology and respect briefly banished her panic. "I never knew you were a doctor. You'll help him, won't you?"

"Yes, Marcy, I will."

Grant took a deep breath. Yes, he was a doctor. He knew how to keep the youngster's pain to a minimum and ensure that no permanent damage was done. He knew how to turn this bloody incident into nothing more than a bad memory. As he looked at the gradual return of reason to Marcy McDonall's face, his knowledge seemed nothing less than miraculous. He was no antiseptic god, no arrogant figure of awe. He was just a man, but a man who carried within him a mighty power.

Grant made a quick but careful survey of the boy's injuries. Besides the broken arm, he had two gashes on his skull that needed stitches. The cuts weren't bad, despite all the blood. He checked Robby's pupils for signs of a concussion. So far so good.

"Chantelle," he said briskly, "take Marcy into the trailer and see if you can find her husband."

"Jeff's gone to his brother's place in town," Marcy said in a small voice.

"Phone him," he ordered. "Tell him to meet us at the clinic." Grant smiled at Marcy reassuringly. "Are you all right?"

"That's not important," she replied as she ran a gentle hand across her son's wet, red hair. "Do what you need to do, Grant. Please." She stood suddenly and ran toward the trailer.

"Phone the clinic, too," he called after her. "Tell them I'll bring Robby there, and they should be ready to set a broken arm and give him stitches."

"Thank you, Grant." Marcy sounded as if she was going to cry.

Chantelle knelt beside him and patted Robby's good hand. The boy was still crying, but less frantically. He squeezed her hand.

She looked at Grant. "How can I help?"

A half smile struggled through Grant's professionalism. Strange to think that only minutes ago they were breaking up. Those feelings seemed so far away. "In the cabinet under the bathroom sink I have a first-aid kit."

"Anything else?"

"A clean, damp cloth to wipe away the blood. And bring a few of the cookies you baked the other night. I bet you'd like a cookie, wouldn't you, Robby?"

The boy just sniffled.

Chantelle was halfway across his garden before he realized he should have thanked her for reminding Marcy, and himself, that he was a doctor.

Years of training took charge from then on. Traction on Robby's arm would help relieve the pain by pulling the sharp bone ends out from muscles and other tissues, but what was the best way to apply and maintain traction under these crude circumstances? When Chantelle handed him his first-aid kit he immediately opened packets of sterile bandages and had her press them firmly to the cuts on the boy's head. Then he began molding metal-mesh splints to Robby's arm. The boy whimpered at Grant's touch.

"The doctor will put a cast on that arm when we get to the clinic," Grant said to distract the boy. "Do you know what a cast is?"

Robby shook his head.

Grant folded a triangular bandage as padding and placed it on the opposite side of the arm from the misshapen bulge where the bone was fractured. "A cast is a hard white sleeve that will help your arm heal and keep it from getting hurt again."

Robby sniffled, but looked at Grant with interest on his face. "My cousin Timmy had one of those last winter. He said it didn't hurt when they took it off, like a bandage does. I drew on it with felt pens. It itched him."

"I want to be the first one to write my name on your cast. Is that a deal?"

"I guess so." After a few seconds, Robby sat straighter so he could watch what Grant was doing. "Can I have a cookie now?"

Marcy returned, but Chantelle kept her occupied. She had Marcy take over applying pressure to the head cuts, realizing that the woman needed to be doing something to help her son. Chantelle would have made a good nurse. Grant wondered if she would favor him with her pride-peeking-through-reserve smile when he told her that, later.

He had Chantelle help him apply traction by pulling slightly on Robby's arm while he put on the splint. Her face was pale, but she never hesitated to do what had to be done. He tried to catch her eye with a smile, but her gaze was on the boy.

Sooner than Grant would have expected from a rusty physician, the boy was splinted and bandaged and ready to go to the clinic. When Robby was in the back seat of his mother's car, Grant hurried back to Chantelle and took her hand in both of his. "I'll drive them to the clinic."

Chantelle returned the pressure of his grip and smiled. "I knew you would."

She watched the car till it disappeared, then hugged her arms as she turned back toward her car. She was glad Grant was helping his neighbors. But what of all the other Robbys he could help, but never would? What of his own children he might nurture and heal, but never would?

In the garden she stopped to pick a handful of raspberries. She could almost picture Grant here, digging and then playfully chasing her. That image melted into another image, that of Grant carefully cradling the injured boy. He would never hold *their* child in a protective embrace of love and comfort. The thought stabbed her heart and brought tears close to the surface.

Chantelle stuffed the warm raspberries into her mouth, then wiped the red spot on her palm heedlessly against her slacks. She left the garden with a long glance over her shoulder and got into her car.

She headed the car into the driveway, then braked for another last look. With her forehead resting against the glass, she saw Grant's balcony directly above the porch where she'd sat with her mother. The front door was open. Unlike her, Grant had intended to come right back.

The least she could do was close the door for him. Besides, it would give her a final chance to savor the house where she'd spent the happiest days of her life.

Once inside, though, she realized she'd made a mistake. Even the cast-iron wood stove made her throat catch and her eyes burn. By its light they'd shared wonderful moments....

Chantelle walked through the house toward the kitchen, trailing her hand along furniture where Grant had sat or countertops where they'd cooked together. He had a habit of not waiting for baked goods to cool before he sampled them, and she'd learned to have ice water handy when they baked. She poured herself a glass of water, got three ice cubes from the freezer, then held the cold glass to her forehead.

She wandered from room to room, occasionally sipping from the glass but mostly just letting the cold seep into her hands to remind herself that she was alive in the present and not just in memories.

The utility room, where they'd embraced while washing her clothes.

The downstairs bedroom, with so many interesting books still unread. Grant was like a book she'd started but now would never finish. Just as well, she chided herself as she slowly mounted the stairs. She hated unhappy endings.

His bedroom was the hardest room to visit, since it was the most intimately his. She tried to brand every detail into her memory. Half-burned candles sat atop the dresser, making her smile in remembrance of Grant's love of candles and mood lighting in general. In one of his still-surprising flights of poetry, he had claimed that she looked different in candlelight, sunlight, firelight, at dawn and at dusk, with shadows and colors playing magic across her features as if even Nature could never tire of her beauty.

A sob tore from Chantelle's lungs as confusion overwhelmed her. Her attempts to staunch her tears were as useless as a stop sign in the path of an avalanche. Surrendering to the inevitable, she threw herself onto Grant's bed, and cried.

Grant wheeled Robby into the clinic on the wheelchair that a nurse brought out to the car. With the resilience of youth, the boy made motor noises as he rode.

Grant knew the layout of the clinic from Bob Isaacs's efforts to convince him to practice, and so he headed directly for the examining room. Adrenaline coursed through his veins, making everything look sharper and more real.

He had wrapped Chantelle's ankle, but that took no great skill. This was the first time in two years his skill had really made a difference, and he had thrilled to it.

Furthermore, helping Robby hadn't felt threatening, as he'd assumed practicing would. It wasn't as if he had wielded a knife and hacked through skin and muscle. He hadn't risked the boy's life. All he had done was help a friend.

Bob hurried to meet them at the examining room. He put his hands on his knees and smiled down at the boy. "What's your problem, young fellow?"

Envy stabbed Grant. Bob helped his friends and neighbors every day, without taking godlike risks with their lives.

When Robby hung his head shyly, Grant answered for him. "Fractured humerus and a few scrapes. He'll be all right once I put a cast on him."

Bob stood up. "Once *you* put the cast on him?"

"You don't think I'm going to let you have all the fun, do you?"

"Mommy," Robby said, "I want Grant to cast me."

A huge grin split Bob's face—but not as big a grin as Chantelle would have when she heard about this later. Bob waved Grant grandly into the examining room. "Be my guest—*Doctor*."

An hour later, when Grant finally got out of the clinic after being thanked repeatedly by Marcy and her husband, and congratulated and cajoled by Bob and several nurses, he was surprised that Chantelle wasn't outside waiting for him. He'd assumed she'd be there, though she'd never said she was coming.

He longed to tell her how it had felt caring for the boy— good and warm and so unlike the megalomania he used to thrive on—but being without a car meant delay. When he finally arranged a ride back to his house, Grant shifted around on the front seat in eagerness to confront Chantelle and take care of unfinished business.

Her car was still in the driveway, though it had been moved. Grant let out a held breath. He hadn't consciously wondered whether she'd left, but the possibility must have been nibbling at him. And she'd come close to leaving. The car was pointing away from the house.

Grant absently thanked his ride and stumbled toward Chantelle's car. His eyes began burning as he fingered the small dent in the hood.

When he'd slammed his fist on her car something had been broken inside him. And now, the knowledge that she still planned on leaving brought back the pain. The pain, and the realization that had been on the verge of discovery when Robby fell.

He *couldn't* lose her. All his problems and his fears were reduced to that one simple fact. He couldn't lose Chantelle, no matter what he had to do to keep her.

Even if he had to marry her.

And suddenly—though he still felt no certainty that he wouldn't hurt her in some small way—marriage seemed better than an act of desperation. Much better. More like a life sentence in heaven, instead. He shrieked in delight.

As his ride disappeared in a dust cloud, Grant turned slowly around with his hands on his hips. He may have just changed his life, but Chantelle was nowhere in sight. The car door was open and the keys were in the ignition, so surely she was close by. The seat was cold to the touch, though.

Grant walked through the garden, then toward the blood-darkened dirt near the logging truck. He came back through the woods to the house.

Nothing. He cupped his hands around his mouth. "Chantelle?" He forced the call into the wind again, but got no answer. He headed to the house.

"Chantelle?" Pausing for an answer in the middle of the living room, Grant was struck by the utter emptiness of his haven.

"Chantelle?" Still no answer. He took the stairs two at a time, but a quick glance told him the upstairs was as empty and lifeless as the downstairs. He walked to the middle of his bedroom, where a glass lay in the middle of a dark splotch on the carpet. The pillow and covers of the bed were rumpled in the long, slender shape of a beautiful young woman.

Grant stroked the imprint of Chantelle's body with reverent fingers. Cool. She had been here, but had left a while ago. Where had she gone, though?

As Grant hurried down the stairs, impatience consumed him. She had to be around here somewhere—how far could she have gotten on foot? But if she was playing hide-and-seek at a time when he needed her presence desperately, he would . . .

He would what? Kiss her? Tell her he loved her? Some punishments. Tightening his jaw till his teeth hurt, Grant charged outside.

"Chantelle?" He studied the road, shielding his eyes from the sun as he turned toward the south. He turned more, then paused when he faced the mountain a quarter mile behind the house. Just like her childhood home, she'd told him.

Chantelle, he realized with a certainty that drove all other options from consideration, was at some vantage point, looking down on his property and thinking. Alone.

He couldn't trust any solitary deliberations. She'd been threatening to leave him, and though he couldn't believe she really would—not now!—he had to find her. He had his faults and, heaven help him, he would probably always fall back into arrogance from time to time. But she had to let him fill the silence of her heart. She had to.

Chantelle was up there somewhere. Grant didn't know where, but he would join her if it took the rest of his life.

* * *

Chantelle, sitting with her arms around her raised knees and chin resting on her forearms, rocked slowly from side to side on the moss cushion covering her Thinking Place. Grant's house was no more than a slice of shake roof seen through the trees, but the rest of the valley spread out like a living postcard.

Everything seemed different from up here, as she'd known it would. Even the breeze was stronger here, tousling her hair with a sudden gust that spread tickling hair across her face. She didn't bother to brush the hair out of her eyes, but studied life down in the valley through its curtain.

For the first hour that she'd been here, she'd done little. She had paced this small promontory perched a hundred feet above the valley bottom, then sat as peace and solitude finally began to seep into her. She had wound dried grass stems into finger-size circles with her remaining nervous energy.

Now she was absorbing as much serenity as possible, emptying her mind so she could catch thoughts as they wandered past. Solitude was the best place for thinking, even about a relationship. Was that ironic, or merely wrong?

She could picture Grant's face as vividly as if he was sitting in front of her. Grant grinning with boyish delight. Grant studying her with smoldering passion alight in his eyes. Grant standing proud, expressionless, upright.

She could be arrogant and rigid, too, of course. She was so arrogantly, unshakably certain he loved her, for example, though he'd never said so. How could she know if his feelings ran as deep as hers? That might be the kernel of the problem right there.

Fiddlesticks. Grant loved her.

Chantelle shoved the hair out of her face with an impatient gesture. She smiled as another image of Grant came to her, Grant the lover. He was fantastic, incredible, beyond any woman's dreams. He was a stunning human being: intelligent, charming, inventive, caring, masterful.

Okay, Grant was marvelous. Why, then, hadn't she been able to accept him the way he was? She *had* been trying to change him, she realized with a stab of guilt. There was no surgery for the soul. All she could do was nurse duty. No ultimatum would ever force him to enjoy medicine or to change his mind about marriage.

Chantelle stretched her legs and lay back with her hands behind her head. The bumps and irregularities of this rocky bed anchored her in reality and kept her from floating off into the clouds as her mind involuntarily returned to shared passion. From a purely physical viewpoint, this relationship simply had to be one of the best possible for any woman, anywhere.

She chuckled and wriggled into a more comfortable position as she followed the soaring spiral of an eagle. Arrogance, again.

Besides, she knew that even if she never made love to Grant again, she would still love him. Forever. And she knew with equal certainty that he would love her forever. Her attempt to run from him back at the Robson River had nearly killed them both. If she ran from him now, it would kill her, on the inside at least, but she would still love him.

She jerked to a sitting position. The breeze funneled into her ear, setting up a cascade of white noise that drowned out her thoughts. She turned her head so that the wind was a whisper through the evergreens, the same murmur that always seemed so close to comprehensibility. A murmur that seemed to say, "Chantelle—" the word was whisper faint but so distinct that her eyes went wide "—I love you."

A shiver raced down her spine. Was she dreaming?

She shook her head, fully alert now to the outside world instead of her own thoughts. On hands and knees she crept to the precipice of her Thinking Place, and listened.

"Chantelle, where are you?"

A whole series of shivers rippled down her spine, leaving her arms quivering slightly. She wasn't losing her mind. Somewhere, hidden in the trees of the slope, Grant was searching for her.

She spied movement in a spot of thick brush. Chantelle cupped her hands around her mouth. "Up here, Grant." She waved her hands till she saw him return the wave, and then sat back and waited, her eyes closed and her lips trembling.

He loved her. He'd just said so.

Grant's lungs burned, but he increased his pace to a near run. Now that he'd found Chantelle he refused to stop for anything, no matter how dense the underbrush or how steep the climb. How did she manage to reach these places? She was as bad as Robby.

Pride in her determination, daring and ability warred with frustration. Chantelle, he vowed, needed someone to watch over her and keep her out of trouble.

When he finally pushed aside the last shrub and emerged into the clearing, Grant was too winded to speak immediately. As he sat and filled his lungs, he watched Chantelle. Her eyes had opened to slits when he first arrived. Now they were closed again, but her face nonetheless seemed alert, alive, about to burst with barely suppressed emotions.

When his breathing had slowed she finally spoke, as if she'd been waiting for the sounds of normalcy with a patience he didn't begin to possess at the moment. Her eyes remained closed. "How is Robby?"

"He'll be fine. He wasn't injured seriously. I mean, a broken arm is serious but not life threatening."

"I suspect it won't be his last broken bone."

"Not the way he plays." Grant closed his eyes, voluntarily slipping into a shared darkness.

Chantelle said nothing for a minute. Her next words sounded casual. Too casual. "Did you set his arm?"

Grant took a deep breath. "Yes."

"How was it?"

He knew she didn't mean the arm. Holding his hands up as if they could help him find words, Grant spoke slowly. "Different. It was very different from the surgery I used to do."

Chantelle emptied her lungs and slowly turned to him. "I'm glad."

"Maybe you were right about general practice. Maybe. But, Chantelle, I have to do this my way. When I eventually go back to medicine, in my own good time, it will be because it's my idea, not because you pressured me."

"I understand. And I'm sorry."

"Just because you were right this once doesn't give you a license to run my life. No more meddling, Chantelle."

She nodded solemnly. She'd never looked more beautiful, more intense, or more vulnerable. "No meddling."

"Promise?"

She nodded again, then made a cross over her heart.

"Good." Grant linked his hands behind his head and leaned back to look at the sky. "Then I think I'll start a practice here in town as soon as I possibly can."

With a small yet humble exclamation of happiness, Chantelle squeezed Grant's hand. She closed her eyes again and tried to subdue tears. This was a time for celebration, not crying. She surreptitiously wiped at a solitary tickle dribbling down her cheek.

"When I was young," she said, "my mother used to scold me for my temper."

"Is this going to be an apology? If so, you don't have to bother."

"It's an explanation." She paused. "And an apology, too. Anyway, my temper was the main thing that kept me from getting completely walked on by my older brothers. I

thought I'd left my temper behind when I grew up—until I
met you, that is."

"Are you trying to tell me I bring out the worst in you?"
Grant's voice was light and teasing. "If so, that isn't much
of an apology."

"I think—I hope—I can avoid losing my temper now that
I understand. You see, the attraction I feel for you is so
strong that I guess I was afraid of losing myself."

Grant moved to sit beside her, then put his arm around
her and drew her against him. "Apology accepted."

Chantelle snuggled as close to him as possible. Being in
Grant's arms felt so *right*, as well as so good. It was where
she belonged, forever, even if that meant risking everything. She turned her head and lifted her face. Grant met her
halfway with a kiss that treasured and cherished and promised. The taste of him whet her appetite for a lifetime of
kisses.

When the kiss ended, he held her close as they both lay
back and watched the clouds drift past.

"So," Grant said, "your sister is getting married."

Chantelle's heart skipped a beat.

"Will the wedding be soon?"

She took her time answering. "They haven't set a date."

"I see." When he paused, the pleasurable, anxious silence yearned to be filled, yet Chantelle let him string out the
silence as long as he wished.

"If their wedding is soon," he said slowly, "would you
like to have a double wedding?"

A tear slipped from Chantelle's eye.

"You aren't saying anything." Grant sat up and looked
down at her. "Is that silence supposed to mean yes?"

Another tear tickled its way down her cheek. All she could
do was nod.

Grant picked something off the front of her jeans. At first
she thought he meant to caress her, but instead he held up

one of the grass rings she'd woven earlier. He looked at her for a long time, still holding the ring, till Chantelle felt herself melting under his gaze. And then, with a slow grace that took Chantelle's breath away, he took her hand and held it toward him. When she realized what he was doing her wrist suddenly felt so limp she had to struggle to hold it up.

Grant slipped the grass ring onto her finger. His gleaming blue eyes promised more, much more, but Chantelle knew she would treasure this simple grass circle forever.

With Grant watching her every move, Chantelle carefully wove another stem into a circle, then slipped it onto his left hand. She said nothing. If she opened her mouth she didn't know what would come out, and she didn't want to sob through the happiest moment of her life.

Still holding hands, they looked at each other for a long time. More tears trickled down her cheeks. She didn't bother to wipe them away.

Grant spoke in a voice so intimate that the sound slipped into her bloodstream and roused her whole body to instant feminine awareness. "Do you, Chantelle Marie Du-Maurier, take Grant to be your lawfully wedded husband, to love, honor and cherish in sickness and in health, till death do you part?"

"I do." Chantelle closed her eyes against a rush of love so strong that she felt dizzy. Taking a deep breath, she gazed at Grant and spoke in a voice that rang clear and triumphant. "Do you, Grant Pieter Van Arden, take Chantelle to be your lawfully wedded wife, to love, honor and cherish through richer and poorer, in sickness and in health, till death do you part?"

"I do."

He leaned forward to kiss her, but Chantelle stopped him with gentle fingers laid against his lips. "Uh, since we're doing this ourselves, do you think we could change the wedding kiss into something a bit more...well, a bit more?"

Grant's face warmed her with his radiant love. "From now on, anything you wish."

Chantelle lay back on the moss. "I love you."

"And I love you, Chantelle."

* * * * *

SILHOUETTE·INTIMATE·MOMENTS®

NORA ROBERTS
Night Shadow

People all over the city of Urbana were asking, Who was that masked man?

Assistant district attorney Deborah O'Roarke was the first to learn his secret identity . . . and her life would never be the same.

The stories of the lives and loves of the O'Roarke sisters began in January 1991 with NIGHT SHIFT, Silhouette Intimate Moments #365. And if you want to know more about Deborah and the man behind the mask, look for NIGHT SHADOW, Silhouette Intimate Moments #373.

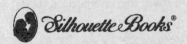

Silhouette Books®

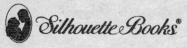

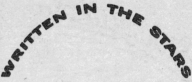

WRITTEN IN THE STARS

**Star-crossed lovers?
Or a match made in heaven?**

Why are some heroes strong and silent . . . and others charming and cheerful? The answer is WRITTEN IN THE STARS!

Coming each month in 1991, Silhouette Romance presents you with a special love story written by one of your favorite authors—highlighting the hero's astrological sign! From January's sensible Capricorn to December's disarming Sagittarius, you'll meet a dozen dazzling and distinct heroes.

Twelve heavenly heroes . . . twelve wonderful Silhouette Romances destined to delight you. Look for one WRITTEN IN THE STARS title every month throughout 1991—only from Silhouette Romance.

STAR

Silhouette Books®

SILHOUETTE'S "BIG WIN"
SWEEPSTAKES RULES & REGULATIONS
NO PURCHASE NECESSARY TO ENTER OR RECEIVE A PRIZE

1. To enter the Sweepstakes and join the Reader Service, scratch off the metallic strips on all your BIG WIN tickets #1-#6. This will reveal the potential values for each Sweepstakes entry number, the number of free book(s) you will receive and your free bonus gift as part of our Reader Service. If you do not wish to take advantage of our Reader Service but wish to enter the Sweepstakes only, scratch off the metallic strips on your BIG WIN tickets #1-#4. Return your entire sheet of tickets intact. Incomplete and/or inaccurate entries are ineligible for that section or sections of prizes. Torstar Corp. and its affiliates are not responsible for mutilated or unreadable entries or inadvertent printing errors. Mechanically reproduced entries are null and void.

2. Whether you take advantage of this offer or not, on or about April 30, 1992, at the offices of Marden-Kane Inc., Lake Success, NY, your Sweepstakes numbers will be compared against the list of winning numbers generated at random by the computer. However, prizes will only be awarded to individuals who have entered the Sweepstakes. In the event that all prizes are not claimed, a random drawing will be held from all qualified entries received from March 30, 1990 to March 31, 1992, to award all unclaimed prizes. All cash prizes (Grand to Sixth), will be mailed to the winners and are payable by check in U.S. funds. Seventh prize will be shipped to winners via third-class mail. These prizes are in addition to any free, surprise or mystery gifts that might be offered. Versions of this Sweepstakes with different prizes of approximate equal value may appear at retail outlets or in other mailings by Torstar Corp. and its affiliates.

3. The following prizes are awarded in this sweepstakes: ★ Grand Prize (1) $1,000,000; First Prize (1) $25,000; Second Prize (1) $10,000; Third Prize (5) $5,000; Fourth Prize (10) $1,000; Fifth Prize (100) $250; Sixth Prize (2,500) $10; ★ ★ Seventh Prize (6,000) $12.95 ARV.

   ★ This presentation offers a Grand Prize of a $1,000,000 annuity. Winner will receive $33,333.33 a year for 30 years without interest totalling $1,000,000.

   ★ ★ Seventh Prize: A fully illustrated hardcover book published by Torstar Corp. Approximate Retail Value of the book is $12.95.

   Entrants may cancel the Reader Service at anytime without cost or obligation to buy (see details in center insert card).

4. This Sweepstakes is being conducted under the supervision of an independent judging organization. By entering this Sweepstakes, each entrant accepts and agrees to be bound by these rules and the decisions of the judges, which shall be final and binding. Odds of winning in the random drawing are dependent upon the total number of entries received. Taxes, if any, are the sole responsibility of the winners. Prizes are nontransferable. All entries must be received at the address printed on the reply card and must be postmarked no later than 12:00 MIDNIGHT on March 31, 1992. The drawing for all unclaimed Sweepstakes prizes will take place on May 30, 1992, at 12:00 NOON, at the offices of Marden-Kane, Inc., Lake Success, New York.

5. This offer is open to residents of the U.S., the United Kingdom, France and Canada, 18 years or older, except employees and their immediate family members of Torstar Corp., its affiliates, subsidiaries, and all the other agencies, entities and persons connected with the use, marketing or conduct of this Sweepstakes. All Federal, State, Provincial and local laws apply. Void wherever prohibited or restricted by law. Any litigation within the Province of Quebec respecting the conduct and awarding of a prize in this publicity contest must be submitted to the Régie des Loteries et Courses du Québec.

6. Winners will be notified by mail and may be required to execute an affidavit of eligibility and release, which must be returned within 14 days after notification or an alternate winner will be selected. Canadian winners will be required to correctly answer an arithmetical skill-testing question administered by mail, which must be returned within a limited time. Winners consent to the use of their names, photographs and/or likenesses for advertising and publicity in conjunction with this and similar promotions without additional compensation. For a list of our major prize winners, send a stamped, self-addressed ENVELOPE to: WINNERS LIST, c/o Marden-Kane Inc., P.O. Box 701, SAYREVILLE, NJ 08871. Requests for Winners Lists will be fulfilled after the May 30, 1992 drawing date.

If Sweepstakes entry form is missing, please print your name and address on a 3" ×5" piece of plain paper and send to:

In the U.S.	In Canada
Silhouette's "BIG WIN" Sweepstakes	Silhouette's "BIG WIN" Sweepstakes
3010 Walden Ave.	P.O. Box 609
P.O. Box 1867	Fort Erie, Ontario
Buffalo, NY 14269-1867	L2A 5X3

Offer limited to one per household.
© 1991 Harlequin Enterprises Limited   Printed in the U.S.A.

LTY-S391D

Silhouette Romance®

LONG, TALL TEXANS

HARDEN
Diana Palmer

In her bestselling LONG, TALL TEXANS series, Diana Palmer brought you to Jacobsville and introduced you to the rough and rugged ranchers who call the town home. Now, hot and dusty Jacobsville promises to get even hotter when hard-hearted, woman-hating rancher Harden Tremayne has to reckon with the lovely Miranda Warren.

The LONG, TALL TEXANS series continues! Don't miss HARDEN by Diana Palmer in March . . . only from Silhouette Romance.

LTT-1